THEY WERE BROUGHT TOGETHER BY WAR,
TORN APART BY PASSION. . . .

Ben McQueen—Heroic descendant of the patriot Kit McQueen, he has lost all memory of his heritage and his past. But the gleaming silver medal he wears around his neck—and his inborn honor and courage—will drive him to put his life on the line in the name of truth and justice.

Josefina Quintero—A proud and beautiful widow alone in a harsh, unforgiving land, pursued by the henchmen of a powerful Mexican general, she would seek the help of a ragged Anglo stranger who had come to conquer her adopted home.

General Najera—Cruel, arrogant, and shrewd as a snake, he holds the countryside in an iron grip of fear with his hardcase army of brigands and banditos. What he wants he takes and who dares to oppose him . . . dies. Now he wants the pretty Josefina—and the man standing in his way is Ben McQueen.

Zion—Escaped from slavery in Texas, he has made a new life as foreman on the Quintero ranch. Now once again he must be ready to fight, even to die for what he believes in and those he loves, so long as he dies a free man.

Snake-Eye Gandy—A rugged, one-eyed Texas Ranger with a lust for battle and a warrior's heart, he now has a sing... betrayed his bro... back in bloody k...

D0802798

★ THE MEDAL ★
Book 7

SCORPION

Kerry Newcomb

BANTAM BOOKS
NEW YORK • TORONTO • LONDON • SYDNEY • AUCKLAND

SCORPION

A Bantam Book / May 1994

ISBN 0-553-29447-4

Published simultaneously in the United States and Canada

Bantam Books are published by Bantam Books, a division of
Bantam Doubleday Dell Publishing Group, Inc. Its trademark,
consisting of the words "Bantam Books" and the portrayal of a
rooster, is Registered in U.S. Patent and Trademark Office and
in other countries. Marca Registrada. Bantam Books, 1540
Broadway, New York, New York 10036.

PRINTED IN THE UNITED STATES OF AMERICA

OPM   0 9 8 7 6 5 4 3 2 1

This novel is for Patty, my wife and best friend, and for my children, Amy Rose, Paul Joseph, and Emily Anabel who fill our house with noise and our lives with love.

To Tom Dupree and Tom Beer and the Bantam team, I can only express my gratitude for your faith in this humble storyteller. Heartfelt salutes to my indomitable agent Aaron Priest, who keeps me off the streets and at the computer. To my parents, Ann and Paul Newcomb, and brother Jim, I can only say that every day I realize how blessed I am to have you on my side. And lastly, a special thanks to Louis L'Amour for words of encouragement long ago in Dallas. I was just starting down the trail then. Mister L'Amour, if you're seated around that celestial campfire with the likes of the Duke and Wild Bill; Colonel Tim, Gabby and the Mesquiteers, may I say "Vaya con Dios" . . . and I hope you're pleased.

SCORPION

Chapter One

May 1, 1846

The body began to pick up speed the farther down the incline it rolled. Arms splayed out, legs kicked high. A boot went sailing off into the spiny embrace of an ocotillo. The falling man's coarsely woven brown serape snagged on a prickly pear, but the momentum of the corpse pulled the plant out of the earth and carried it along with the tumbling body that no longer resembled anything but a rag doll, a toy man that someone in their haste had discarded.

The dead man, a ranchero from the look of his tattered clothes, started a small avalanche as he made his way down the hillside, head over heels, sliding on his belly in the brown rubble, then inevitably twisting, one shoulder up and the other down, loose-limbed and blood-smeared, until he came to rest against a tangle of creosote bush about twenty yards above the floor of the arroyo. The ranchero was joined there, a few seconds later, by another equally ragged man with red hair, who had spied the dead Mexican's ungainly descent from the ridge and stumbled forward to examine the serape-draped figure.

Red Hair looked down at the lifeless form whose features, streaked by thorn and briar, had become a garish death mask with only the merest hint of how the ranchero had appeared in life. Had he been young or old, fair of face or homely as a wart? Was he a man of brave deeds, a coward, a proud man, or humble as a saint? Questions without answers . . . And perhaps most important of all, Red Hair thought as he lifted the man's serape and gazed down at the gaping hole left by an exiting bullet, who shot the poor bastard in the back?

The front of the ranchero's shirt was matted with blood, and now that he was still, the wound had already begun to attract flies. For a few seconds the buzzing of the insects was the only audible sound as they hovered in the hot stillness above the dead man on the hillside. Red Hair reached down and brushed sand from the man's cheekbone. It was an oddly tender gesture, an act of pity for this battered corpse seeping the last of its fluids into the thirsty earth.

Gunfire cracked like thunder and echoed down the broken battlements of the ridge. Red Hair winced and ducked forward, the sudden exertion causing him to groan. He gingerly prodded the lump on his forehead and cursed. The scalp wound had been there since he had climbed out of the Rio San Juan a couple of days ago. Something had struck him but he didn't know what. The pain had lessened to a dull ache that only bothered him when he touched his scabbed flesh. Thirst plagued him now, and a lingering nausea that had returned after only a few hours lapse. He glanced up the slope as the gunfire continued to echo down the long-dry hills, and he realized with no small relief that the shots weren't meant for him. He glanced again at the dead man at his side.

"Friends of yours? Well, it's none of my business," he muttered. But then what was? He noticed a familiar bulge beneath the ranchero's sticky red-stained vest, and lifting a fringed flap, discovered the worn walnut grip of an Allan pepperbox revolving pistol tucked in the man's belt. The six-barreled, .32 caliber percussion pistol was loaded and primed. The weapon's walnut grip had suffered a crack at one time, but someone, perhaps the ranchero, had bound the wood together with sinew and hardened glue. The gun butt was as sturdy as new.

Red Hair leaned back against the baked hillside and, after turning on his side, glanced longingly at the east end of the arroyo. Common sense told him to avoid the gunfire. Every weary aching fiber of his being told him this much . . . that he was courting trouble the longer he remained in Mexico. For two days Red Hair had been working his way north and east as best he could, keeping to the high country as much as possible and avoiding all contact with the locals. Mexico and the United States were at war, and here in the foothills of the Sierra Oriental, a wounded Anglo was the intruder. After checking the loads in his second weapon, a Patterson Colt holstered at his side, Red Hair paused a moment to examine his own sun-browned, callused hands. They seemed like alien appendages to him. He could learn nothing about himself from them other than the fact he appeared to have a trace of Indian in him. Two days ago he had examined his features, mirrored on the surface of the Rio San Juan: red hair; a blunt, square jaw; a youthful, good-natured face offset by his sad-eyed gaze. He was a big man, six-foot-two when not stumbling along, long arms dangling and his whole carriage stooped over by thirst and a throbbing headache. He had studied his own reflection but was staring into the dark green eyes of a stranger. Lying here on the hillside with a corpse for company, Red Hair ruefully confronted his own conscience and made a decision.

"Well, one thing's for sure, whoever I am I must be a damn fool," he croaked. This man with no name knew he could not walk away from the gunfire. He must climb the ridge and see for himself, no matter the risk. Five rounds in the Patterson, six in the Allan. He was ready for trouble. His bravado caused him to mirthlessly laugh, which in turn started his head hurting. He laughed anyway and rode out the pain.

When the delirium passed, the man with red hair rolled onto his belly and began to work his way crab-legged up the hillside, dragging himself along from one clump of creosote to the next and bruising his knuckles on the bleached rocks. Sweat stung his eyes and streaked his features, leaving a crisscross of trails upon his dust-caked cheeks and forehead. The sand felt like hot ashes in his boots as the climb began to take its toll, yet the sound of gunfire drew him on like a moth to firelight.

"Isabella! Get down!" the black man shouted. He hauled the ten-year-old girl back behind the wagon bed as a flurry of bullets struck the wooden siding, ricocheted off the coffin on the wagon bed, and spattered the two with splinters as they dropped to the creekbank. Zion's strong right arm held fast the struggling child. Isabella Quintero was a high-spirited girl with too much courage for her own good. She lifted her face, spat out a mouthful of muddy water and tried to stand, but the former slave at her side pulled his charge back alongside him.

Isabella was a pretty girl, even with muddy features. Her black hair was gathered for the most part in a bun on the back of her head, although several strands had escaped to lie against the side of her neck. She had soft dark eyes and lips the color of cherry wine.

"Are you all right?" Zion asked. At five-foot-six, he didn't stand much taller than Isabella, who had started to gain her height at an early age, but Zion was wider by several inches. His shoulders and arms were corded with muscles, and his ebony flesh, where his coarse cotton shirt was damp with perspiration, moved with sleek and supple grace. A little over a decade ago he had escaped his former masters in East Texas and crossed the Rio Grande to freedom. Half starved and desperate, he had been taken in by Don Sebastien Quintero, Isabella's father. Now, at thirty years of age, he had risen to the position of foreman and the don's trusted segundo, Quintero's second in command. It was not a responsibility Zion took lightly.

He rose up, sweat beading his close-cropped black hair, and brought his shotgun to bear on the boulder-strewn hillside that swept sharply up from the east bank of the creek. The shotgun boomed and belched black smoke, sending a load of buckshot toward the three shadowy figures who had ambushed the Quinteros' wagon. One barrel was for the two men hunkered down to the right of the wagon about twenty-five yards up from the water's edge. The second barrel of buckshot caused the lone gunman to Zion's left to yelp and drop behind a limestone ledge. A plume of brownish-yellow dust erupted from the front of the ledge as the darkskinned man in a scarlet and black serape vanished from sight. At about thirty yards the spread of pellets wouldn't be fatal, but they'd sting like hell.

"Oh stop. Please. Stop this!" a woman with pale yellow hair fine as cornsilk shouted from up near the singletree at the front of the wagon. Josefina

Quintero, Isabella's stepmother, was holding the reins to the team of bay mares that had hauled the wagon along the road from Monterrey. Although distraught by the attack, she had enough presence of mind to keep the team from bolting.

"Stay down, Miss Josefina," Zion called out as he rested his back against a wagon wheel and proceeded to ram another charge down the twin blue-steel barrels of his shotgun. The woman gave him a wide-eyed stare and nodded as if she understood, but Zion doubted she did. The sound of gunfire and the proximity of violence had left her visibly shaken.

Josefina had been Don Sebastien's paramour for several years. Only fourteen months ago the widower had defied his country's current political climate and taken the norteamericano governess to be his wife. Publicly, the wealthy landowners around Saltillo roundly criticized Don Sebastien's choice of a bride. Privately, it was difficult for the hacienda-do's friends to find fault with his choice, for Josefina was fair of face and her skin looked as soft and cool to the taste as sweet cream. She was slender and graceful. Sensitive and reclusive by nature, the gentle Josefina had grown utterly devoted to her husband and his child, displaying a loyalty that even Don Sebastien's untimely death had not curtailed.

Josefina stood and reached toward the coffin with an imploring look on her face, her hands outstretched as if to summon the spirit of her deceased husband to shield her and Isabella from harm. Unfortunately, the killers among the rocks harbored no respect for the dead. They did not fear ghosts. But Zion and his shotgun was another matter. So far the segundo had kept the men on the hillside at bay.

Every time Josefina pressed her cheek to the side of the coffin and pleaded to the man within, the hackles rose on the back of Zion's neck. The only way they were going to escape this trap was through blind luck and their wits. And damn it all, the widow was losing hers.

Zion knew he would have to hold off their attackers until night. He hoped they would be able to slip away and escape under cover of darkness. He intended to backtrack and return Josefina and Isabella to Monterrey. If the ambushers were Comanches, as he suspected, they probably wouldn't shoot the mares. Zion didn't want to consider the possibility of losing the horses. Afoot, he might still avoid capture, but the women wouldn't stand a chance.

Zion's worst fears were suddenly realized as a rifled musket spoke from the hillside and one of the bay mares staggered on its hind legs, fought its traces, neighed pitifully, and collapsed into the creek. Zion cursed and grabbed a revolving pistol from his belt, loosing a furious volley of gunshots at his attackers. His pistol was a .45 caliber Allan pepperbox, a heavy-barreled weapon with a kick like a Mississippi mule. He didn't hit anything, but the burst of gunfire gave the men on the hillside something to worry about. Zion squatted down in the creek and winked at Isabella.

"You got me all wet," she complained.

"Better than getting shot," Zion retorted.

"Not so much better. I don't think you hit a thing." She shook her head in dismay. "Carlos is much more reliable with a pistol."

"Carlos, if you remember, senorita, is not here. He scampered off like a frightened rabbit at the first sign of trouble. Right up the hillside he went after they shot his horse out from under him." Zion glanced ahead at the carcass of Carlos's prized nut-brown gelding, which lay on its side in the creek.

Sure were a lot of horses getting killed for the attackers to be Comanches. Most bucks would go out of their way, even to the point of risking their lives, to secure the likes of the two dead animals. He'd never heard of a war party of Comanches that wasn't on the lookout for remounts.

The segundo finished loading the pepperbox and handed the heavy-looking weapon to the girl in the mud. "Perhaps you'd like to try your hand at them red devils, senorita."

Isabella studied the weapon as if genuinely considering whether or not to take the gun which looked about as long as her arm and twice as heavy at least to her exaggerated first glance. Finally she shook her head.

"No thank you," she said. "Not that I couldn't use it. My father taught me to shoot. But after all, I pay you to defend me against these savages."

"Indeed?" Zion replied. "You pay me?"

"Now that papa is . . ." Isabella glanced toward the coffin lying in the wagon. Her eyes grew red and she quickly averted her gaze. She refused to give in to her emotions, fearing she might unleash an uncontrollable flood of tears. Don Sebastien had raised his daughter to be strong. In that respect she was much like her father. "Dead," the ten-year-old finished. "And now that he is dead . . . someone has to pay you." She sniffed back a tear and wiped a forearm across her nose, leaving a smear of mud on the tip. Zion grinned and wiped it off with the coffee-colored bandanna he wore around his neck.

"And what will you pay me for saving your life, senorita?"

"Nothing," she replied matter-of-factly.

"Nothing? So little?"

"A gentleman always saves the *lady's* life. That's expected," Isabella patiently explained. Didn't Zion know anything? she silently wondered. She did not want to hurt his feelings if he really didn't know.

"Oh . . . then I best get on with it," the segundo replied.

"Well, I should say so," Isabella concurred. A couple of geysers erupted from the shallows as gunfire continued from the hillside. Bullets filled the air like a swarm of angry bees, forcing the black man and his two charges to squirm even lower in the cold creek and hug the sides of the wagon. Josefina began to moan, then she stifled her outburst, aware at last of frightening her threatened stepchild.

Zion glanced at his own mount, a sturdy, hammerhead gray with a deep, powerful chest and tapered legs. The animal was tethered to the back of the wagon, and every time a bullet ricocheted off into the sunlight, the gelding would whinny and tug violently against the lead rope securing him.

"Easy," Zion softly cooed. "Easy now." If worse came to worst and the red heathens charged, he'd put Isabella on horseback and send the sturdy gray galloping on its way, leaving himself and Josefina to take their chances. It was his job to rescue the "lady," Isabella had said. That might take a bit of doing, he thought. Well, sir, he lifted his eyes heavenward as he spoke the words in his heart, if my name hasn't come up in that book of yours . . . I could sure use some help.

Zion squinted over the sights of his shotgun and waited. He didn't put much stock in praying, but a man never knew. And alone with the lives of two innocent women depending on him, anything was worth a try. So he rested his cheek on his gun stock and waited, watching the sky for some heaven-sent sign. He should have set his sights lower, to the crest of the ridge above the ambushers, where a worn and battered man with red hair prepared to answer the segundo's desperate prayer.

The coin reflected the burnished brilliance of the yellow sun burning against an azure backdrop of sky. Red Hair caught the silver disk in the palm of his hand and tucked the shiny object back inside his shirt before its gleaming surface caught the attention of the three men below. He counted two men on his left and another solitary figure draped in a black-and-scarlet-banded serape off to the right. All three men were about ninety yards below the ridge line. Red Hair studied the valley floor, where countless wagons had worn a rutted road among the hills. Directly below, the road dipped down and cut across a creek whose wide banks showed signs of flooding in the past, but today the silty stream looked about a foot and a half deep.

Trails of powder smoke drifted in the air over the heads of the men on the hillside and curled in sooty tendrils above the wagon and its defenders. A black man rose up to fire at the attackers and immediately ducked down. Shading his eyes against the glare, Red Hair also made out two women behind the wagon. The three were pinned down and obviously in need of help. He took a moment to study the situation and to catch his breath.

Two of the men on the hillside wore dusty, colored shirts and faded buckskin leggings. They appeared to be armed with muskets and pistols and to be taking orders from the lone gunman in the scarlet and black serape. A broad-brimmed sombrero hid this man's features, while the other two were hatless, their long black hair gathered back from their eyes by strips of cloth. Even as Red Hair was appraising the situation, the men on the hillside loosed another volley at their intended victims behind the wagon. Chips of wood exploded from the lid of the coffin lying on the wagon bed. A woman with blond hair began to scream at the gunmen to leave her poor husband alone. Her pitiful voice carried up the hillside, and her sobbing lingered long after the gunshots had faded.

Red Hair cautiously studied the rubble-strewn path that would take him right behind the Comanches and the man in the serape. The path ended roughly thirty-five feet from the gunmen and just a couple of yards above them. Red Hair assessed his chances. For one final fleeting instant he considered turning his back on the wagon and the people in the creek who were in such a desperate predicament. But somehow he could not bring himself to walk away. They needed help, and he was elected.

"So be it," he muttered, and moved shakily toward the path. The going looked simple enough, but Red Hair hadn't counted on the lingering effects of his wounds. The ground suddenly began to spin and grow spongy as he set foot on the path. The head wound he had suffered—how long ago, he could not remember—and the hunger gnawing at his belly had taken their toll. Yet he managed to will the world into place and steady himself on his feet. For one horrid moment the ridge seemed to writhe like a snake. Then it ceased, and Red Hair continued down the path.

"Nothing to it," he said through gritted teeth. One step at a time, one after the other, he was careful not to disturb a single stone. He was a man of skill, stealth came naturally to him. Unfortunately, the ridge chose that moment to buck and toss one last time. Red Hair sucked in his breath and tried to suppress the surge of nausea that swept over him. He struggled to keep his balance and ride out the dizziness. All of a sudden his boot heels slid in the rubble and his legs went in two directions at once. He was falling, sliding, bruising his shoulder and rolling over and over, then onto his backside. He started a small avalanche of gray rocks and chunks of hard-packed clay. The noise of his arrival not only halted the fight below, but caused every eye to turn in his direction as the wounded man tumbled down the path.

Down behind the wagon, Zion had finished reloading, and watched with mouth agape as this stranger joined the fray. "Who in the hell . . ." he muttered. For a moment he thought it was Carlos returning to help those he had abandoned, but he changed his mind after catching a glimpse of the man's red hair. Well, whether friend or foe, the fellow sure knew how to make an entrance. Too bad it appeared to be his exit as well. Of course, this new arrival might be some renegade come to join his compadres on the slope. The segundo took up his rifled musket and sighted on the falling man. Why take chances? Perhaps it was best to put a bullet in him as soon as he came to rest. He waited to take the shot he was determined not to miss.

The ground leveled out and Red Hair came to rest lying flat on his back against the slope. The world settled into place as rubble continued to rain down around his shoulders. The slope had clawed his shirt to tatters, but somehow he had managed to hold onto the pepperbox. The Patterson Colt was still holstered at his side. A quick assessment of his arms and legs told him he was bruised but not broken, though his rear end hurt like hell where he'd slid over a prickly pear cactus. Still, he was alive, and that was good. He grinned, realizing he had cheated death again. He didn't have long to relish his victory. A Comanche war whoop shattered the silence.

Bullets fanned the air near his head. A geyser of dirt erupted inches from his thigh. He flattened against the earth as the leader of the trio, the man in the serape, snapped off a shot from a double-barreled pistol. The braves on the left came forward at a run, ignoring their intended victims behind the wagon in the creek for this new threat. It was plain to see they intended to quickly dispatch him before returning their attention to the besieged travelers below.

Red Hair moved instinctively. His bleeding fingers curled around his holstered gun while he raised the Allan pepperbox in his left hand and squeezed off a shot. The two Comanches were short, with sloping shoulders and dark features framed by stringy black hair that hung in ponytails past their shoulders. Though on horseback they were without peer, afoot the two seemed devoid of any natural grace. And the time it took them to traverse the hillside and reach Red Hair proved their undoing. The first shot from the pepperbox missed by a yard. Red Hair turned and fired his Colt at the man in the serape, just to keep him honest.

The leader of the ambushers howled as a lead ball creased his thigh. He changed his course and leaped back behind the limestone ledge he had so foolishly abandoned when he thought he had an easy kill. This unwanted intruder lying on his back on the slope was nothing like Carlos, the ranchero who had tried to escape. No, Carlos had been a coward at heart, and it had taken little enough effort to follow him up the hill, shoot him in the back, and leave him to die in his own juices.

A second bullet from the Patterson Colt wasn't as lucky as the first, but it kept the gunman on his right pinned down, allowing Red Hair to return his attention to the Comanches. The path they followed across the slope bunched the two of them together, the older of the two braves in the lead. He carried a brace of double-barreled percussion pistols. The scowling warrior a few paces back brandished a pepperbox revolver that spewed gun smoke as he fired past his companion.

Red Hair rose up to snap off another shot from the .32 caliber pepperbox. The pistol seemed to explode in his hand. A blinding flash of fire erupted from the muzzle as the remaining five barrels ignited almost as one and loosed their loads in a deafening blast. The recoil tore the gun from his grasp and nearly dislocated his shoulder. It was a miracle the pistol didn't explode and blow off his hand. Even so, the simultaneous discharge of the remaining five gun barrels left the man's arm numb. Bullets from the pepperbox trimmed the spindly outstretched limbs of an ocotillo and ravaged flesh and bone. The Comanche in the lead went flying backward through the black smoke as if hurled from a catapult, trailing an arc of crimson from his ravaged chest. He slammed into his companion, who managed to brush the dying man aside and press his attack. The two combatants were scarcely a stone's throw apart when a bullet from Zion's musket buzzed the Comanche and distracted him from his intended prey.

From his vantage point behind the wagon, the segundo had seen enough to realize the "bricktop" who had stumbled into the fray was not of the war party. Zion tossed the musket aside and, taking the pistol from Isabella, ordered the women to remain under cover, then he charged out of the creek and clambered up the limestone slope toward the ambushers.

The Comanche hesitated, seeing Zion come on at a run, then returned his attention to Red Hair. Too late. The brave leveled his pistol, but the Patterson Colt spoke first. The brave rose up on his toes, fired into the air while his free hand clutched at his skull. He twisted, pitched to the side, and rolled down the cactus-dotted incline to splash facedown in the shallows. A trace of bubbles escaped his lips, a tenuous trace of life . . . ebbing . . . ebbing . . . ended.

Red Hair scrambled to his feet and charged the limestone ledge the man in the serape had retreated behind. Any second he expected to dodge a hail of lead. Red Hair stumbled, cursed, regained his balance, thumbed the hammer of his Colt. Fifteen feet, then ten, a leap and a bound and he rounded the ledge, his finger tightening on the trigger.

Nothing. The man in the serape had vanished along a boulder-lined path that wound upward and away from the arroyo, disappearing into a thicket of mesquite trees. As sweat stung his eyes and dripped from his jaw, Red Hair found himself staring at a scorpion scuttling over sun-baked stone. He sighed and almost relaxed. Boots scraped the rocks behind him, and the man with the Colt swung his weapon around to confront this new threat.

Zion immediately held out his hands. *"Muchas gracias, mi amigo."* It took him a moment to realize the dusk-caked, bruised figure standing before him was a norteamericano. The segundo tucked the big .45 caliber Allan in his belt, then wiped his hand on his vest before extending it in an offer of friendship. "You came along at a mighty opportune time, my heaven-sent friend. The name is Zion. Maybe you've heard of me. I ride for the Quinteros. You've heard of Ventana . . . Don Sebastien's ranch . . ." The segundo's voice trailed off as he spied the uncertainty in the norteamericano's eyes.

"Who is it?" Isabella called out. The girl had completely disobeyed Zion's orders, left the protection of the wagon and crossed the stream to the other side, taking care to avoid the dead Comanche in the creek. Zion glared at her, but the girl's question was one that was foremost in his mind as well, and he looked back at their benefactor for an answer.

The man with red hair shrugged, holstered his gun, and wiped the sweat from his eyes with the back of his hand. His brow furrowed in thought, but even the attempt hurt. He had a Patterson Colt, the remnants of a uniform, and a silver coin dangling from around his neck. The coin, which he wore like a medal, bore the curious initials GW scrawled across the face of some monarch etched on the shiny surface.

"I don't know," he said. Benjamin Bittercreek McQueen shook his head and abandoned the effort. Desperation sounded in his voice. "I . . . don't . . . know."

Chapter Two

Zion overturned a flat slab of chalk-colored stone and with the toe of his boot nudged a scorpion out into the sunlight. The brown insect scuttled across the white dust, its pincers raised, the curved, barbed tail arched threateningly.

"They're always where you least expect them," observed the segundo, tormenting the defiant insect with a mesquite twig. "In your boots, under a blanket, right where you choose to, uh . . . squat." The barbed tail struck at the offending stick. "And they pack one hell of a sting." He looked over at the red-haired young man seated across the campfire. "Like you."

They were camped in a grove of scrub oak a couple of miles from the arroyo. Josefina, too shaken to continue on throughout the afternoon, had insisted that Zion find a place to make camp. She was hoping to rest the remainder of the afternoon and evening and calm her nerves. Zion hadn't objected all that much. One of the axles could use some repair. The former slave had grudgingly hitched his gray to the singletree after cutting the dead mare loose. It was a shameful waste of a damn good cutting horse, but necessity demanded the sacrifice.

At least the timber and overgrowth of brush offered plenty of cover, and a spring, bubbling up in the center of the grove, provided plenty of sweet water. It was as good a place as any for the women to recover from their harrowing ordeal.

"*Alacron* . . . the scorpion," he continued. "I think it suits you, Senor Alacron."

"Alacron," Ben wearily repeated. The name spilled from his lips as Isabella stepped around the campfire and handed him a tin cup of steaming coffee. Well, he had to be called something, and the name would do until he made his way across the border and rejoined the United States Army, where he hoped to discover his true identity. Ben glanced down at the ragged remains of his uniform. Either he had been or still was a soldier. Perhaps he was a deserter. In that case, returning might place him in front of a firing squad. Now there was an unsettling notion.

"Bet I can count on my fingers higher than you," Isabella said, interrupting his thoughts. "Want to see?"

"Leave the poor man be, Isabella," the girl's stepmother called out. "The very least we can do to show our gratitude to Senor Alacron is to give him a moment's peace." Josefina Quintero spoke while peeling a jicama root and placing chunks of the root's white meat into a cook pot, along with strips of dried beef and peppers. She brushed a blond strand of hair back from her features and smiled wanly. Behind the mask of grief was a very pretty face. The late Senor Quintero had shown good taste in his choice of a bride.

"It's all right," Ben said. He set his coffee aside, reached out and examined the girl's hands.

"What are you doing?" she asked.

"Just checking to see if you had twelve fingers or something," Ben said with mock seriousness.

Isabella shook her head. "You count first."

"One, two, three, four . . ." He continued on to ten.

When it was her turn, Isabella raised her hands high above her head and counted on her fingers. With Ben seated on the ground, she was indeed counting "higher" than her ragged benefactor. With a squeal of triumph she scampered off to help her mother.

"That's Isabella." Zion chuckled. "I've seen twisters get into less mischief." He sighed and ran a hand across his weathered features. "But there's nothing I wouldn't do to see that little spitfire safe and happy. I owe her daddy a powerful lot." Zion's gaze seemed to watch events from his past unfold in the tangled shadows of the grove. "I ran off from a plantation in East Texas, over by Washington on the Brazos. I reckon it's been ten years now since I seen the place, and I don't miss it. No sir. I outran dogs and the overseer and crossed the border with nothing but the shirt on my back and a gnawing in my belly. Don Sebastien found me half starved and near dead and brought me back to Ventana. I learned to ride and rope cattle. Don Sebastien gave me a home." His head turned slightly as he shifted his attention to the coffin in the wagon bed.

"What happened to him?" Ben asked. "Comanches?"

Zion shook his head. "His sister passed away. He hadn't seen her in a long time. She lived in Linares. Don Sebastien hoped to straighten out her affairs and locate some papers he was missing that he thought she had. One night he didn't return to the hotel and I went looking for him. I found him lying facedown in the middle of the plaza, with his back broke and skull caved in. A freight wagon ran him down. Witnesses said the driver had lost control of his horses. I don't imagine Senor Quintero knew what hit him." Zion stretched out a leg and rubbed a sore calf muscle, but it was his heart that was really aching. The memory was still vivid in his mind and caused him pain. As the segundo, it had been his responsibility to watch out for Don Sebastien.

Ben could sense Zion's turmoil, but in a way, he envied the former slave. At least Zion had a memory, no matter how painful. But to have nothing but a blank . . . Well, not nothing. Ben knew the United States and Mexico were at war; but what part, if any, he was playing in the conflict, lay beyond his grasp.

His thoughts drifted back to the aftermath of the fight in the arroyo. They had left the two Comanche braves where they had fallen. The carrion birds had already begun to circle, and neither Zion nor Ben saw any reason to deny the buzzards their feast. The Comanches were a part of the wild and untamed country, so now the land was reclaiming its own.

However, Zion seemed especially upset that the third man had escaped. Ben suggested that perhaps the three were not part of some larger raiding party, otherwise the main force of warriors would have arrived at the arroyo at the first exchange of gunshots. Zion had agreed.

"Tell me, Alacron, did you get a close look at the one in the serape?" he asked.

Ben stared at the former slave, wondering if the man had somehow read his thoughts. "No," he sighed. "I was pretty dizzy, and the gun smoke stung my eyes." He could picture a flash of color from the gunman's serape, a band of black and scarlet. As for the man's features, everything had happened so fast.

All Ben could discern was a patch of shadow beneath the man's sombrero. Judging by his garb, he was no full-blood. Perhaps he had been a breed, hoping to turn a profit on the deaths of three innocent people with the help of a pair of renegade Comanches.

Half an hour later, Josefina stepped around the campfire and brought a plate of food over to Ben, who managed to stand as the lady approached.

"I can get that, ma'am," he said.

"Nonsense. I was the governess and teacher in the Quintero household for many years following the death of the first Senora Quintero. Just because Don Sebastien took me to wife doesn't mean I have forgotten simple courtesies. It is always an honor to serve a friend."

"You hardly know me, ma'am," Ben said. Their eyes met, held, then she looked away.

"You risked your life to help us. My husband says that makes you a friend." The woman did not notice how Ben's expression changed, and the furtive glance he snuck toward the coffin. She handed Ben his plate of food. "And I still throw together a stew when our cook allows me in the kitchen."

"Yes, ma'am," he said, inhaling the mouthwatering aroma that wafted from his plate. Hunger was all the seasoning he needed. And if the events of the past week had left her a little crazy, what the hell. He met Josefina's eyes with a look of heartfelt gratitude. She was an attractive woman whose physical attributes—her laughing brown eyes, a well-rounded figure, and flaxen hair—were enough to set a man's blood racing and put fire in his veins. She handed a second plate to Zion and then returned to the campfire, where Isabella had already helped herself.

"Sit here with me, Josefina," Isabella said, making room on a log for her stepmother.

"No. Thank you, dear. I'm not hungry just yet," the widow replied in a voice tinged with a sense of loss. Lifting the hem of her embroidered riding skirt, she climbed up in the wagon bed and sat alongside the coffin, her hand resting upon the lid. She remained there throughout the afternoon, although gradually her head lowered and came to rest upon her arm. She closed her eyes and fell asleep. Ben, however weary, could not bring himself to rest unless he had pulled his share of the night watch. Zion was impressed when the young man put his empty plate aside and announced he would keep an eye on their back trail and the mesquite-dotted hills they had left behind.

"Maybe you better take care of a more pressing matter, amigo," Zion suggested. He stood and walked over to the wagon, retrieved a pair of saddlebags and brought them back to Ben. "You can't walk around with your back end hanging out. Hell, there's not enough of that uniform left to make a proper set of clothes." Zion dropped the saddlebags into Ben's outstretched arms.

The man called Alacron untied the rawhide strings and opened the saddlebags, to find a pair of coarse denim pants and a faded gray shirt, both of which had belonged to Don Sebastien Quintero. The haciendado's work clothes looked a close fit and certainly preferable to running around Mexico with the seat of his britches torn away. And the sooner Ben was rid of the remnants of his uniform, the better. At least until he crossed the Rio Grande into Texas, several days to the north.

"What about . . ." Ben looked toward Josefina.

"It was her idea," Zion replied.

Ben walked out of camp and ventured into the thicket until he was hidden from the widow and her daughter, then he quickly changed clothes. As he had no hat, he hid his red hair beneath a bandanna. Fortunately, the shirt fit with only a modest effort to tug it into place. Lastly, he buckled the gun belt around his waist. The Patterson Colt rode at his side. A leather pouch of shot and a brass powder flask also dangled from the belt. He had handed the Allan .32 caliber over to Zion. And he could keep it as far as Ben was concerned. The weapon had proved too untrustworthy in the arroyo and nearly blown off his hand. The man they knew as Alacron wasn't taking any chances; his fingers were still numb. Ben wearily returned to camp carrying the remains of his uniform rolled up underneath his arm.

"Think you can stay awake, mi amigo?" Zion asked. Sweat beaded like pearls on the segundo's ebony features. His own eyes were pouchy from lack of sleep.

"Watch me," Ben stated flatly.

"Not hardly. Reckon I'll hunker down and take a siesta." Zion passed a rifled musket to the Anglo, who cradled the long gun in the crook of his arm and took up his position alongside the wagon, where he could keep a watchful eye on the narrow winding trail they had followed into the grove. Ben decided that waiting here at the campsite wasn't the best of ideas. If Comanches pursued them into the thicket, it would be better if Zion and the women had some warning. They might be able to make good their escape. Ben sauntered off toward a natural barricade of fallen timber he had spied about twenty yards from camp.

"Can I come with you?" Isabella asked, anxious to escape another boring late afternoon with nothing to do but sit around and watch the dragonflies and mud dawbers.

"You stay here with me, little one," Zion said.

The girl glared at him. "I won't get in his way."

"You already have," Zion told her.

"You need to be with your mother in case the Comanches show up again," Ben said, pausing among the scrub oak.

"But I want to know all about you. We don't get many visitors at Ventana." Isabella sighed. "It's lonely talking to the wind."

"I know nothing about myself," Ben tried to explain. What was there to say? That he had been wandering around the Sierra Orientals for God only knew how long?

"Oh, that's quite all right," Isabella enthusiastically replied. "I can make things up."

And despite his sense of loss and terrible confusion, Ben almost smiled. Almost.

At the ripe old age of seventeen, Raul Salcedo had already killed five men, "not counting Indians," as the gunman liked to say. His first kill had been the result of an argument over a chicken. Raul had roasted the scrawny hen and enjoyed his dinner over the body of the bird's former owner, a bellicose farmer who had the misfortune of fathering Raul and raising him for the first twelve years of his life.

Raul was slender, with hard brown eyes and narrow, pinched features that women often laughingly described as weasely behind his back. No one derided him to his face, for Raul's quick temper made him as dangerous as lightning.

He lifted a smooth, tapered hand to his face to examine the pockmarks made by the scattershot from Zion's shotgun. His fingertips came away tipped with dots of crimson. The bullet crease striping his thigh had ceased to bleed. He had stanched the wound with a paste of spiderwebs and mud, and tied a bandanna around his leg to hold the makeshift poultice in place. A quarter of a mile from the grove and on high ground, Raul had easily located Zion's campsite. But that knowledge was of little value. Alone and across open ground, he would not last a minute against the guns of Zion and the stranger who had come out of nowhere to ruin his best-laid plans. The loss of the Comanche renegades was hardly a tragedy. As far as Salcedo was concerned, the two had not even been worth the whiskey he had plied them with. Still, the gunman was unaccustomed to failure; and even less so was General Najera, the man who kept the seventeen-year-old killer employed.

The palms of Raul's hands were as smooth as a courtesan's. The hard gritty toils of ranch life were none of Raul's concerns. His duties were more suited to his considerable talents. His skills were with pistol, rifled musket, or throwing knife, like the thin, finely balanced blade he kept in his boot sheath. Raul shook his head and cursed. He didn't look forward to admitting failure to Valentin Najera, *El Jefe*, who commanded the troops garrisoned around Saltillo. Najera was not a forgiving man. But Raul had served the general well in the past, and this whole mission had not been a total failure.

Raul opened his saddlebag and rummaged through the contents until he found a twist of beef jerky. His yellow teeth clamped down on the dried meat and gnawed a morsel free. He chewed the dried, peppery beef and studied the tendril of white smoke that drifted above the post oaks and mesquite trees. Well, there's still time, he thought to himself. Senor Quintero's gringo whore hadn't reached Ventana yet. At the rate they were traveling, Raul calculated he still had four or five days to redeem himself. The gunman pictured other places along the way where he might pick off Zion and the stranger if the man were foolish enough to tag along.

Raul smiled and ran a finger along the pencil-thin moustache he wore as an affectation, hoping it made him appear older. His brown eyes took on a dreamy look as he played out his course of action. He intended to ride past the thicket under cover of darkness, and range a couple of miles ahead of Zion's wagon. The next time they met, Raul vowed the blood spilled would not be his own.

The man called Alacron nodded, caught himself, but his eyelids were so damn heavy. His head drooped forward until it rested on his forearm. He caught himself again and abruptly straightened, embarrassed and hoping no one had noticed him. He glanced around and found Zion standing a few feet away, framed by moonlight. In his fatigue, Ben had not heard the telltale crackle of the dry grass and creosote bush at Zion's approach.

"Reckon you're about played out," Zion said. "Senora Quintero spread a blanket for you over by the campfire. And there's some beans and side meat left."

"Sounds good to me," Ben replied sheepishly. He didn't like being caught unaware. He doubted it was even midnight yet, but he knew he'd reached his limit. Ben shoved clear of the makeshift barricade of fallen timber he'd been crouching behind and crossed to the segundo. Zion's arm extended, and Ben caught the gleam of a metal flask gleaming silver as the moonbeams played across its shiny surface. Ben voiced his thanks, tilted the flask to his lips, swallowed twice, and returned the flask to its owner.

Tequila is a hard-bracing drink taken straight, but it cuts the dust and can warm a body against the cool arid nights of the Sierra Oriental.

"I apologize for the lack of salt or lemon," Zion said in a voice that seemed to have its origins somewhere in the man's barrel chest.

"Fine the way it is," Ben gasped, starting past him. Zion caught him by the arm and gently restrained him.

"Hold a second, Alacron. I've got a proposition to set out for you." Zion glanced over his shoulder to the campfire, where Josefina Quintero continued to rock Isabella in her arms and sing a soft lullaby, her bleak stare fixed on the leaping flames. Zion cleared his throat.

"Now, the way I see it, you don't know who you are or where you ought to be heading. You might stay a blank all your days. As for me, I've got a ten-year-old girl that I've got to keep a constant rein on, and a woman so torn up by grief that half the time she doesn't even make sense." Zion tilted the flask to his lips and poured a shot of liquid courage down his gullet. He wiped his forearm across his mouth. "You've already shown me you're a man to stand alongside of in a fight. Come on with us to the Senora's ranch outside Saltillo. I've got another four days ahead of me, and on my own, well, let's say I'd rest a mite easier with another gun." Zion hooked a thumb in the pocket of the fringed wool vest he wore to ward off the chill. "You'd be welcome to stay on the ranch and make a place for yourself."

Ben studied the camp. He doubted that they were in danger. Two of the robbers had already been killed. And the third had run off like a frightened rabbit. Still, he might have accepted Zion's offer but for the nagging feeling the answers he sought lay to the north. And he was desperate for answers. Having not only his name, but his entire life become some immense void, was quickly becoming unbearable.

"I can't." Ben looked away. He couldn't find the words to articulate his feelings, the horror of not knowing, of being . . . empty. Who was he? What was he doing there? What had happened to him? "I'm sorry . . . but I can't."

Zion did not reply. He hid his displeasure behind a curtain of silence, nodded and took up the position at the barricade that Ben had abandoned. "Suit yourself," the segundo finally replied without emotion, and turned his attention to the wheel-rutted path that cut through the heart of the thicket. The scrub oaks, like scrawny sentries, guarded the trail, spindly branches extended to form a canopy above the path, which seemed for all the world like some night-darkened hall. Fireflies winked aglow then vanished in its depths. "Suit yourself," he softly repeated beneath his breath.

By the time Ben returned to the campsite and the warmth of the fire, Isabella was asleep upon a pad of thick blankets, and Josefina was standing alongside the wagon, her eyes on the coffin and her hand resting upon one of the brass handles on the side. She glanced in Ben's direction, and he half bowed in greeting, but she seemed to stare right through him. He might as well have been a vapor or a mist. His skin crawled and goose bumps rose on the back of his neck. In her own way, Josefina appeared as lost as he.

Ben crawled onto his bedroll and turned his back to the fire. Exhaustion settled on him like stone. Tomorrow he would resume his journey north in search of himself. Tomorrow . . . He closed his eyes and in a matter of minutes was fast asleep.

Chapter Three

Chained!

Ben lifted his wrists and found two feet of black iron chain connecting his arms. Another set of shackles joined his ankles. He was tethered to the wagon by a length of hemp rope that looped through his leg irons

Ben hauled on the chains, exerting what strength remained in his rested limbs. He tore at the rope and wrenched his shackles, shouted "Zion!" and struggled in vain to free himself.

Isabella and Josefina, fresh from a morning bath in the spring, heard the prisoner's outcry and came running out of the woods. Woman and child were both frightened, Isabella's eyes were wide with terror. Josefina looked as if she expected to see a horde of howling blood-crazed Comanches descending on them. However, the man primarily responsible for Ben's outrage seemed wholly unconcerned and was helping himself to a cup of coffee. Zion turned to face the chained man and held out a blue-enameled tin cup of coffee.

"Just the way I like it . . . thick as mud, hot as hell, and black as the devil," Zion said, smacking his lips after taking a swallow.

Ben charged him, erupting from the ground and plowing forward with all the speed his hampered limbs would allow. He reached the end of his rope about a yard short of Zion. The line went taut and jerked Ben off his feet. He landed on his face in the dirt, rose up and looked over his shoulder at the rope. For the first time he realized he was tethered to the wagon, by a length of hemp rope that looped through his leg irons. He faced Zion again, managed to stand, and held up his wrists to the segundo.

"What the hell is this?!" Ben growled, his eyes blazing as he towered over him.

"Insurance," Zion replied. "I gave you the chance to come along with us of your own will. As for the irons, they once were mine. I keep them as a reminder."

Josefina cautiously approached the two men. The fury etched upon Ben's scruffy features was not tempered by the proximity of the woman. He assumed she was in accord with Zion's conduct, a suspicion she immediately confirmed.

"I am very sorry, Mister, uh . . . Alacron. Very sorry indeed. But Zion is worried there could be more trouble, and your presence, however unwilling, could prove useful. I must get my husband home. I simply must."

"Your husband is dead, Senora Quintero," Ben flatly told her. He was in no mood to be tactful.

"Of course he is. Quite so. But that really doesn't change anything." The widow dabbed at the perspiration beading on her upper lip. A single tear spilled from the corner of her left eye. It gleamed like a jewel in the arid sunlight. Ben wondered if anyone would weep for him if he never returned from Mexico.

"Please try to understand, we need you. Someone must handle the wagon in order to leave Zion free to fight." Josefina offered her explanation in the same amicable tone of voice one might reserve for a friend.

The chained man lowered his right hand to his holster and discovered the Patterson Colt was missing. Zion cleared his throat, and when he had his prisoner's attention, revealed McQueen's Patterson tucked in his belt.

"I may have saved your lives yesterday," Ben reminded him, hoping to awaken in Zion a sense of gratitude.

"For which we are profoundly grateful." Zion drained the contents of his coffee mug, then refilled the cup with some of the grounds from the bottom of the coffeepot. Using the soggy grounds as a base, he proceeded to add a handful of dried peelings of jicama root, crushed sotol, and water. He mixed his ingredients until he had the right consistency before offering the odd concoction to Ben.

"This stain will darken your skin enough so you'll pass for Mex," he explained. "Where we're going, a gringo like yourself is an open target for every vaquero anxious to settle a grievance with those north of the Rio Grande." Ben's fist clenched as Zion stepped closer, moving within reach. He was tempted to make another attempt at Zion but held back, suspecting the segundo would not be so foolish as to have the keys to the leg and wrist irons on his person.

Zion was no fool. He knew what was going on in his prisoner's mind. Escape had always been in his thoughts when he toiled as a slave in East Texas. Don Sebastien had not only saved his life, but had also restored his dignity. This was not a debt the former slave took lightly. "You're going to help me get the senora and senorita to their home outside Saltillo whether you like it or not."

He sloshed the contents of the cup and offered

the mixture to Ben. "Once I have the women safe, I'll give you a horse from the ranch stock and send you on your way with enough food and water to keep you supplied for a couple of weeks." He placed the cup within Ben's reach. "You want to reach the Rio Bravo alive, Alacron? I'll leave it up to you."

Ben stared at the cup, then lowered his gaze to his forearm. He was damn near as dark as a local. But a little more brown wouldn't hurt, and his red hair certainly had to go. Even if he managed to escape, a disguise could help him safely reach the Rio Grande. As his wrist shackles allowed some freedom of movement, Ben picked up the cup and began to apply the stain to his face and neck. He worked it into his arms, massaging his flesh until the skin turned a nut-brown. Then he started on his hair. Soon his head was topped by a shaggy rust-colored mane that hung to his shoulders.

"Why is Senor Alacron all chained up? Did he do something bad?" Isabella asked. Her stepmother told her to hush and ordered her charge to return her carpet bag to the wagon. Isabella shrugged and did as she was told. However, she did not consider such a demand an answer to her question.

"Best you stay clear of Alacron," Zion cautioned the girl. He returned to the campfire and proceeded to finish his breakfast.

Ben watched him eat, and silently cursed his own carelessness. If he hadn't been so blasted exhausted and dizzy from his head wound, he might have heard Zion bring the leg irons, or at least been roused awake when he fastened the black iron bracelets around his wrists. He sensed Isabella starting toward him, but when he looked in her direction, the girl reconsidered. She backed off and rejoined Josefina over by the wagon.

Within an hour the wagon was loaded and the

horses harnessed. Ben took the reins while Zion sat beside him, a rifled musket cradled in his arms. Josefina and the girl sat on folded blankets alongside the coffin. They rode out of the glade in silence, the only sounds being the jangle of harness rings, the noise of iron-shod wheels glancing off stone, and the rattle of a prisoner's chains as they headed south to Saltillo.

Chapter Four

Two days' ride from the site of his earlier, disastrous ambush, Raul Salcedo crouched beneath a limestone ledge that overlooked a narrow ravine through which the Saltillo road cut a winding path just wide enough to permit a freight wagon. A large, freshly cut post oak had been dragged across the road and left with its branches touching one hillside and the base resting on the loose gravel of the opposite wall. Any wagon entering the ravine would have to stop and wait for someone to lift the log aside. No more than a minute's effort, but long enough to put a bullet through Zion's head. Raul gnawed the last of his jerky, followed it with a few stale tortillas he'd baked over hot coals the night before, and washed his meager meal down with a couple of swallows of tepid water collected from a nearby *tinaja*, a depression in the barren stone where rainwater from five days ago had collected. General Najera's gunman was cramped and tired and disgusted with the way things were working out. This ploy was his last chance at accomplishing the task the general had set for him.

Zion was too clever to be allowed to live. Sooner

or later he would discover the reason why Don Sebastien had been murdered. Of course, it would be so much the better if Josefina and Isabella were also eliminated, fallen prey to "Comanches" in a terrible massacre. That would greatly simplify matters. And Raul Salcedo was the kind of man who liked to keep things simple.

The seventeen-year-old killer stood and stepped out beneath the ledge, and watched the Quinteros progress as the driver of the wagon guided the freight box down a steep grade, the wheels sliding in the washed-out rubble, the unevenly matched team of horses fighting the loose footing as they descended the wooded slope. A pair of mule deer darted from the underbrush several yards in front of the wagon and bounded to safety before either of the intruders could bring a rifle to bear.

"C'mon," Raul muttered. "Come." He fished in his pocket, removed a spyglass and lifted it to his right eye, adjusting the focus until Zion's image appeared in the center of the eyepiece. Raul could almost see the beads of sweat glistening on the man's ebony features. He shifted his view and studied the driver. Was this the same man who had interfered two days ago? The gunman's brows furrowed as he tried to make some sense of what he was seeing. Things had happened pretty fast during the brief gunfight, and Raul Salcedo really couldn't be certain what the intruder had looked like. He shrugged and shifted again, this time to the widow and the ten-year-old girl. If the notion of murdering a woman and a child bothered him, it did not show. In truth, these two meant nothing to Raul Salcedo.

Nothing at all.

"Won't you have one of these biscuits, Senor Alacron?" Isabella asked. "They are very good." She had made biscuits earlier in the day, using a recipe that Josefina had taught her, and had bound up the left-overs from breakfast in a checkered kerchief that she carried in her lap.

"No thanks," Ben replied dourly. His shackled wrists did nothing to improve his mood. Zion had removed his leg irons, but no matter, the man without a memory was still a prisoner.

"You really ought to eat," Isabella told him. "You remind me of a coyote pup I once brought home. He wouldn't eat either."

"What happened to him?"

"Why, eventually he just ran away."

Ben glanced at the man sitting next to him. Zion had betrayed him, and however noble the motives, Ben would not forgive him. The expression on Ben McQueen's face spoke volumes. Like the coyote, he intended to escape at the first opportunity.

"Hold the team up here," Zion ordered. Ben obeyed him, sensing the caution in his voice. He climbed down from the wagon and walked a few paces down the road, came to a halt and proceeded to study the narrow ravine that cut through the rolling landscape. Some of the hills were topped with rocky outcroppings and fringed with scrub oak, cactus, grama grass. All manner of birds swooped and soared through the warm, still air, flashes of redwing and black, pale blue, drab gray, and dull brown gave chase to dragonfly and cicada in an endless pursuit of dinner.

Ben took in the surrounding terrain with appreciation for the harsh but subtle beauty of Zion's adopted homeland. The man called Alacron was another orphan for Old Mexico, a man without a past, whose future—he shook the chains binding his wrists—was seriously in doubt.

"Is the way blocked?" Josefina called out.

"Doesn't appear to be so," Zion said. He sauntered back to the wagon and looked up at Ben. "The earth shook . . . three weeks ago I'd say."

"That's about right," the widow agreed.

"Shook us in Ventana. Folks in Saltillo felt it too. Figured it might have tumbled some of those limestone boulders down into the ravine, so Don Sebastien wanted to take the west road out of Saltillo on our way to Linares. It was longer, but it missed the dry washes and cut-throughs like the one up ahead." Zion licked his lips and dry-swallowed. He didn't relish the idea of proceeding on without checking the ravine. But he wasn't about to leave Ben alone with the senora and her stepdaughter. "You reckon these nags have a run left in them?"

Ben shrugged. "They'll do."

"Then we'll try making it through. You take the whip to these animals when we're about twenty yards from the defile." Zion looked back at his charges. "Senora . . . Isabella . . . you hold tight to the coffin handles and try and lay as flat as possible. I doubt there'll be trouble, but it doesn't hurt to be cautious."

"What about these damn chains?" Ben said, holding up his wrists.

"When the time comes, and I can be certain you won't be taking potshots at me," Zion replied. He climbed back up in the wagon and bounced a pebble off the gray's rump.

The wagon rolled forward, axles creaking, the passengers swaying from side to side as Ben seemed to find every rut in the hard earth. The echo of their progress reverberated off the hills. The noise was unsettling as they neared the ravine. It announced their presence, and with Comanches about that was the last thing anyone wanted to do. When the wagon was about twenty yards from the ravine, Zion gave the word and reached for the whip while Ben flicked the reins and shouted for the horses to run. The animals recognized his tone of voice and knew what was expected of them. Don Sebastien's horses were the pride of Saltillo, bred for stamina and speed, and they rose to the occasion. They went from a canter to a gallop, churning billowing brown clouds of dust in their wake. Isabella squealed with joy. Josefina said a silent prayer, clung to a brass handle on the coffin with one hand, and wrapped her free arm around the ten-year-old's waist and forced her to lie prone among the carpet bags alongside the coffin. By the time they reached the defile, the horses were running flat out. Ben leaned forward, the reins tangled in his hand. Zion's sombrero was flapping behind his head. He would have lost his hat but for the leather tie that fastened beneath his chin.

The sound of the wagon filled their ears as it careened through the ravine, skimming past limestone outcroppings and fallen timber. Suddenly the fallen scrub oak appeared in front of them, blocking their progress as the wagon bore down on it. Ben started to apply the brake, then changed his mind and exhorted the team of horses to even greater speed.

"What the hell are you doing!?" Zion shouted. "You can't be fixing to jump that!"

Ben did not bother to reply. Twenty feet from the blockade, then ten.

"Pull up!" Zion ordered. He clawed for the reins, but Ben fought him off. "Pull up, you son of a bitch!" His eyes widened and he abandoned trying to capture control of the horses. He tucked his rifle beneath the bench seat and held on for dear life. Ben gave the reins a sharp pull and the team responded and started up the slope. For a moment the wheels twisted and slid, the wagon nearly toppling over onto its occupants as Ben came within inches of being thrown from his seat. As the wagon lurched to the left, everyone leaned to the right. They crashed through scrub brush and upturned roots. Dust and grit stung their eyes. For what seemed an eternity the wagon hung poised, inches from disaster. Then they were clear and once more on the relatively level surface of the travel-worn road, the defile was behind them. The hills seemed to be slowly, ever slowly, receding. A couple of miles down the road, when they were well out of the pass, Ben hauled on the reins and slowed the team to a walk, allowing the horses to catch their wind. Only then did Zion turn toward Ben, his features contorted in anger.

"What the devil? You nearly killed us all. I could have moved that tree out of our path. Damn it, man, we've a woman and child with us." Zion tugged the Colt from his belt. "The next time I tell you to pull up, you do as I say or it won't go well, Alacron." Zion jabbed the gun barrel into Ben's side. The man's broad chest rose and fell as he caught his breath. "Just 'cause you saved my life once doesn't mean I aim to let you break all our necks."

"Twice."

"What?"

Ben reached for the segundo's sombrero. Zion flinched back and cocked the revolver until he realized what the man without a memory was after. Ben caught the brim and tugged the hat around to the front. In the crown of the hat was a ragged bullet hole that hadn't been there before.

"Damn," Zion cursed, and looked back through the settling dust at the road winding among the hills. He'd felt the tug on his hat but hadn't heard the gunshot, and assumed it was merely a stone thrown up by the wheel. Someone had tried to kill him . . .

again. If Zion had stopped the wagon to clear the fallen timber from the road, he might be dead.

"Twice," Ben repeated. He had indeed saved his captor yet again.

Chapter Five

Raul Salcedo walked his sodden mount through the rainswept night. Failure didn't sit well with him. But he was young and resilient, and was able to accept what had happened in the defile as something beyond his control. What manner of fool would send a wagon careening across a steep hillside and risk overturning and being crushed beneath axles and spokes and flailing horses?

Lightning flashed and the night shimmered with sheets of pale and ghostly illumination. He halted his mount between two mesquite trees, and looking back the way he had come, searched the briefly lit landscape until he caught a glimpse of a campfire flickering forlornly at the base of a sandstone bluff off to the north. Raul glared at the distant encampment and muttered, "This day was yours, compadres. But there will be other days. We will meet again."

Raul was a proud man, and the mantle of defeat was not something he cared to wear for very long. But he consigned his anger to the back of his mind and concentrated on the things he most enjoyed,

Saltillo's willing whores, tequila, and the luck of the cards. He reveled in the respect he received and the fear he engendered in the townspeople when he'd had too much to drink and the dark mood came upon him and he prowled the *pulquerias* looking for trouble.

The seventeen-year-old killer had wearied of this chase and the discomforts it involved. He knew where to find the Quinteros and Zion—the trail to their rancho, Ventana, was well-marked. Let them think they were safe. One night, Raul Salcedo intended to pay Senora Quintero a visit. And he'd deal with the segundo and the mysterious vaquero who seemed to have only one mission in life—thwarting his plans. Yes, it was time to return to Saltillo, he thought, and await the arrival of General Najera.

Burrowing into his serape and lowering his head to the elements, Raul Salcedo continued down the Saltillo road, his shoulders bowed by his recent failures. The cold spring storm might have chilled him to the bone but for the anger that surfaced anew and warmed his wiry frame, forging his vengeful resolve until it was strong as steel.

Zion was awakened by a groan and reached for the Patterson. He liked the feel of the gun. It was common knowledge that all the Texas Rangers were armed with a pair of such weapons. The Rangers were said to be dangerous as coiled rattlers . . . men who could out-ride and outfight the Comanche on his home ground. Zion rolled over on his side, looked at his restless prisoner and wondered if the man called Alacron was one of those "devils on horseback." He certainly fought like one.

Ben stirred and tossed in his sleep. His head twisted from side to side, and sweat beaded his forehead, but his eyes remained closed, and his breathing, though rapid, did nothing to affect his slumber. Outside the entrance to the cave, the downpour continued unabated. A curtain of water masked the night, a gust of wind drawing tendrils of smoke from the embers of the fire they had built at the mouth of the cave, for lack of any better ventilation. Only a trace drifted back to cloud the clammy air at the rear of the chamber in which the segundo had chosen to ride out the storm.

The gray gelding tethered just beneath the ledge pawed at the rocky floor and shook its mane. The stubborn animal, nervous about being underground, had to be hobbled before it would remain in the cave. Zion had used his bandanna to secure the gelding's forelegs. The mare had also needed to be ground-tethered, and the segundo had tied a rag across the animal's eyes to keep the creature from becoming unnerved by the lightning.

The wagon had been left outside. However, Josefina had insisted the coffin be brought in out of the storm. Zion could not see how it mattered. Don Sebastien was beyond caring. As the segundo's mind turned to thoughts of death, the wind began to moan as it blew across the hillside and the mouth of the cave. The storm's keening voice made Zion shiver. This was an old land. The Comanche, the Lipan Apache, and the Yaqui all had stories of the spirits that roamed these hills, often at night; mischief makers, demons, the haunters of the dark. Zion felt a tug on his arm and nearly jumped out of his skin. Isabella gasped and scooted back before Zion realized who had touched him, and relaxed.

"Lord, young'un, you damn near scared the bejesus out of me," he scolded.

"I just wanted to tell you I heard something," Isabella whispered. She looked past Zion at the man she knew as Alacron. "Is he all right?" The ten-year-old pursed her lips and her brows knotted. "Maybe I ought to wake him? He might be sick."

"Let him be, senorita. Stay clear of him," Zion instructed. "Such men are dangerous, and he has no use for us now. But I did what I had to do, for you and for the brand." Today's events proved to Zion that he had made the right choice in forcing Alacron to accompany them. Had he himself been forced to drive the team, or Josefina for that matter, the race through the defile might have ended in disaster. Alacron had more than proved his worth. The former slave scratched his stubbled cheek and wondered what nightmares plagued his captive compadre. "He must wake himself," Zion thoughtfully observed. "Only then will he be healed."

A black raven spread its wings, took to flight and blotted out the sun, then the wings closed around the man. But the eye of the raven began to glow and pulse with fire and became the sun, molten and burning amber, impossible to watch. Ben was not afraid. But he averted his eyes until he felt the talons on his shoulder, digging into his flesh. He turned and looked into the eyes of the raven and he said, "I am lost . . . lost. . . ."

"I hear you," the raven said. "Poor child. Poor child. My poor child." Ben tried to catch the raven, but when he looked, he found himself alone with nothing but a whisper on the wind for company.

Laughter. Who? Ben searched the plain he was standing on, but the rain obscured his vision and he could only make out two dim silhouettes. Who was watching him?

"Better beware, younker." A voice behind him! Ben turned and saw a grizzled long-armed man with stringy silver-streaked hair. He looked tough as braided leather. He'd been scalped at one time but he wore his lifted hair as a topknot that dangled down the side of his head. The man was dressed in greasy buckskins, and his features were protected from the downpour by a battered sombrero. He smiled, revealing yellowed tobacco-stained teeth. Ben started forward then halted in his tracks and gasped in horror. The man had a rattlesnake protruding from his left eye socket. The snake hissed and its tongue darted out between its fangs. The creature struck the air over and over, as if the rain was the enemy.

More laughter. Ben recoiled from the snake-eyed man and turned to face his tormentors. A patch of darkness in the rain became a man . . . no, two men. The laughter ceased and the silence was worse than what had preceded it. Ben cautiously approached. He called out for the men to identify themselves, but all he heard was the lonely echo of his own voice, hurled across the vastness of the empty plain. He stopped as the two men started forward, walking abreast of one another, slowly emerging out of the rain, drawing closer, ominously closer.

One of the men had a scar running the length of his nose. He was of average height, with stringy blond hair, square-faced, and with a mouth like a gun slit. His companion stood as tall as Ben but carried an extra thirty pounds on his hips and paunch. He was bearded and butt-ugly, with slick brown hair plastered close to his round skull. Whatever intelligence was lacking in his close-set eyes was made up for by the sheer brute instincts Ben somehow knew the man possessed.

Ben warned the pair to stop, but his tone lacked conviction. Their hands dropped to the Colts each man carried. Ben clawed at his own empty holster. He was unarmed and powerless to stop his own execution. The guns came up, the men grinned, the pistols spewed tongues of orange flame and roared like cannons . . .

Bolting awake, Ben sat upright and gasped as the thunder reverberated in the cave. He glanced around, wild-eyed, slow to get his bearings. Isabella, seated at the back of the cave, peered past Zion, who appeared to be asleep.

"Don't worry, Senor Alacron, it was just a dream. Now you are awake and it's over. You're safe. It was just a dream." Isabella settled down in her blankets and flashed him a smile.

Ben dropped his gaze to his imprisoned wrists. The faces, the vision, what was the meaning of it all? Somewhere, hidden in the nightmare, was the key to his identity. He had to find it. Ben settled back on his bedroll, and extending his arms before him, stared at the links of chain. Plunged deeper into Mexico against his will, a prisoner in a land at war, without an inkling of who he was, he knew nothing. No, that was no longer true. The nightmare had given him a piece of the puzzle. At least two men wanted him dead.

"It's just a dream," Isabella said. "You're safe."

And the man without a memory softly repeated the girl's words of comfort, his whisper thick with irony. "Safe."

Chapter Six

General Valentin Najera found Saltillo much the same as when he left it. The neat cluster of white-washed adobe houses, shops, hotels, and cantinas seemed radiant in the sunlight, and he could almost taste the baked chicken and black bean sauce that was the specialty of Casa del Noche, the hotel the general used as his headquarters. The general enjoyed town life, the proximity of friends and the frequent social gatherings, and spent as little time on his ranch as possible.

Saltillo had no fortress, but the cluster of buildings around Market Square allowed him to station over a hundred men in the center of town alone. The remainder of his force, another couple of hundred lancers, were quartered throughout the city, and if need be were only twenty minutes from the hotel. The bulk of his command, almost eight hundred soldiers consisting primarily of infantry, were encamped in the hills outside of town. A brisk march of thirty minutes could bring them into the city.

General Najera had not needed a thousand men for this latest victory. Riding at the head of a column of fifty handpicked lancers, each man a veteran of campaigns against the Apaches and the banditos who plagued the roads to the south, Valentin Najera had trapped and destroyed a matching force of United States Dragoons and Texas Rangers scouting the road to Linares, north of Monterrey.

The general's lancers had suffered only two casualties, while the gringo soldiers had died to a man, leaving Najera to confiscate the U.S. Army–issue weapons and the horses. Najera had even taken a few grisly trophies to commemorate his victory and instill fear in the hearts of the norteamericanos.

The general was by nature a showman, and had sent riders ahead to announce his latest triumph. When he entered Saltillo, the populace turned out to greet him like the conquering Caesar he envisioned himself to be. Indeed, Valentin Najera looked the part. He was a diminutive man, blessed with a booming voice and an aura of command that instilled in his devoted lancers a determination to follow wherever he might lead. Najera was handsome, with a Roman nose, coppery flesh, and jutting jaw. He wore his silver hair brushed forward to mask a receding hairline. He was elegantly attired in black cloth coat and trousers. The coat was embroidered with scarlet and gold thread at the wrists and at the wide lapels that covered his chest. He wore a lancer's metal helmet topped by a brass mortarboard and scarlet plume. At forty-three, Valentin Najera was a vain and forceful individual who recognized that his time was running out and he must seize the day and make his move to garner greatness. Although the don of an estate second only to Ventana, Najera had squandered much of his family fortune outfitting his army. A politically ambitious man, the general had cast his lot with Santa Anna, seeing in the contro- versial ruler of Mexico, the self-styled Napoleon of the West, an opportunity for personal gain. Power was the prize Najera sought, and he would settle for nothing less than the governorship of Coahuila once the invaders from the north were expelled from Mexican territory and driven back beyond the Nueces Strip.

The citizens of Saltillo lined the tree-shaded streets and hailed the conquering hero. The peasants and townspeople waved hats and scarves, and a sweet-faced little girl bounded barefoot across the street to present the general with a bouquet of wildflowers, which Najera accepted with the appropriate show of humility and surprise. No one was fooled, but the citizens of Saltillo appreciated the performance. As for the girl, General Najera seemed to notice a vague similarity between the child and himself, and wondered if he might not be the little one's father. It was a distinct possibility. After all, he had bedded most of the available young women in the town.

The church bells in the tower of Santa Maria Magdalene began to peal at the edge of town, signaling the general's arrival. Najera was not moved. He knew Father Rudolfo was welcoming home the soldiers from Saltillo. There was no love lost between the general and the padre, who despised Najera's penchant for cruelty and lust for power. However, the two men had arrived at an uneasy truce. The padre emerged from the church and, despite his immense girth, moved quickly across the courtyard to stand at the aqueduct wall that carried water from the creek to a circular stone cistern in the courtyard. Father Rudolfo took note of each of the returning riders. General Najera had conscripted just about every available man in Saltillo as well as from the outlying farms and ranchos to serve in his militia. The padre knew every man who had ridden out more than a week ago, and as the column filed past, he counted two empty saddles, but the dead men were some of Najera's handpicked ruffians, and though he deplored any death, Father Rudolfo was grateful that those who had gone to meet their maker were none of his own. As the last of the riders trotted past, the padre mopped the sweat from his bald head and returned to the church, where he intended to light a candle and offer prayers for the living and the dead.

General Najera continued another three blocks and arrived in Market Square, the *mercado,* and headed straight for a two-story adobe structure whose six-inch-thick walls and roof battlements befitted a small fortress. The hand-lettered wooden sign swinging in the breeze in the cooling shade of the porch read CASA DEL NOCHE, and the general sighed and muttered, "Home."

Najera dismounted as the dust of his arrival began to settle. He waved to his men to scatter throughout the *mercado*, where a number of low-roofed, mud-bricked cantinas and brothels offered the promise of a warm fire, a hot meal, and the possibility of a woman's companionship at least for a few brief, heated moments. About half of the riders had families in town, and these men hurried off to be reunited with their loved ones. For them the war was a brutal disruption of their lives, and they were anxious for the hostilities to end as quickly as possible, hopefully with the Mexican Army victorious over the invading forces from north of the border.

Raul Salcedo emerged from the cantina that adjoined the foyer of the hotel, and with a sweep of his sombrero, bowed to the general. "Welcome, *Jefe.* I preceded you by a day."

Valentin Najera clasped the young man's hand

and clapped him on the shoulder. "I trust your undertaking had a successful conclusion."

"Partly, mi general," Raul admitted.

Najera frowned. The gunman's reply smacked of failure. Still, he was willing to give Salcedo the benefit of the doubt. "We will talk later, eh," the general said, and hurried inside, anxious for brandy, a bath, and a shave.

A pair of vaqueros rode up, dismounted in front of the hotel and called out to Salcedo, who recognized Angel Perez and Mariano Rincon, the only men the young gunman considered his friends. Raul, Mariano the mestizo, and Angel had ridden the outlaw trail together before joining Najera's legion. Mariano Rincon, in his mid-twenties, was a potbellied, balding half-breed, dark-skinned and stubbornly devoted to Salcedo. Angel Perez was only a year older than Raul, a lean and hungry young man. His black hair was plastered with sweat, and a scraggly fringe of new beard sprouted along his jawline. Both men wore broadcloth trousers tucked into dust-caked brown boots and homespun cotton shirts. Rincon sported a silver-trimmed leather vest. Angel favored a serape that the proprietress of the Casa del Noche had made for him. Serena Montenez was old enough to be Angel's mother. A comely woman in her early forties, she had never married and for now was enjoying the lusty infatuations of her latest paramour.

"What do you think, Raul?" Angel grinned and ran his fingers over his new growth of beard, relishing the fact that Salcedo's attempts were poor in comparison.

"You call that a beard?" Raul sneered. "I got prettier hair growing in the crack of my ass."

"I told him he better watch himself," Rincon interjected with a wink in Raul's direction. "That stubble is apt to make him look too old for the likes of Senora Montenez." Salcedo and Rincon chuckled as Angel scowled at them both.

"Laugh while you can, amigos, but tonight when the desert chill settles on your bones and you huddle close to your fires, think of me, warm between my senora's thighs, eh?" Angel hitched his gun belt and tilted his sombrero back off his coppery forehead. He tugged a pouch from his belt and removed a cigarillo, black and dry and knobby as a twig, but he rummaged in vain for a match.

"Here, Mex," a gravely voice called out as another pair of riders dismounted in front of the hotel. Unlike the other men who had ridden in with General Najera, these two were norteamericanos, men who had chosen to ride for Najera and the money he paid. The man who had just offered the match was a hard-looking pistoleer of average height, with shoulder-length blond hair. His nose had been split by a Mexican bayonet during the battle of San Jacinto back in '36, and bore a white ridge of scar tissue from where his wire-rimmed spectacles rested to the tip between his nostrils. His name was Ned Tolliver, and when he held out a packet of matches, his eyes, behind his round lenses, locked with Raul Salcedo's steely stare. It was plain that neither man had any use for the other. Angel sensed the animosity and tried to defuse the situation. After all, the majority of Najera's personal guard were aware that if it had not been for Tolliver, the Mexican casualties would probably have been much higher.

Angel ignored Raul's look of displeasure, accepted the matches, and then enjoyed a smoke. "Ah, you should have seen it, Raul. Senor Tolliver led the americanos and their Ranger escort right into our trap. We waited until they were under our guns, and

then"—he clapped his hands together for effect—
"we let them have it!" He shook his head, and his
face all but beamed when he spoke of the slaughter.
"We cut them down. Within minutes it was finished
and they were all dead. No prisoners." He glanced at
Mariano Rincon for substantiation. The mestizo
shrugged and glanced at Salcedo.

"We killed them all," he concurred.

Tolliver's partner, Lucker Dobbs, looped the
reins of his mount over the rail. Dobbs, at forty-one,
was a steady hand in a fight. He'd spent a lifetime
hitting and getting hit. It showed in his battered, ugly
features and in his sloped shoulders and shuffling
gait, which made his six-foot frame appear smaller.
Lucker had a fondness for whiskey and women and
other men's gold. A seasoned Indian fighter, he had
chased Comanches from the Big Bend to the Staked
Plains and was wholly fearless. He was older than
Tolliver by more than a decade, but frequently followed Tolliver's lead. Both men had joined the
Rangers less than a year ago, and in that time had
come within a hair's breadth of being expelled for
their lack of basic virtues—honesty, integrity, and
devotion to duty. However, the war had a use for
such men of violence, and when the Rangers headed
south with General Zachary Taylor's army, Lucker
Dobbs and Ned Tolliver tagged along.

Dobbs's cheek was usually swollen by a plug of
tobacco that he continually chewed, and he often
punctuated his brief remarks by spewing a brown
stream of tobacco juice into the nearest spittoon
whenever one was handy. The ground, the base of a
hitching post, or the nearest anthill also served as
targets for his foul habit from time to time. The big
man's beard was stained dark from his spittle.

Dobbs dismounted and sauntered up to stand
alongside Ned Tolliver. Each of the two gringos was

armed with a pair of Patterson Colts, and each had a
bowie knife tucked in a belly sheath at his midsec-
tion. Thanks to their perfidy, General Najera and
several of his men were similarly armed, though they
had acquired their weapons from the bodies of the
deserters' slain comrades.

"Well, it looks like this here place is home,"
Dobbs said, eyeing the word "cantina" at the corner
of the building. He appeared unaware of Salcedo's
distrust and immune to the young gunman's dislike.
Lucker Dobbs was thirsty, and that occupied his
attention.

"It's where the money is," Tolliver added, noting
that Najera had disappeared within the doors of the
hotel. He gestured to a tousle-haired boy standing off
to the side, a dark-featured youth not yet in his teens.
"Take these two horses to the stables, boy. See
they're watered, fed, and brushed down." He
thumbed a silver coin toward the boy, who caught
the money in mid-flight and hurried to take the reins
of the two horses.

"Come, senors, I will buy the first drink in honor
of our friendship," Angel said, and led the way into
the Casa del Noche.

Raul shook his head in disgust as the trio disappeared into the hotel's cool interior. Mariano Rincon
scratched his belly and then patted the walnut grip
of the Colt he had taken off a Ranger's corpse. He was
delighted with the weapon and wore it tucked in his
belt in cross-draw fashion, butt forward on his left
thigh.

"You worry too much, amigo. The gringos will
be gone before long. General Najera hopes to build a
troop of norteamericanos with Senor Tolliver as their
captain and then use them against their former
compadres. The gringos will lose heart when they
find themselves confronted by other gringos, eh?

Maybe General Taylor's whole army will decide to join us when they see how well Senor Tolliver has been treated." The mestizo mopped the sweat from his high forehead with a bandanna. In the glare of the afternoon sun, his features reflected the Aztec heritage that was the legacy of his forebears.

Raul Salcedo glared at his friend, making no effort to hide the fact he was mightily unhappy, but he kept his objections to himself, saving them for Valentin Najera and the confrontation to come.

The first bath was the best, after a week spent along the dusty border trails. Najera motioned for the fifteen-year-old girl attending his needs to bring another kettle of hot water from the kitchen at the rear of the hotel. Marita Two Ponies was a dark-skinned lass, slim-hipped and buxom, with a coquettish way about her. She had the eyes of a woman twice her age. A prostitute since the age of twelve, Marita had run away from Father Rudolfo's mission and been seduced by the amount of money to be made plying her considerable charms in Saltillo's cantinas. She had been wise enough to pick and choose her paramours, and had at last attracted the attention of none other than General Najera. Now she was his consort, and he insisted she share a blanket with no one else. It was common knowledge that Najera could be as jealous as he was cruel. Marita was only to happy to oblige the general, though a man like Raul was more to her liking. She had even deluded herself into thinking one day the general would take her to wife.

The girl leaned down over the tub and kissed Najera, who laughed and bit her neck and reached beneath the bodice of her peasant blouse to cup a brown breast. He blew on her neck and chuckled, then sent Marita on her way with a pat on the derriere. He watched her leave before he turned to Raul, slouched against the wall. The gunman was staring at the prostitute. For a fleeting second Najera thought he saw something more than indifference as the gunman and prostitute exchanged glances.

"She's got an ass like a boy's. Flat. That's my only complaint." Najera sighed. He dismissed his suspicions. Raul would never be such a fool. Using a porcelain bowl, he poured water over his head to wash the soap away and settled back in the tub. Smoke curled from the tip of his cigarillo. He reached for a glass of brandy on a nearby table, inhaled the bouquet and took a sip. He sighed and smiled, then his gaze rested on Raul, who shifted uncomfortably beneath the general's scrutiny.

Salcedo had recounted the entire episode from the time he climbed into the freight wagon and ran down Don Sebastien in the streets of Linares, to his final failure, when Senora Quintero escaped his trap for the second time, thanks to the interference of the stranger. Raul explained how he had decided to abandon the attempt and wait for another opportunity to present itself after the widow had arrived at Ventana.

"Still . . . one complaint is not all that much," Najera said, still thinking of the girl. The general was in a forgiving mood. After all, he had won a great victory. "She is only a woman. Alone, without her husband to act as her champion, there will be none to speak for her. All of Ventana will be mine."

"It will be as you say, *Jefe*."

"But only with your help, my loyal one." Najera blew a cloud of smoke into the air. "The situation is far from hopeless. Senora Quintero will probably be arriving tomorrow or the next day. Keep watch on the roads. I think we will ride out to Ventana and welcome her home, eh? Send riders to watch for them, and keep me informed."

"I know just the men," Raul replied. Angel was acting far too friendly toward the turncoats, Tolliver and Dobbs. It was time to put a stop to such behavior. The gunman turned to leave, then hesitated. Najera could tell his lieutenant was troubled by something else.

"What is it, mi compadre?" Najera said.

"The gringos who rode in with you. General Najera, such men are without honor. I ask you, can such as these be trusted?"

"Of course not." Najera settled back in the tub and folded his hands behind his head. "But they can be used." He grinned and winked, and Raul suddenly realized that Najera shared his opinion of the turncoats. "I'll pay them their blood money. Let them run our whores and drink in our *pulquerias*. And when the invaders are driven from Mexico . . ." Najera raised a hand as if holding an imaginary pistol. The "gun" recoiled, its implication clear. Raul nodded, satisfied with the general's response. The door to the hotel room opened and Marita reentered, bearing a large kettle of hot water. Steam curled from the curved spout as she pointedly ignored Raul and carried her burden to the high-backed washtub. Najera tucked his knees to his chin while the girl added the hot water to the tub. When she had finished, he straightened, then caught her wrist and pulled the girl into the tub. Marita squealed and pretended to struggle with her suitor, splashing water onto the hardwood floor. Raul departed as the laughter turned to sighs of ecstasy.

The Casa del Noche Cantina was adjacent to the hotel lobby and occupied a corner formed by the junction of Market Square and the Paseo de Caballo, a tree-lined side street at whose end was a series of corrals and pens holding well over two hundred horses, remounts for the dragoons, confiscated from the surrounding rancheros.

The interior of the cantina was brightly lit, thanks to the wall-length windows that opened onto both streets and permitted a cross breeze as well as sunlight to enter the room. Fully a dozen tables, each one circled by three or four chairs, were provided for the customers. A bar ran the length of one of the walls, and men were crowded before the row of glasses and dark brown bottles of whiskey, tequila, and other spirits concocted by Senora Montenez, the proprietress of the hotel and cantina.

She could be seen hurrying among the tables, dispatching her young serving girls from customer to customer with all the finesse of a commander in the field. Senora Montenez genuinely enjoyed her work. It gave her pleasure to see a man eat his fill or unwind from a hard ride with a bottle of tequila while one of her girls entertained him, singing soft love songs or dancing to the strains of a flamenco guitar. It was understood that Serena's women were not to be trifled with. She hired them to serve and look pretty and to remind lonely men of loves left behind. If a man wanted more, let him visit one of the brothels, where he might find some *puta* to service his needs.

Raul remembered the last man to try and force himself on one of the senora's "songbirds." He left the cantina minus an ear. Serena Montenez noticed Raul as he descended the back stairs that led from the rear of the upstairs hall. The senora, a buxom black-haired woman whose thick features were hidden beneath a layer of rouge and powder, crossed the room to stand at Raul's side.

"Is the general ready for his dinner?"

"I think he is having dessert first," Raul icily replied. The proprietress had offered Raul her favors just that morning, but he had declined. He wanted nothing to do with this woman. He pictured Najera and Marita in the tub together, locked in one another's embrace, and scowled. Senoritas . . . they lured men into taking unnecessary chances, then demanded too much. Marita was playing with him, flaunting her relationship with Najera to drive him crazy. As for Senora Montenez, if he had taken the senora to bed, sooner or later Angel would have discovered what they had done, and then Raul knew he would have to kill his friend. With but two compadres, Raul Salcedo had no wish to lose one.

"Marita is with him."

Senora Montenez understood. She started to return to work, then paused and glanced over her shoulder. "You should have had me while you had the chance, little one. Now Angel is already waiting for me in my bedroom out back."

"See you please him, senora," Raul said. "And soon. For he will be gone before dark." The gunman flung his black and scarlet serape back across his shoulder. "Tell him to meet me within the hour down by the horses. The general has work for him."

The woman scowled. "That is not enough time for me. I have waited all week. I see your hand in this."

"You would have had more than my hand this morning." Raul chuckled. "And if Angel were to find out, he might mark that homely face of yours. And maybe leave you for a younger, prettier senorita. One who doesn't show how much she has been used."

Senora Montenez's hand shot up to slap his face but Raul's reflexes were quicker and he caught the woman by the wrist and bent her arm back until she winced. Then he motioned for her to attend Angel.

The proprietress met his malevolent gaze and glimpsed enough dark madness in his eyes to chill her to the bone. Though unafraid of most men, the hotel keeper recognized here was someone to give a wide berth. She hurried off and did as she was told. Raul heard laughter and noticed Ned Tolliver and Lucker Dobbs watching him from the bar, leaning back on their elbows. One man held a jug of whiskey, the other a thick, clear tumbler of the same.

"You havin' a lover's spat?" Dobbs said. His grin revealed a row of broken teeth.

Raul moved quietly over to the former Rangers at the bar, but ignoring the bigger man, turned to Ned Tolliver, whose owlish gaze behind his spectacles was unwavering. He was not afraid of any man, especially this Mexican kid with the somber expression.

"Keep a tight rein on your fat friend," Raul said softly. "Before his big mouth talks him into a shallow grave."

"I'd not want to be the man to try and lay him down," Tolliver replied.

Lucker grabbed a tortilla, folded the flattened bread around a helping of refried beans and began to eat. A full mouth didn't stop him from talking, though.

"Lookee here, Ned. Seems this pup is trying to bare his fangs. From where I'm standing, I don't see nothing but a mouth full of milk teeth." His speech was muffled by the food he'd packed into his cheeks. A trickle of brown beans and grease dribbled from the corner of his mouth. Dobbs wiped it away on the sleeve of his buckskin shirt. He looked to be the epitome of an uncouth, slovenly oaf, solid as a brick, with half the brains.

But Ned Tolliver had not sided with the big man for his intelligence. Tolliver recalled Dobbs at the battle at San Jacinto, ten years earlier. The man had been marked by bayonet and gunshot, yet he stood tall amid the carnage of that Texican victory and prowled the battlefield with knife in hand. Then, Lucker Dobbs had been stained crimson to the elbows with the blood of the Mexican soldiers he had slain in battle. No, Tolliver did not envy the chili eater if Dobbs lost his temper.

Raul glared at both of the gringos, then turned away and sauntered through the sunlight and tobacco smoke. Several men called out to him, inviting Najera's lieutenant to join them for a drink, but Raul was anxious to leave the cantina and the gringos behind. He emerged through the bat-wing doors, scattering a trio of children who fled like startled mice. He stood with his hands on his hips and studied the *mercado*. The merchants were arriving at their stalls, lured to the square by the arrival of the soldiers and hoping to hawk their wares for a tidy profit. A man walked past him balancing bolts of cloth on his head. Another man in the wake of the cloth merchant led a burro laden with two large clay cisterns of goat's milk. A woman was rolling out tortillas, slapping them into shape with her hands and baking them on a flat sheet of hammered iron placed over a cook fire. Another woman was stringing chorizo, highly spiced homemade sausages, and dangling them from the pole roof of her stall. She accomplished this task under the watchful scrutiny of a pack of mongrel dogs, a mangy assortment of mixed breeds varying in size but sharing a common ailment—hunger. The senora noticed her unasked-for audience and took up a straw broom to chase them from her stall. The dogs ran off a few paces, then returned to the very same spot. The woman was not about to allow them to remain. She hoisted her skirts and assailed the mongrels yet again. This time she continued her pursuit down a length of stalls and over to the edge of the *mercado*. Suddenly the dogs scattered, and led by a particularly scruffy-looking mixed breed, a cross between a sheepdog and a coyote, charged past the woman and raced pell-mell toward her stall. Realizing she had been duped, the woman howled, swung the broom in an arc above her head and bolted to the rescue. But the pack beat her to the stall, and in a matter of seconds the dogs had dragged off several strings of sausages and escaped down the nearest side street, leaving the senora to shake her fists in the air.

Raul chuckled. Mariano Rincon appeared at his side. A trace of liquor was on his breath but his hands were steady. He held a cup of pulque, fished a fly from the surface of the milky liquid and tossed it out into the dusty road. Pulque, fermented juice extracted from the agave cactus, was a strong, bitter drink capable of sneaking up on the unwary and leaving a man to bay in the moonlight with the wolves. Rincon drained the contents of his cup, and motioning for a boy to approach, instructed the youth to return the cup to the bar inside. A few centavos was more than enough compensation for the orphan to oblige the mestizo. Rincon fished a couple of peyote buttons from his pocket and held one out to Raul. The gunman declined.

"We will not be staying the night in Saltillo," Raul said. Mariano Rincon shrugged and shoved the nut-brown roots back in his coat for another day.

"Where are we going?" the mestizo asked. "Will we need fresh horses?"

"Three horses. Angel will join us as soon as he can escape Senora Montenez."

Rincon chuckled and remained at his friend's side. The two men watched as seven of Najera's lancers unloaded as many jars from a string of pack mules they had procured from a farm north of Monterrey. Raul immediately guessed the contents of the jars when he noticed how the pack train had been slowed by the curious inhabitants of Saltillo, who had crowded around to peer beneath the jar lids at General Najera's grisly trophies, preserved in oil.

There had been seven of the hated Texas Rangers leading the column of gringo soldiers, Rincon explained. Najera, to show his contempt for them and to put fear in the hearts of those who might come after, had cut off the heads of the Rangers and placed them in the jars. Fourteen months ago, Najera had given the same treatment to a party of cattle thieves he had caught in the act. The general's stock had not suffered a theft since.

The dragoons had made the rounds of the cantinas and brothels surrounding the *mercado*, displaying the general's "spoils of war." Arriving back at the Casa del Noche, Najera's men prepared to place the jars alongside their counterparts in a niche in a courtyard wall fronting Market Square. Counting the cattle thieves, there were eleven jars now. The general's collection was mounting. Raul had to admire Najera's audacity. Mutilating the corpses of the Texas Rangers was an act akin to hurling a gauntlet in the faces of these border riders who had proved such a nemesis to the Mexican populace. By his actions, Valentin Najera showed he was unafraid. He was even daring the Rangers to come and avenge themselves. Indeed, Valentin Najera looked forward to such a visit. After all, jars were plentiful in Saltillo, and the courtyard of the Casa del Noche had space to spare.

Chapter Seven

Ventana, true to its name, was a window onto the stark, vast beauty of the Sierra Oriental, the east arm of the Sierra Madre, eight hundred miles of wooded ridges and wind-scoured peaks running from northwest to southeast. The hacienda was a single-storied adobe structure whose roof was topped by a wall tall enough for several men to hide behind and, if need be, fire down at any attackers. The main house, the barn and corral, the stone bunkhouse, and the low wall that formed a square around the site, dominated the center of a gap in a grass-covered ridge that rose like a barrier four hundred feet from the valley floor. Here was the only approach to the Orientals for many miles. Don Sebastien's land grant encompassed the entire valley, spanning the gap and reaching all the way to the cordilleras, more than thirty miles away. Quintero's cattle, bearing a double slash Q brand, should have been grazing the wild grasses that carpeted the meadow.

Several miles to the north the desert took hold and the landscape became stark and ancient-looking, home to the spirits of the Old Ones, whose passing had preceded the coming of Cortez and the conquest of the Aztecs, and foretold the demise of the mountain tribes and the death of their culture.

Here in Quintero's valley, bright yellow trumpet flowers heralded the advent of summer, and warm breezes wafted through the chino grama grass, stirring swarms of bees and dragonflies and lifting hawks to lofty heights. But the ranch that should have been bustling with activity sat strangely silent. The mid-afternoon heat of July and August was weeks away. It was not hot enough to warrant taking a siesta, yet the bunkhouse, barn, and hacienda appeared abandoned. Where were the vaqueros, where were the housekeeper and her husband?

Zion muttered his concerns to the disguised man sitting beside him on the wagon seat as they halted the wagon before the thick heavy-looking front doors of the hacienda. Even more puzzling, there was no sign of any trouble.

"What are you waiting for?" Isabella asked. "I'm tired of this wagon." She climbed over the side and hopped down onto the hard-packed drive that circled in front of the hacienda. Zion started to caution her, but when Josefina joined her adventurous daughter, he realized there was no holding them back. The women were home. They felt safe here. The fact that the ranch appeared deserted did not seem to faze them in the slightest.

"We'll bury my husband in the family plot after we've all refreshed ourselves with a cool drink." She wasn't wasting any time. And judging from the heat and the condition of the casket, that was all to the good. They'd plugged the bullet holes as best they could, but despite their efforts, Don Sebastien's earthly remains had begun to smell a little ripe.

Ben didn't care if the place was a ghost town. All

that mattered to him was that they had safely reached their destination. Zion no longer needed his skills. The women were home, and the sooner Ben could quit their company, the better. As for the coffin, let the dead bury the dead. A scruffy-looking herd dog poked its head around the corner of a hog pen, and recognizing the new arrivals, darted past a chicken coop, took a shortcut through the empty corral, and came loping toward Isabella, who greeted the excitable animal with open arms.

"Nino!" she called out, and the dog placed its front paws on the girl's shoulders and proceeded to lick her face while she laughed. The front door of the hacienda opened and an unusual couple in their mid-fifties emerged from the cool interior of the house and stepped into the sunlight. Elena Gallegos was the housekeeper, a tall rail-thin woman. Her long hair hung in two thick braids in the fashion of the Comanche women she had lived with during an eleven-year captivity that had robbed her of her childhood. Her plain features, burned brown from the sun, brightened with a smile as she recognized the wagon.

"My little ones . . . my poor little ones," she exclaimed, and left the shade of the porch to gather Josefina and Isabella in her embrace.

Pedro Gallegos, Elena's husband, held back at first sight of the coffin in the wagon and the stranger in chains clambering down to stand alongside Zion in the yard. He was carrying a shotgun. His sombrero was tilted back to reveal a shock of steel-gray hair. Shorter than his wife by six or seven inches, Pedro looked to have been a feisty ranchero in his youth, and still pulled his own weight about Ventana, despite an injury that had left him with a permanent limp and too stove-up to earn his wages astride a horse.

"Looks like we made it," Ben said. He held up his manacled wrists, but Zion, preoccupied as to the whereabouts of the other ranch hands, ambled across the yard to join Pedro in the shade of the tile roof that shaded the front windows of the hacienda. The flooring beneath the overhang was a layer of crushed stone that crunched beneath Zion's boots as he approached the man with the shotgun. "Hey!" Ben called out, to no avail. He turned and found the three women staring at him. Elena appraised him with measured concern.

"And who is this?" the housekeeper said.

"A friend who helped us," Josefina replied.

"His name is Alacron. That's the name we gave him," Isabella interjected. She shook her head and sighed. "He doesn't know his real name."

"Ma'am," Ben said, reaching up to touch the brim of his sombrero as he faced the housekeeper. The chain fastened to the black iron links about his wrists rattled as he raised his hands. Elena's eyebrows arched, her gaze fixed on the manacles.

"A friend?" she asked incredulously. Then the housekeeper's expression changed and she moved past Ben to stand alongside the wagon. Oddly enough, Elena did not seem surprised by the presence of the coffin and what it implied. "Then it is true," she said. The housekeeper reached out and gripped the iron wheel rim for support. When she turned to face the newly widowed mistress of Ventana, her eyes were moist with tears.

"You knew? How?" Josefina asked.

"Father Rudolfo came to dinner two days ago and told us the terrible news. The cousin of Juan Medrano, the blacksmith, came through Saltillo on his way. He came from Linares and brought word of the accident. Juan told the padre and the padre told us." The housekeeper blessed herself with the sign of the cross.

"I prayed to Our Lady that the good padre was mistaken. Yet I knew in my heart he spoke the truth."

Zion, after a brief interchange with Pedro, stalked away from the hacienda and headed for the barn. Ben rounded the wagon and tried to head him off. His long-legged stride quickly brought him abreast of the black man.

"You forgetting something?" Ben asked.

"I'm not forgetting anything," Zion growled. "You can bet on it!" His eyes blazed with anger. He reached the side of the barn where someone had leaned a pair of shovels, a spade, and a pickax against the weathered wall. "C'mon." He tossed a shovel to Ben and selected one for himself.

"Not till you take this iron off," Ben snapped. "Get your vaqueros to dig the grave."

"Not a man on the place," Zion said. "General Najera's taken every rider for his army. Left a bunch of worthless damn vouchers for over a hundred head of cattle, too. And said he'd be back for more." Zion retraced his steps to the wagon. "You'll help me with the burying or by heaven I'll toss the keys to those shackles down the well." The segundo spoke without slowing his stride. He was furious at this turn of events. Ben supposed he couldn't blame the man. After all, from what McQueen had seen of Ventana and heard Zion tell, a twenty-man crew would have their hands full running the spread. A man alone was in a bad way.

But Ben reckoned it was none of his concern. All that mattered now was Don Sebastien's grave. Then the man called Alacron would be on his way, to his own journey's end.

They buried Don Sebastien beneath a purple sky. While the sun teetered on the crest of the Sierra

Oriental, faint wisps of clouds fine as angel breath gleamed an incandescent gold. Soon would come the bats to dive and dart and sweep through the fading light, feasting on insects and nightcrawlers. But for now, the mourners at the gravesite had Ventana to themselves.

Josefina read from Psalms over an ever-increasing mound of fresh earth. Ben and Zion shoveled the last of the soil into place, closing the final chapter in the life of Don Sebastien Quintero.

"The Lord is gracious and merciful, slow to anger and abounding in steadfast love. The Lord is good to all and His compassion is over all that He has made." Josefina spoke the words with care. The newly widowed woman struggled with "gracious and merciful" as if she doubted the veracity of her own words. She faltered for a moment, then regained her composure and finished the psalm. Then she closed the worn leatherbound Bible that had been her mother's and looked around at the people at the gravesite.

Elena and Pedro were standing alongside one another, their elbows touching as if connecting for support. Worry lines creased their features, their spirits numbed by grief and uncertainty. What would happen to them now? The ranch was stripped of its vaqueros and the haciendado who had ruled their lives with a just and firm hand. What did the new senora know about running the ranch? With the current state of war, she might just sell Ventana and return to the Estados Unidos, leaving the loyal housekeeper and her husband to fend for themselves. These were bad days to be without some means of support. Ventana had been their lives for more than three decades. It was difficult to even consider being anyplace else.

Zion leaned on his shovel, his coarse cotton

shirt matted to his compact, well-muscled physique. In the fading light he looked to be made of iron. Ben McQueen waited in respectful silence. Nearly a foot taller than the black man, with eyes that flashed with green fire, Ben intended to allow these people their time of grief. He hadn't known Quintero, but there was something to be said for a man who could inspire devotion like Zion had exhibited. Still, Ben's patience was at an end. The chains were coming off now or blood would flow.

Isabella was absent from the gravesite. The ten-year-old had not attended her father's burial. She had flatly refused, and nothing Josefina could do or say had changed her mind. Even Elena had tried to win the girl over, but she had resisted the kindly house-keeper's best efforts. At last Josefina had recognized an impossible situation and abandoned her attempts to change Isabella's mind. She allowed the girl to choose for herself just when and how she would bid her father farewell.

The widow brushed a strand of hair fine as corn silk away from her features and glanced around at the others who had gathered to pay their last respects. She thanked them all. It did not faze her in the least that one of the four, the man called Alacron, had certainly not attended of his own free will. She took no notice of his chains.

The Quintero family plot was located southwest of the hacienda, just within the low wall that encompassed the ranchyard. A lone oak tree offered its shade to those good Christian souls awaiting resurrection beneath the sod of Old Mexico. Josefina turned away from the gravesite and started across the empty yard. The others fell in step.

"Pedro, fetch a ham from the smokehouse," Elena said, and the vaquero nodded and limped off toward the barn. The smokehouse was located on the north side of the barn, the chicken coop and hog pens on the other. Ben figured that way the hogs wouldn't have to look upon their eventual fate, all day, every day, till the butcher came. "We've bread and wine left over from yesterday's meal. I should have had something better ready. . . ."

"Nonsense, Elena, that will be fine," Josefina replied. She looked over her shoulder at the two men behind her. "Please join us, Zion. You too, Senor Alacron."

"We'd be happy to, ma'am," Zion said.

"We have some unfinished business, segundo," Ben said, catching the smaller man by the arm.

"I reckon we do, amigo." Zion nodded and motioned toward the wagon. "The key's in my saddlebag."

The two men walked side by side toward the wagon and the pair of horses they had tethered just beyond the stone wall that bordered the burial ground. The women left them and continued on to the hacienda while Ben waited for Zion to climb aboard the wagon and return with his saddlebags. A moment later he had the key in hand.

"I'm sorry I had to do this. But the woman and the girl were my responsibility. I had to see them safely home. You understand?"

"Sure, I would've probably done the same thing if I had been in your boots." Ben held out his wrists.

"Glad you see it my way." Zion worked the key in the iron lock and twisted. For a moment the catch refused to turn and Ben experienced a momentary panic. Then suddenly it clicked, the iron wrist cuffs opened and the chains fell away. Ben sighed and rubbed his wrists where the shackles had irritated the flesh.

"No hard feelings," Zion said, offering his hand in friendship.

"None," said Ben. "Well, maybe just a few . . ." His fist shot out in a vicious uppercut that caught the segundo beneath the chin and snapped his head back. The force of the blow lifted Zion a foot off the ground and deposited him on his back in the dirt alongside the stone fence. Ben leaned down and retrieved his Patterson Colt from the prone man's belt.

Zion groaned and lay there, staring silently at the deepening dusk. He eventually sat upright and waited for his vision to clear and his eyes to focus. Then he sat there rubbing his jaw. He leaned forward and spat blood. "Sonuvabitch! I think I bit half my cheek off." He looked up at the man he had aptly named Alacron. Zion had seen a blur of motion, and the next thing he knew, the fist had connected with his jaw. "You feel better?" he dourly inquired.

"Much better," Ben said, satisfied. He held out his hand. Zion caught hold and Ben hauled him to his feet.

"Then I reckon that evens things between us. We better wash up for supper," Zion said. "We best be on time for eats. Senora Gallegos expects folks to show up when she sets out the food."

Zion steadied himself, then, taking his hammerhead gray by the reins, walked the wagon team back toward the barn. The horses would need a quick rubdown and fresh hay before anyone else sat down to dinner. Ben agreed to help. Ambling along in step with the segundo, Ben could not help but notice how empty the corral seemed, and made his observation known to Zion, who had promised him a horse and supplies enough to reach the Rio Grande.

"You can thank General Valentin Najera for this," Zion said as they unhitched the horses and led them into the shade of the barn. He lit a lantern and hung it from the nearest beam. The interior of the barn was partitioned into twenty stalls, ten to a side and all of them empty.

"Don Sebastien kept his breed stock in here. The corral held a string of thirty-five more, all of them prime."

"He stole them?"

"Requisitioned." Zion's tone was full of irony. "There's a war on and Najera's a damn general. Personally, I think the best mounts will wind up on his ranch to the south of here, closer to Saltillo." Zion spat another stream of blood. It wasn't as coarse red as before, but his jaw still hurt. He took some small satisfaction in the bruised condition of Ben's knuckles.

Ben tended to the bay mare, leaving Zion to curry and feed the bad-tempered gray gelding. The bay was bred for hauling. It was thick and sturdy but hardly the mount for the back country Ben would have to travel to avoid the Mexican patrols. The gray was obviously a one-man horse and no doubt would fight Ben every step of the way to the border.

"Looks like I've got a long walk home," Ben predicted ruefully.

Zion shook his head and began tossing hay into both stalls with a pitchfork. "Ventana is as good as anyplace else if you ask me. Maybe even better. It's all the home I've ever needed. You might wind up feeling the same way if you gave it half a chance."

Zion had argued his case before. But Ben wasn't buying any of his arguments. He was convinced the answers to the question mark that was his life lay to the northeast.

"I'm no vaquero," he said.

"How do you know?" Zion reached out and turned Ben's hands palm upward. His skin was callused and rough, and in places streaked with scar tissue, the legacy of a rope burn. "You've worked cattle, horses too, I'll warrant."

"Maybe so," Ben said. "But I didn't work them here."

"Hell, I give up," Zion said in mock disgust.

"It's about time." Ben grinned. "And don't try the trick with the shackles again. Tonight I aim to sleep light." He patted the Colt.

"You win, Senor Alacron," Zion said. "We'll ride into Saltillo tomorrow." Ben visibly stiffened. The segundo chuckled. "Don't worry. You can pass for a Mex. Just keep your sombrero pulled low, eh?"

"Why the blazes Saltillo?" Ben asked, his eyes narrowing as he searched the black man's expression for a glimmer of duplicity. Zion appeared to be totally forthright.

"Juan Medrano owes me many favors. If there are any decent saddle horses left in Saltillo, the blacksmith will know about them."

"I have no money."

"I don't think that will be a problem," Zion said. "Don Sebastien had a saddle with a silver pommel. Juan Medrano's always wanted to own it. Tomorrow I'll give him his chance. But it will cost him. Come." Zion headed up the center aisle of the stall. "If we're late, Elena will be angry."

"Go on. I'll be along."

Zion gave him a quizzical look but continued out through the double doors. A fading wash of amber, lavender, and cobalt-blue painted the western horizon where the sun had vanished beyond the cordillera to a chorus of coyotes howling in the distance. The ranchyard was eerily quiet. The segundo was deeply troubled by Najera's latest actions. By requisitioning the horses and pressing Ventana's vaqueros into service, the general had dealt the ranch a death blow. Cold fury welled in the former slave. Don Sebastien's family deserved better. Zion had never trusted Najera, despite the fact that Don Sebastien and Josefina considered the man a friend. The segundo had seen past Najera's platitudes. As in a deck of cards, Najera, like the one-eyed jack, had always kept one side of his face hidden. Until now.

Ben McQueen chose the nearest ladder and climbed up into the hayloft. Half an hour ago, while coming across the ranchyard from the Quintero family plot, he had glimpsed movement in the shadowy reaches of the loft and thought he knew who had been watching as the coffin was lowered, the words read, and the grave covered over. He squeezed his broad shoulders through the hole in the floor and stood silent and watchful as his vision adjusted to the glow of the lanterns that filtered up from below. Isabella Quintero, dressed in a plain cotton dress with a cream-colored shawl wrapped about her shoulders, sat near the loft window at the rear of the barn, from where she was watching the sunset. Her knees were drawn up to her chin, her arms folded before her. She studied Ben as he approached and squatted down on a sack of grain a respectful distance away.

"What do you want?"

Ben realized he had no answer. Yet he was filled with tenderness for the girl, parental feelings that left him puzzled, and he wondered if they could tell him something about his own past. He smiled at the girl, his eyes full of compassion, but the shadows hid most of his face.

"Perhaps I thought you might need someone to talk to."

"Well, I don't," Isabella replied. A shadow stirred at her side, and Ben realized it was the girl's dog, Nino. The animal rose up, walked a tight circle, stretched and then settled alongside its owner once again.

"I understand," Ben said, and prepared to leave. He had just begun to retrace his steps when Isabella spoke, halting him with another question.

"Why did you come up here? I don't even know you. You're a stranger without a name."

"Sometimes strangers are the easiest people to talk to." Ben faced her again. "I understand the hurt you're feeling. I've lost someone too."

"Who?" Isabella shifted uncomfortably. She continued to struggle to hide her emotions.

"Myself. And it makes me feel as if there's a hole, here." He placed his hand over his heart. "And every night feels like I'm carrying the darkness on my back."

The girl sniffed and wiped a forearm across her eyes. Before she could reply, Josefina's voice drifted on the night air, calling her stepdaughter to the dinner table. Isabella craned her head past the edge of the loft window. "I'm coming," she called out. The girl climbed to her feet and dusted the straw from her dress. Her hair fell long and straight and black across her shoulders, in stark contrast to the shawl. "You may escort me to dinner," she said.

Ben marveled at her composure. This was a strong little girl. And yet he felt sad that she dare not allow herself to weep for her father. He bowed, quickly descended the ladder and waited at the bottom for Isabella to join him. A carriage at the rear of the barn allowed Nino to leap from the loft to the carriage top and then to the packed earth floor.

Isabella looked up at Ben. "I hardly knew my mother, and there was always Elena and then Josefina, so I guess I didn't miss her so much. But I will miss papa very much. Do you think he's in heaven?"

"I'm certain of it," Ben replied.

"I think so too. I saw lightning flash in the north. It was very far away, but that was papa. He loved the rain. He's told the angels to make it rain here at Ventana. Just wait and see." Isabella spoke as if she were trying to convince herself. "Do you believe me?"

"Yes." The big man placed a hand on her shoulder. They stood in silence.

"Senor Alacron . . . what you said, about the darkness, it's the same with me. Promise me you won't tell."

Josefina appeared in the doorway, her blond hair pinned back with a mantilla. A silk veil framed her pale, high-boned features. "Oh. You both are here. I was worried, my dear." She raised her arms, and Isabella hurried down the aisle between the stalls and into her stepmother's embrace. She glanced questioningly at Ben.

"Zion said you are leaving us."

Isabella looked back at him. She had forgotten the conversation she had overheard between Zion and the gringo, and had begun to like this norte-americano and think of him as a friend. Surely he wouldn't leave now.

"Yes, ma'am, in the morning."

"Oh . . . I had hoped . . ." Josefina stammered.

Isabella jerked as if stung. A slight gasp escaped her lips. The look of betrayal she cast in Ben's direction nearly wilted his resolve. But parental feelings aside, this was something he had to do.

"I cannot thank you enough for all your help," Josefina said. Ben wanted to grab her by the shoulders and shake her and scream in her pretty face, "Your man chained me! I had no choice!" But what was the point? The experience had cost him a week of his life, precious little for a man whose past was a blank.

"You're welcome," said the man called Alacron.

"Please join us, then. A decent meal is small payment for all your help." With a wave of her hand, Quintero's widow led the way to the hacienda where Elena waited in the dining room by a table she had laden with the bread and *pan dulce*, the smoked ham, the beans and spicy salsa that comprised the funeral meal.

Chapter Eight

Josefina Quintero heard Nino barking and realized the men were leaving for Saltillo. The widow set the bottle of laudanum aside, though its contents had served her well since Don Sebastien's fatal accident. Her husband had used the opiate to deal with a chronic back ailment that had plagued him for the better part of two years. More recently, the bitter-tasting liquid had helped to ease the woman's pain and unbearable sense of loss during the long ride home.

Josefina glanced at the table by the bed where a worn leatherbound volume of Dickens's *Oliver Twist* lay. Don Sebastien's bookmark, a slim, gold-plated tab crafted to resemble a writing quill, had been left undisturbed despite Elena's dusting. She sighed and drew the bookmark from its resting place, the first step along the road to acceptance of her husband's untimely death.

Quintero's widow padded across the bedroom floor, left her quarters and proceeded down the hall to the broad, high-ceilinged living room with its dark, heavy furniture, hand-hewed and -crafted from sweet gum, oak, and even maple wood harvested from the forests to the east, nearer the Gulf. The living room dominated the front of the hacienda's interior. She glanced to her left at the study and felt a catch in her throat. Don Sebastien always went to his study after rising. The room's corner windows allowed him a view of the sunrise, and he liked to sit in his leather-backed chair and watch the dawn. She would never find him there again.

Josefina averted her eyes and continued on to one of the front windows. The shutters were thrown back and sunlight flooded the room. A blur of motion to her right caught her attention, and Isabella, in her cotton sleeping gown, appeared in the doorway leading off to the long rectangular dining room that ran the length of the hacienda's west side.

The girl held a couple of pieces of *pan dulce*, crisp rounds of fried bread coated with a dark caramel-flavored glaze. Caught off guard by Josefina's presence, she started to retreat. Then, as if deciding retreat meant losing face, Isabella left the doorway and continued on into the living room. She and her stepmother were alone in the house. Josefina could hear the housekeeper's voice drifting in from outside, scolding her husband for some infraction. Elena and Pedro lived in quarters that were attached to the outdoor kitchen at the rear of the hacienda, across a breezeway shielded from the elements by a roof of woven vines and branches. Elena's domain was the kitchen, and there her word was law. She reigned with an iron hand. Pedro often suffered the brunt of his wife's temper, especially when she caught him pilfering a scoop of custard or a handful of fried bread, wrapped in cloth and cooling in a wicker basket.

Isabella crossed to the woman who had been her tutor for many years and now was the only parent she had. The girl held out a sweet roll, and Josefina, who had a sweet tooth to rival the ten-year-old's was happy to oblige. Then Isabella returned to the window in time to see Zion and the man called Alacron, astride the gray and the mare respectively, ride out of the ranchyard. Nino, usually much too lazy to pay the coming and going of humans any mind at all, had taken it upon himself to herald the segundo's departure.

"People are always leaving." Isabella sighed. "First Mama, then Papa, now Zion and Alacron."

"Zion will come back. And he will hopefully have some horses for us." Josefina reached out to the girl. "And I won't leave. I have never expected nor wished to take your mother's place, but we have been friends ever since I came here. I hope we can always be friends."

Josefina felt a rush of guilt for the way she had handled her husband's death. While poor Isabella had persevered and hidden her grief behind a mask of stoic resolve, her stepmother had numbed herself with an opiate and transformed the entire journey home into a plodding procession of hours that finally concluded at Ventana. Don Sebastien's burial had been the final act of a tragedy begun in Linares.

The enormity of the task that lay ahead was enough to quash even the bravest spirit. How could she run a ranch the size of Ventana? Even with Zion's expert guidance, they would need vaqueros. One man alone could not possibly hope to gather what cattle General Najera had missed and drive them to market. Summoning her courage, Josefina turned and crossed the room to the doorway of the study. A ledger book lay closed upon Don Sebastien's rolltop desk, a stack of notes and letters stuffed into compartments and drawers. The walls of the room were lined with crowded bookshelves and adorned here and there with artifacts from Quintero's past: Comanche war clubs, a quiver and arrows, a porcupine quill breastplate trimmed with eagle feathers and clay beads; and on the wall just behind the desk, a bull-hide war shield, a prize Don Sebastien had personally taken in battle. In one corner of the room a suit of Spanish armor kept silent vigil. Its iron visage was etched with whorls of detail, swans and griffins upon a backdrop of polished steel. Josefina smiled, recalling how once, years back, just after her arrival at the hacienda, a sound like ghostly rattling and wailing had issued from the armor. She had entered the room to investigate, only to have the "knight" come crashing down at her feet. Isabella had dropped a cat into the armor and hidden herself behind her father's desk to watch the fun. She had howled with laughter as Josefina nearly jumped out of her buttoned boots.

The widow smiled and shook her head. Isabella had certainly tested her in those first few months. Then Josefina steeled herself and turned toward the massive desk. She slowly exhaled with relief, for she had half expected to see some ephemeral image seated at the desk, hard at work, laboring over the ledgers. But no, the chair was empty and waiting for Josefina Quintero to take her place.

Clouds of dust like smoke from a brushfire concealed the southern approach to Saltillo. Zion and Ben skirted a herd of cattle, about five hundred head in all, and rode on into town. With a southerly wind, the dust churned by the herd blanketed a corner of town, forcing the two men to eat grit until a few blocks into Saltillo.

Ben studied the town as he approached and

noted how the cluster of white adobe businesses and haciendas that comprised it was surrounded by a dry, rolling landscape of thorny brush-choked ravines and eroded gullies. The spring that dominated the center of Market Square was the reason for the town's existence. It provided a constant source of sweet, cool water for all the inhabitants. As Saltillo grew, other wells had been sunk to tap into the shallow water table, while Franciscan missionaries had guided Indian laborers into building an elaborate series of aqueducts which made water even more accessible.

Zion guided them through the town, taking care to use the less-traveled streets, choosing alleys when he could. Ben kept his head low, unable to shake the feeling that he was placing himself in the jaws of a trap. They rode past street vendors hawking hastily prepared food, frijoles, tamales wrapped in corn shucks, and links of chorizo. A group of brown-faced children burst from hiding like a covey of quail and raced directly into the street past the two men, who had to struggle to keep their horses from bolting. The gray reared and pawed the air as an eight-year-old boy darted beneath the animal's flashing hooves. Seconds later the children had dashed out of sight, leaving the horsemen shaken, but eager to reach the blacksmith shop of Juan Medrano.

Ten minutes later Ben was relieved to hear the clang of a pounding hammer. The ring of metal on metal, the sound of a bellows pump, and the smell of red-hot iron struck a familiar chord, as if they were all pieces of a puzzle he had yet to put into place. Zion dismounted and tied his horse at the hitching post before Juan Medrano's smithy, on the eastern side of town a few blocks from Market Square. The norteamericano, in disguise, followed suit. Ben recalled an earlier warning from Zion that the *mercado* was frequented by Najera's dragoons and he did not intend to press his luck by going there.

The blacksmith seemed relieved to find an excuse to leave his forge. He left the horseshoe lying on a bed of coals, wiped his hands on a soot-streaked apron, and ambled up the aisle to greet his customers. Juan Medrano was a man of average height, dark brown, with a bushy black moustache concealing his upper lip. Perspiration glistened among the sparse strands of black hair matted to his skull. He was thick-chested and heavyset. His eyes were pouchy from lack of sleep, a common state of affairs in his household, which was located just across the alley behind his shop.

Zion quickly introduced Ben as a newly hired vaquero and explained that Najera had requisitioned all but two of Quintero's horses from the ranch. Juan listened but continued to scrutinize Ben, who shifted uncomfortably beneath the blacksmith's sleepy stare.

"Alacron . . . what sort of name is this for a man?" Medrano gruffly inquired.

"It is name enough for a blacksmith who is too curious for his own good," Ben answered in passable Spanish.

"Bueno," Medrano replied with a chuckle. He was not afraid of this *Senor* Alacron, but the blacksmith had spent his entire life avoiding trouble whenever possible, and he saw no reason to alter his habits at this late date. Suddenly a woman's brassy voice bellowed from the alley behind the shop.

"Juan . . . do not forget to go to the *mercado.* Nita has told me Old Bustamente has slaughtered a pair of goats. Tell him he can repay the money he owes you with one of his plump carcasses. We will have *cabrito* tonight, si?" A buxom *mamacita* filled the doorway at the rear of the smithy. Two little dark-eyed twin girls, toddlers really, clung to their mother's skirts.

"Now?" Juan asked.

"Of course now! Before he sells the goats or Valentin Najera takes them. Go!"

"Maria . . ."

"Vamonos!" She ducked back and herded her unhappy urchins toward the house. The toddlers vociferously protested, loud enough for all the surrounding neighbors to hear. One of the girls had a particularly piercing squall.

"Caramba. The woman gives me five daughters. Five daughters and not one son. Who is she to order me about?" Medrano shook his head in disgust.

"No man in Saltillo has prettier daughters, and you know it, old friend," said Zion with perfect timing. The compliment achieved the desired results. Medrano wiped a forearm across his features and nodded proudly.

"This is true, segundo. Nor louder. And I would not trade a one of them for all Ventana." Medrano untied the apron, pulled it over his head and draped it across the gate of a nearby stall. The horse within, a chestnut gelding, tossed its head and whinnied.

"I had better find Bustamente."

"But first, my friend," Zion said, "tell me of your horses. We need at least four." The black man blocked the entrance with his squat, wide frame. "Najera has made soldiers of our vaqueros and confiscated our horses. Alacron and I have nothing but the mounts we rode in on."

"These two are not mine to sell. They are owned by Najera's men. This gelding belongs to one of the gringos who ride for the general." Medrano held up his hands in a gesture of helplessness. "I wish I could help . . ." Zion turned and exited the shop, returning a few moments later with Don Sebastien's silver-inlaid saddle.

Zion placed the saddle on the singletree of a nearby freight wagon whose wheel rim the blacksmith had been ordered to repair by one of Najera's lieutenants, the young gunhawk, Raul Salcedo. Medrano knew he would not be reimbursed for his efforts, and intended to procrastinate as long as possible. But the blacksmith's eyes lighted up with renewed interest as he beheld the saddle he had prized for many years.

Ben stood off to the side, allowing Zion to do the bargaining. He only hoped the segundo's efforts would result in a good mount capable of carrying him back across the Rio Grande. He paused near a pail of water in which Medrano had been cooling the iron he was working. Ben stared down and didn't recognize his own reflection. His beard had grown in, completely altering his features. He had darkened his jaw growth with the same stain he had used on his hair. His eyes seemed haggard, the windows of his soul were closed and defying his desperate attempts to unravel his past. Despite his size, he appeared no different from any of the other townspeople. He kept his gaze lowered, like many of the cowed residents of Saltillo. It was not healthy to attract undue attention. Too tall, he cautioned himself, and bowed his shoulders to cut his size. A patched serape covered his homespun shirt and nankeen trousers. The Patterson Colt was tucked in his waistband and concealed against the small of his back beneath the serape. He surveyed the shop and experienced a sense of belonging that was almost painful.

"Alacron," Zion called out. Ben turned and acknowledged him with a wave of his hand. "Senor

Medrano has remembered the whereabouts of some horses he has hidden in another part of town. I will look at them, and if they are fitting, the saddle will be his."

"All my horses are of excellent breeding, sold to me by comancheros who only stole from the best rancheros," Juan said indignantly. He carried the saddle into a vacant stall and buried it under a mound of hay. "If Najera should ever discover I did not turn over all my stock as he ordered . . ."

"You will have to tell him yourself," Zion said. "I owe the man neither my life nor my loyalty." To Ben, Zion said, "Wait for us here."

Ben nodded and turned away from the two men in the doorway. "Gladly," he muttered beneath his breath. He heard the crunch of their boots on the gravel outside, the voices of Zion and the blacksmith fading until nothing remained but the crackle of the glowing coals and the hum of a mud dauber tending to its nest up where a splintery-looking wood pillar forked to join one of the roof beams. Sunlight filtered down through gaps in the roof. A flock of sparrows used one for both entrance and exit, darting among and through shimmering rods of golden light and swirling ribbons of faint gray smoke.

The forge chimney wasn't drawing properly, Ben thought. He suspected one of the sparrows had at one time built a nest up past the damper. He began to pump the bellows. The wooden handle creaked and rasped as he exerted his strength. Flames danced above the coals as they throbbed with renewed life, fiery and crimson. He held up the horseshoe and examined Medrano's handiwork and knew he could duplicate it. He replaced the horseshoe on its bed of fire, sauntered over to the gelding and, raising one of its forelegs, examined the hoof. The animal turned to nip at him, but Ben slapped the horse across the nose just hard enough to sting, giving the bellicose animal fair warning not to try anything funny. Returning to the forge, he removed the glowing red horseshoe from the flames, placed it on an anvil and began to pound the metal into shape. He could feel the heat on his face. Sparks flew from beneath his hammer and winked out in the shadows.

He knew this work. He stopped and stared down at his hands. Yes, here was something from his past. The forge and iron were somehow a part of his life. The sensation of being in touch with a part of himself he had thought lost gave him hope. Perhaps it began like this, the revelation of his life, first a feeling, then a brief memory, then another, and finally the rediscovery of who he was and what had precipitated his loss of self.

"Hey Medrano, you seen to my horse yet?" a voice said from the aisle behind Ben. "What—you ain't Medrano. Where's your boss, Mex?"

Ben McQueen froze. He had been so engrossed in his work, he hadn't heard the man enter. He considered bolting toward the door but dismissed the idea immediately. Now was not the time to panic. He turned to face the man. He kept his head lowered and eyes hooded as he studied Medrano's gringo customer. The moment Ben set eyes on Ned Tolliver, he recognized the man as one of the haunters of his sleep. The same stringy shoulder-length hair, the scarred nose, and the round lenses in the man's wire-rimmed spectacles. There was no mistaking him. Ben shifted his gaze to Lucker Dobbs, standing just inside the entrance. The paunchy, grizzled turncoat hooked his thumbs in his gun belt and kicked a clod of dried dung across the floor. Ben recognized him as quickly as he had Tolliver.

"I don't reckon he speaks American," said Dobbs.

"Where's Medrano, eh, hombre? Medrano!" Tolliver said. Clearly he hoped that if he increased his volume he might somehow be able to make the fool understand. He repeated the question in halting Spanish.

Ben shrugged, although it was only with a superhuman effort that he managed to conceal the emotions raging in his breast. The men were linked to him, but how and why? An innate sense of caution warned him to remain quiet and to continue his charade. He understood none of this, yet he believed with all his heart that if these men so much as suspected the truth, they would kill him where he stood.

So he endured Tolliver's insults and more of Dobbs's broken Spanish. As if he were deaf and dumb, Ben ignored the gringos and concentrated on his work. Out of exasperation Tolliver took it upon himself to inspect his own horse.

"Looks like he's got one shoe to go," the former Ranger growled. He emerged from the stall. "Let's have another drink. Ain't no telling how long this dumb sum'bitch is gonna take." Despite his own command, Tolliver remained by the stall, his shrewd eyes focused on the tall silent Mexican.

"What is it?" Dobbs asked.

"Funny. For a moment I thought I seen this greaser before," Tolliver remarked.

Ben, laboring over the coals, felt a tightness between his shoulder blades, the same feeling a man gets when he thinks he's about to be shot. He forced himself to continue to work. He dunked the horseshoe into the water bucket. The submerged metal sizzled and sent a column of steam rising up into the disguised man's face. A bead of sweat rolled down the tip of his nose and dropped onto the back of his hand. With horror, Ben realized he had worked up enough sweat to cause his disguise to streak. He concentrated on keeping his back to the two men and maneuvered himself deeper into the shadowy recesses of the stable.

"Seen him before?" Dobbs chuckled. "Hell, how could you tell? All these chili eaters look alike to me."

"I suppose you're right," Tolliver admitted, softly laughing. "C'mon. I'll send a kid over later to fetch the gelding." The two men vanished into the afternoon sunlight. Dobbs paused by the olla outside, quenched his thirst, then dropped the gourd dipper back into the water and sauntered off after his companion. Alone at last, Ben headed for the nearest three-legged stool and slumped onto the seat before his legs completely gave out. The encounter had left its mark upon him. He lifted his hands and found them trembling, as if he were standing in a north wind in the dead of winter.

Bodies falling, tumbling from horseback. Gunshots from all sides. Men and animals screaming, but there is no place to run. Run, yes. Run! It's a trap! Damn your black hearts!

Ben leaned forward, elbows on his knees, his head drooping. The vision lasted but a few brief seconds. But that it came at all spoke volumes. These men had played a part in whatever had happened to him. They might even be the key to unlocking a past he just might wish had stayed buried. He sat there, head bowed, staring at the dirt. He lost all track of time. A wasp hovered in front of him and alighted on the toe of his boot then sailed off on a blur of wings, circled the silent man and rose upward to join its sisters in the nest above his head. Eventually the tremors subsided and Ben sought solace in the work at hand. He finished the horseshoe and left it on the anvil, then returned to the stool, where he awaited the arrival of the segundo.

Half an hour later Zion and Juan Medrano returned from their excursion to the *mercado*. The blacksmith carried the carcass of a goat over his shoulder and would have headed straight through the shop and into his house had he not immediately realized that someone, no doubt Ben, had taken a turn with his tools. Juan Medrano scowled, set the goat aside and without speaking walked down the aisle to the anvil and forge. He noticed his tools had been properly put away and were none the worse for wear. That took the edge off his anger. He picked up the horseshoe from the anvil and stepped into the sunlight streaming through one of the unshuttered windows. After a few moments of examination he nodded, satisfied. Then he hung the horseshoe on a peg near the chestnut gelding's stall and proceeded to retrieve the goat carcass and head for his house. He paused in the doorway to the alley.

"Alacron, if chasing cows is not to your liking, you can come work for me."

"Gracias," Ben said. "Any luck?" He glanced up at Zion, who waited for the blacksmith to leave before he answered.

"Four horses. All of them mountain bred and strong." The segundo rubbed his hands together in satisfaction. "But we better round them up and get out of town before General Najera learns about them."

"Where are they hidden?"

"The last place Valentin Najera would ever go nowadays." Zion grinned. Then he frowned and stepped in close to Ben. "You all right?"

"Yes," Ben lied. His encounter with the two men from his nightmares had left an indelible mark on his soul, ravaging his already wounded mind. Still, he kept his horror private. Ashamed of his fears, Ben resolved to deal with them as best he could. "Let's go find your horses."

The shadow of a hawk drifted across the sun-baked yard of the church of Santa Maria Magdelene, circled the square whitewashed bell tower, and glided off toward the wood-lined wash just beyond the church. Zion and Ben gave their mounts a drink from the spring-fed cistern in the center of the yard then walked them over to the rectory, where the rotund, brown-robed priest was busily stringing dried chilies from the thatch roof above his porch.

Again Zion made the briefest of introductions, but the priest proved far more observant than Medrano the blacksmith. Father Rudolfo's features grew wide-eyed with alarm and he ushered both men into the shade of his porch.

"What mischief are you up to, Zion? This is the vaquero you spoke of? A norteamericano?" Father Rudolfo appeared truly alarmed. "Najera is looking for a reason to add my head to his collection. Bad enough I allowed Juan to conceal his horses in the church stable. Now you bring a spy into our midst."

"I'm no spy, padre," Ben said. He briefly explained his presence in town, taking care to include just who had forced him south in chains. Zion squirmed uncomfortably and interrupted.

"Don't bore the padre with such a long story. What matters is, we have come for the horses as I promised."

Father Rudolfo glared at the segundo. "You chained this unfortunate one and forced him to accompany you to Ventana? Shame on you." He took Ben by the arm. "Josefina has been a good friend. She has helped me with the children many times during the feast days. I am grateful you helped her, even if you had no choice." The padre looked to weigh about four hundred pounds, and his cheeks were flushed from the heat. The fringe of close-cropped gray hair that circled his skull was dappled with perspiration. And yet, despite his girth and sixty-plus years, the Franciscan marched along at a brisk clip. He issued orders to a Christianized Yaqui dozing against the wall of the priest's house and instructed the man to finish hanging the chilies. The Yaqui, a bow-legged wisp of an old warrior, with skin the color of dulled copper, struggled to his feet, brushed the dust from his homespun garments, and shuffled across the porch to finish the work begun by the priest. The Yaqui gave a start as he drew closer to Ben. Zion turned and for the first time took a close look at his companion. In the sunlight, Ben's features were two-toned and streaked from sweat. Ben also seemed to be aware of his problem.

"Don't worry, Esteban won't talk. But the sooner you leave town, the better for all of us." The padre continued on to the stable. Ben did not relax until he was engulfed in the dusty interior of the stable. Once concealed, he removed a clay bottle from beneath his serape and immediately applied Zion's mixture to his nose and forehead, darkening the skin until he could pass unnoticed among the residents of Saltillo once again.

Zion led Ben past the stalls, in which were kept the four mounts he had paid for with Don Sebastien's silver-inlaid saddle. The horses—two mares, a stallion, and a roan gelding—all looked to be excellent mounts.

"We'll have to wait the day out," Zion said. "And bring these animals out under cover of night, or else we might attract too much attention."

"As you wish," Father Rudolfo halfheartedly replied.

"The padre sets an excellent table," Zion said. "And as you can see by his belly, there is seldom enough for guests." He noted the priest's scowling look of disapproval. "Cheer up, Father Rudolfo, after all, you have God to protect you."

"There are no strangers in the house of the Lord," the padre admitted. He turned to Ben. "I bid you welcome." He flashed a warm smile. "Forgive me my lack of hospitality."

The priest walked to the door of the stable and perused the churchyard. Four dragoons rode through the gate and brought their horses over to the cistern. A few minutes later the animals had drunk their fill and the riders circled the churchyard so that they might ogle a trio of Yaqui maidens who were bringing firewood up from the dry wash. The expression on Father Rudolfo's face was anything but saintly. His broad fleshy hands closed into fists. Tension filled the stable. A chorus of gruff laughter erupted from the horsemen, and the maidens giggled, for they were young, relishing their beauty and youth, and were impervious to the darkness in such men as these. Thankfully, the four horsemen had business elsewhere. They wheeled their mounts and rode from the churchyard, promising to return.

The padre stared at the settling dust. "Sometimes God seems far away and General Valentin Najera much too close."

At dusk Saltillo began to shake off the vestiges of the sleepy afternoon and come alive. The land shed the warmth it had collected all day long, and the temperature began to plummet, becoming cool and arid. Lamp light beamed from windows and flooded through open doorways. The residents of the town streamed into the street to socialize and gossip. With the soldiers in town, the cantinas and brothels surrounding the *mercado* were awash with activity. The music of flamenco drifted out among the alleys and streets. Everywhere Ben looked, people seemed to be enjoying themselves. They were certainly oblivious to him. The tall, serape-draped stranger in homespun garments and down-at-heel boots was but one of many among the throng of townspeople and soldiers.

Ben knew Zion would be horrified to discover his absence. In truth, he had never intended to risk discovery by venturing any farther into town. But after his encounter with Tolliver and Dobbs, Ben McQueen was determined to wait for dusk and then brave the streets. He did not feel the risk was all that great as long as he avoided the brightly lit cantinas, kept his sombrero tilted low, and didn't do anything to call attention to himself.

The two gringos plagued his thoughts. He had to see them again, in hopes that another meeting might jog his memory and cause the pieces of his past to fall into place. It was worth a try. Father Rudolfo, to whom many of the servants reported, was the eyes and ears of Saltillo. Little happened without the padre being informed. So it was that Father Rudolfo had known the names of Najera's norteamericano hirelings—Ned Tolliver and Lucker Dobbs. For now, the names meant nothing to Ben, but he was determined they would.

He reached Market Square and cautiously wandered among the vendors who were busy closing their stalls, as had the proprietors of the shops throughout the town. Ben circled the spring, where several uniformed dragoons lounged against the stone walls of the well, smoking their cigarillos and passing bottles of tequila from one to the other. Their dark blue and scarlet jackets were open to the waist. They wore their leather-brimmed caps at jaunty angles and bragged of their conquests, lying to one another and wishing they had enough money for one last good poke. Alas, money was scarce and the whores in the brothels across the square demanded payment in cash. Nary a "soiled dove" had any use for charity when it came to business. A prostitute's beauty was a temporal thing, and their hearts were rarely made of gold.

A soldier bumped into Ben and growled at him in a drunken voice to get the hell out of the way. Ben pointedly took no offense and hurried past the drunkard, anxious to put some distance between himself and trouble. He recognized the name Casa del Noche. Father Rudolfo had described the hotel as the headquarters of General Najera. The hotel's cantina was a good place to begin his search. He made his way around to the bat-wing doors and was forced to sidestep a trio of swarthy-looking lancers, sabers sheathed at their sides, when they brushed him aside and cut across the square. They paused to purchase the last of the tortillas an old woman was selling from a pushcart. She filled the tortillas with the last of the *barbacoa* spooned from a clay pot. The finely shredded pork was a delicacy to which she added hearty amounts of her fiery salsa, topping the meat until the juices ran out the ends of the tortillas. The lancers gorged themselves on the old woman's cooking, satisfying one appetite before heading off to the brothels to tame the fires burning below their belts.

Ben rounded the corner and peered through the window at the smoky interior of the cantina. Something brushed against his leg and he nearly jumped out of his boots, but looked down to find it was only a cat. The feline arched its back and purred. Ben nudged the creature on its way with the toe of his boot. A bottle shattered within the cantina, and Ben looked up in time to see a young man in a black and scarlet serape break up an altercation.

The two would-be combatants were a rough-looking pair, one a potbellied mestizo, the other a bold-talking, lean young man with a scruffy beard and a chip on his shoulder.

"You take back what you said, Mariano!" the younger of the two blurted, his speech slurred.

"We are compadres, Angel. Would you let the widow put knives in our hands and set us against one another?" the mestizo said. "Raul, see if you can talk some sense into this one before I carve him like a trussed-up sow."

The mediator, Raul, placed himself in harm's way and confronted the irate man named Angel. "The Widow Montenez . . . you have much feeling for her, eh?"

"Si." Angel nodded as his hand crept to the pistol tucked in his belt.

"Good. I would not wish to kill you for a trifle. Better you die for love, for *pasión*." Raul's gaze narrowed. "Leave the gun. Pulque has been the death of many a good man. Think, amigo. Think well."

Every eye within the cantina and without was focused on the two friends. Soldiers, serving girls, townspeople, and vaqueros were ready to dive for cover if gunplay erupted. The seconds crept past with agonizing slowness. Conversation faded. Even the bartender froze, with a bottle of his home brew tilted up and suspended above a clay cup. At last, to the relief of all present, Angel shrugged and slumped into his chair. The mestizo leaned forward and poured him a drink to show there were no hard feelings.

As tensions eased, Raul glanced up and spied

Ben watching him through the unshuttered window. The gunman frowned, obviously struggling to place the stranger framed by the windowsill's weathered wood. There was something about the hombre, but Najera's lieutenant couldn't make the connection.

Ben instantly recognized the gunman as the leader of the attack on Senora Quintero's wagon. He stepped back into the safety of the shadows. He hoped to avoid calling attention to himself, but failed to check the ground behind his heels. The cat had returned, and Ben's left foot came down on the feline's tail. The animal screeched, Ben jumped, and half the cantina turned to look in his direction. The disguised man spun and dashed down the side street away from the *mercado.*

"You! Hombre! Wait!" Raul shouted, and lunged for the doors, but the room was crowded, and even though Senora Montenez's customers struggled to get out of the gunman's path, he still lost precious seconds. By the time Raul reached the Paseo de Caballo, Ben was one block down and half a block over, his long legs taking him at a dead run back to Santa Maria Magdelene.

It was a rare moment when General Valentin Najera attended church. Of course, he picked a dark night to come calling on the Lord. Father Rudolfo was kneeling before the statue of the Blessed Mother, his lips moving, allowing the merest whisper of a prayer to escape. Esteban, the Yaqui, and his three brown-eyed granddaughters, the comely girls who had attracted the interest of the dragoons earlier that afternoon, knelt a few pews behind the priest. When the door creaked on its hinges, Father Rudolfo stirred and glanced over his shoulder. His lower jaw dropped when he identified the visitor.

Valentin Najera wore his dress uniform. The black coat with its scarlet-and-gold-stitched sleeves and wide lapels looked elegant even in the dimly lit interior of the church. Najera was followed by Marita Two Ponies, who dutifully walked behind the general. From the sound of the horses in the churchyard, a number of riders had accompanied the general. Two of his personal guard, dragoons armed with pistols and sabers, stood at attention to either side of the double doors. No doubt they were handpicked and could be counted on to keep silent about Najera's peculiar behavior. The general motionod for the Yaquis to depart. Old Esteban rose up on his aged legs and left with his granddaughters by the side door. Esteban paused but once, and that was to stare past Najera at Marita, the one granddaughter he had not seen or spoken to since she ran away from the Church. The girl could feel her grandfather's sad stare but refused to meet it, nor would she look at Father Rudolfo.

Najera cleared his throat as a signal that Esteban was pressing his luck. The Yaqui slowly turned and followed his remaining granddaughters into the night. The general caught his consort by the arm and guided her forward.

"Do not be afraid, *querida,* the padre is nothing but a harmless, fat old man." Najera glanced around the empty church. The whitewashed walls on either side of the sanctuary bore frescoes of the martyred saints. A row of candles, for the most part unlit, surrounded a poor box on three sides. Here a special offering might be made and a candle lit to symbolize the prayer.

"Why have you come here?" the priest asked. "If you wish to frighten me with threats and insults, so be it, I do fear you. I also fear you will one day overstep the bounds of decency and forever place yourself beyond the reach of Christ."

Najera removed a buckskin pouch from his coat pocket, shook out a single silver coin and placed his donation in the box. He hefted the box and jostled its contents, saw that Marita was watching him, and returned the box to its place among the candles. He took one of the lighted tapers and proceeded to light an entire row of candles.

"You cannot buy the grace of God, my general," said Father Rudolfo. "Nor is there a price on heaven. It must be earned."

"Fortunately, I have you to pray for me," Najera replied. "You do pray for me, don't you?"

"Every day."

"*Bueno*. I am in your debt." Najera turned and walked back to Marita's side. He lifted a few strands of hair and let them fall through his parted fingers. "As for earning heaven, what more can I do than shoulder the responsibility of defending my country against General Taylor's army? I have made many sacrifices. My soldiers love me. And why? Because I am a river to my people." The diminutive officer motioned for Marita to kneel at the altar rail. "She has come for Communion."

Father Rudolfo glanced at the girl, who met his gaze for an instant then hurried down the aisle and knelt at the wooden rail separating the sanctuary from the rest of the church. In truth, the priest had been expecting the girl. Marita's grandmother, old Esteban's wife, had died three years ago to the day. Each anniversary of her death, the Yaqui and his granddaughters had made a special point of receiving Communion.

The priest joined the girl at the altar. He took her hand. "My child, do you seek absolution for your sins?"

"Si, padre," she answered. Her youth and beauty filled the priest with regret. Better she had been born homely as a cow than to be sought after by men like Valentin Najera.

Father Rudolfo bowed forward and spoke softly. "There is a place for you at Santa Maria Magdelene."

"I am dead to my grandfather."

"Even Lazarus returned to life through the will of God."

Fire flashed in Marita's eyes. "Return to being just another mission Indian? No! General Najera has made me much more. He loves me."

"He has made you just another *puta*." The moment the words escaped his lips, the priest regretted them. But once spoken, they could not be called back. Marita's hurt expression moved him to pity. With a rustle of his brown robes, the priest left the railing, climbed the shallow steps to the altar, genuflected, opened the tabernacle and removed the chalice. He turned in time to see Marita hurrying up the center aisle. The door banged against the adobe wall and then creaked shut.

Najera clapped his hands together. "Bravo, padre."

Father Rudolfo frowned and stared down at the chalice in his hands. His reflection danced across the gold surface. Confronted by his own failure, he returned the chalice to the tabernacle and left the altar in defeat. Najera slowly started up the aisle, but paused to look at the dejected priest.

"Now you see, if there is any villainy here at all, it lies within each of us."

"I saw the jars. I know what they contain. Such cruelty is spawned by an evil heart."

"It will teach the gringos the wages of fear, and they will think twice about bringing their armies against us." Najera's chest swelled with pride. The victory he had won on the road to Linares was but the first of many. "All that I do . . . I do for Mexico."

"For yourself, don't you mean?"

"One and the same, padre. When I have driven the norteamericanos back across the Rio del Norte, who can say what the future holds. Santa Anna is sure to receive me with honor. In such times, a man can go far and accomplish much for himself." Najera blessed himself with holy water, then barked an order to the men stationed by the door for them to rejoin their compadres in the churchyard. The dragoons saluted and vanished from sight. Najera dabbed his fingers in the water dish and smoothed his hair in place.

"That water has been blessed," the priest said, lumbering up the aisle, his wide expanse brushing the pews to either side. "It is holy water. This church is holy ground. It is the house of God, yet you treat it with such contempt."

"There is no 'holy' ground, no 'holy' water. And as for God . . . !" Najera quickly surveyed the interior of the humble church. "There is no one here but us." Najera turned with a flourish and strode purposefully up the aisle, away from the priest. His parting remarks drifted back: "Rejoice, padre . . . the day may come when all of Mexico receives me as El Presidente."

"On that day, I think Saltillo and Marita Two Ponies will be far from your thoughts," the priest muttered.

"Continue to save souls, padre, and I will save the country." The general disappeared through the doorway, determined to have the last word.

Poor Mexico, besieged from without and within, thought the priest. He braced himself on the back of a pew, his short, stubby fingers bloodless where he gripped the wood. "And who will save the country from you?"

Ben McQueen reached the barn just as General Najera emerged from the church and climbed into his carriage alongside Marita. The general and his dragoons wheeled their horses, Najera took his place in the lead, and Ben slipped quietly into the darkened doorway. He immediately sensed Zion's presence as the black man shifted his vantage point and crossed over to him.

"Christ almighty, you scared me plumb to death. Where'd you take off to?"

"I went looking for someone," Ben whispered.

"Who?"

"Me."

"Have any luck?"

Ben shook his head. He watched as the soldiers trotted past. The moonlight illuminated the interior of the carriage, and he was able to make out the imperial countenance of Valentin Najera as he turned and glanced toward the barn, his features pale and bloodless. Though the general had not played a role in his dreams, Ben felt he knew this man. He retreated with Zion farther into the barn and remained there until the entourage had departed the churchyard.

Then Zion trundled over to the gray gelding and proceeded to saddle the animal. Ben examined the mounts they had bartered for and chose a solid-looking, mountain-bred roan mustang. He saddled the animal and led it out of the barn. Zion appeared leading his gray and a string of four horses. He would cut them free when they were clear of Saltillo. The two men turned and saw the padre outlined by candlelight in the church doorway. Ben and Zion rode across the yard and up to the priest, who raised his hand and blessed them.

"Thank you for your hospitality, Father," Ben said, touching the brim of his sombrero.

"Be well, you old Bible thumper," Zion added.

"God be with you, old friend, whether you want Him or not," the padre said. He looked at Ben. "And God be with you, my son. May He heal your mind and grant you a safe journey back to the States."

"Thanks, padre," Ben said. "But I don't reckon I'll be going north after all."

"What!?" Zion exclaimed.

"You can't work Ventana by yourself. However many cattle Najera missed will have to be chased out of the brush. And you said it's at least a two-man job. So I suppose I'll hang around."

"Madre de Dios!" Father Rudolfo blessed him. He had taken a liking to this man Alacron and broken bread with him. The padre could see that he was someone lost. And Father Rudolfo had a soft spot in his heart for the lost. It was said the priest of Saltillo had the soul of a shepherd, a quality that had endeared him to the local populace. "If Najera discovers the truth—my son, do you know what the general keeps in those jars in the courtyard outside the hotel?" The priest clapped his hands together. "You risk a terrible death, senor."

"I'll stay." Ben was adamant.

"I don't believe you have any love for the ranch," Zion said, "but so be it, vaquero. My offer still stands. I can use the help." Zion touched his quirt to the gray's flank and the gelding headed for the street. Ben took up the rear, keeping the string of horses from lagging back. They rode through the moon shadow and lamp light. Sentries challenged them on the outskirts of town, but the two men leaned low over their mounts and soon were clear of

Najera's soldiers. On the outskirts of Saltillo the road branched to north and south. Zion glanced around to see if the norteamericano would reconsider his choice, but Ben never gave the road home a single glance. He had made his decision and was determined to confront his nightmares no matter what the cost. The answers he sought were here in Saltillo. And like the man said, it was indeed . . . his own funeral.

Chapter Nine

Part curly wolf, part mountain lion, deadly as a rattler, and unpredictable as a Texas twister, that was Snake-Eye Gandy. There wasn't one of his fellow Texas Rangers who'd deny the description fit. These days Gandy was a sergeant . . . again, a rank he rarely held longer than a few months before being broken back to a regular Ranger for insubordination. Rank didn't much matter to a man like Gandy. And it didn't much matter to the men who rode with him. From the blood-soaked Nueces Strip to the Big Bend, the crusty, battle-scarred Indian fighter had earned the reputation of a man to ride the river with, an hombre the younger Rangers wanted on their side when the chips were down.

To say Snake-Eye Gandy was ugly was like calling the sky blue. It didn't do it justice. This long-armed range buster had seen thirty-one winters, stood five-foot-seven with his boots on, and carried a pair of Patterson Colts riding high on his hips. His silver-streaked black hair covered only part of his skull. The rest was a wrinkled plateau of scar tissue, the legacy of a Comanche who had tried to scalp his victim before checking to see if the man was dead. Gandy had killed his red-skinned assailant and pried his own bloody hair from the dead warrior's grasp. Later Gandy wove his severed locks into a braid which he sported as a topknot.

Some years back Snake-Eye Gandy had been blinded during a skirmish with Mexican raiders. His left eye was glass now. A coiled rattlesnake had been painted on the orb, and Gandy had mastered a wide-eyed stare that inevitably caused both friend and foe alike to shiver and recoil in horror. A life lived for the most part outdoors had left his features weathered and wrinkled as the Texas hills.

Three days out from Matamoros, with General Zachary Taylor's warning still ringing in his ears, Gandy knelt beside his gelding and studied the scuff marks on a headstone-sized chunk of limestone, and shading his eyes, scrutinized the dry wash leading up the wooded hillside. He glanced over his shoulder at the two dozen Rangers who had followed him out of occupied Matamoros in direct disobedience of Army orders. Like Gandy, they were men "with the bark on" who didn't give a damn about such things as orders. Some of their own were missing. They aimed to find them or learn their fate. Gandy motioned for his second in command, Cletus Buckhart, to bring the goatherd forward. Buckhart was a dark man clad in buckskin breeches and a loose-fitting Mexican shirt, standard dress for most of the Rangers, who avoided uniforms whenever possible.

Buckhart was nineteen and already the veteran of several border skirmishes. He could ride like a Comanche and fight like the very devil, the basic requirements of any man who wished to join the Texas Rangers. Buckhart cast a slender shadow, for he was a lean man, almost scrawny-looking, but tough as rawhide. At the age of fifteen he had seen his parents slaughtered by bandits from south of the Rio Grande. The experience had hardened him against all people of Latin descent. For him the war was an opportunity to avenge his parents. The battle for Matamoros had been just the beginning for Cletus Buckhart.

Buckhart's prisoner was a white-haired hermit the Rangers had chanced upon by a spring a couple of miles back down the trail. Buckhart gave the bearded goatherd an extra shove that sent the old man sprawling. Gandy frowned and walked back to help the fallen man to his feet.

"That will be enough, Cletus."

"I ain't doing nothing, Snake-Eye."

"Just back off and leave him be." Gandy proceeded to dust off the frightened goatherd, then spoke to the man in Spanish. "We mean you no harm, Grandfather. My compadre has much anger in him, but he will do as I say."

"He is not the first rude young man I have ever met, and I doubt he will be the last," said Jesus Cavasos as he struggled to stand on his bruised limbs. The venerable hermit seemed old as the wonderful country in which he had chosen to live out his days. His eyes were bright, though tinged with sadness, for he had known war and revolution and the evil that men do in times of violence. For that reason he had chosen to live apart from others. "Personally, I prefer the company of goats," Cavasos added.

"So do I, from time to time." Gandy chuckled. "But today I must find my friends. Two weeks ago they left to scout the road to Linares, and now you tell me they have all been ambushed and killed by General Valentin Najera." Gandy kicked at the loose gravel beneath his boot. "I go to see with my own eyes."

"Would that I had not, sir," Cavasos said.

"Do we go up the wash?"

The goatherd nodded and pointed a bony finger straight up the gradual incline, where a rockslide had carved a path through the trees, leaving a swath of cleared, broken ground about seventy feet wide. The rockslide had blocked the road to Linares and dammed a creek several hundred yards down the slope, forcing the waters to carve a path around a jumble of fallen timber.

"You could hide a small army among the trees on this here hillside. Anybody caught in that open ground would be cut to ribbons," Buckhart dryly interjected.

"They were," Cavasos said in English.

Gandy flashed a look of disbelief at the old man. *So* he could speak English after all. "Lieutenant Ben McQueen was no pup," he said in his own language. "He'd have checked the trail before leading his men up it, and that's for damn sure."

"I watched from the hilltop," the goatherd said. "The gringo officer sent two scouts ahead . . . two *Rangers*," he pointedly added. "They rode up ahead of the column."

"And failed to see this Najera and his men?" Buckhart asked.

The Rangers accompanied the goatherd up the hilltop.

"This is where they saw them," Cavasos said, pointing down the slope. "Then the two Rangers waved the others forward and got out of the way. General Najera and his men handled the rest." He closed his eyes and cupped his hands over his ears. "The noise. So many guns. They frightened my goats."

The slope was crisscrossed by a swell of land, an irregular series of outcroppings that blocked a view of the entire slope from below. Gandy's instincts told him he could trust the goatherd. He looked at the snowy-headed old-timer and knew the answers lay farther up the hillside, beyond nature's barrier of rocks and the curve of the slope. He took up the reins and began to lead his horse up the hill.

"You want us to come along, Snake-Eye?" asked another of the Rangers, a boyish, good-natured man in his mid-twenties. Leon Pettibone was handy with both pistol and tomahawk, but preferred the Colt Revolving rifle cradled in the crook of his arm. He mopped his round face with a bandanna and gazed suspiciously at the woods bordering the cleared swath of hillside. Gandy waved his men forward.

"You're coming with us," Buckhart muttered to the goatherd, and waved his drawn Patterson Colt in Gandy's direction. "I still don't trust you. Just follow Snake-Eye."

The old man shrugged his shoulders and obeyed. He never argued with guns or nature. It was his way to bend with the storm and to survive.

Fifteen minutes later they found what the scavengers had left. Several of the corpses had been picked clean. The rest had been worked over by vultures, wolves, and coyotes. What flesh remained had already begun to decompose. The stench had lessened, thanks to the carrion birds, but the sight, especially the seven headless bodies of the dead Rangers that had accompanied the Army detail, caused several of the men behind Gandy to double over and retch.

A hot wind tugged at Gandy's topknot and moaned as it fanned the hillside with its hot breath. The Ranger sergeant closely observed the lay of the men and the skeletons of the horses that had been killed, and reconstructed what had happened. Trusting in the honesty of his scouts, Ben McQueen would have hurried his men up the slope in an attempt to cross the hill and pick up the Linares road on the other side of the slide. Najera's men must have had him in a cross fire. The first volley must have toppled half his command. The rest would have fallen in the confusion as they tried to make a stand. The entire melee could not have lasted more than a few minutes. Then silence.

Gandy could tell by the tattered remnants of their blue uniforms which of the dead were Ben's dragoons. Judging from their buckskins, the seven mutilated remains were indeed Rangers. That left two Rangers unaccounted for. Cavasos had spoken the truth. The traitors . . . but which ones? Gandy mentally reviewed the roster that had accompanied Lieutenant Ben McQueen into Mexico. He smiled sadly, remembering how Ben had insisted General Taylor allow him to bring a half dozen or so Rangers along with his dragoons, despite the Texans' reputation as troublemakers. Ben had openly expressed his admiration for the Rangers. He had spent so much time riding with Gandy and his men prior to the outbreak of hostilities that the Rangers considered McQueen one of their own. Gandy had taken young Ben McQueen under his wing and had developed an almost paternal fondness for the young officer who had the heart of a Ranger despite his brass buttons and Army uniform.

Snake-Eye Gandy surveyed the scene of battle and prowled through the carnage searching for some indication that Ben was among the fallen. His boots crunching gravel and bone made a sickening sound. Gandy shuddered. Inured as he was to horror, this was something special, and it was all he could do to remain a part of this grisly scene. Blank eye sockets seemed to stare as if with round black orbs. Silent accusations rose from the dead. Was that the wind, or ghostly voices moaning betrayal? Gandy reached the edge of the killing ground and stared down at the broken, scattered remains of McQueen's command, sprawled in death and bleached by the sun.

"You Mex bastard!" Cletus Buckhart growled in a venomous voice, and thumbed the hammer back on his Patterson Colt. Old Cavasos retreated as the gun swung in his direction. Something in Buckhart had momentarily snapped; the butchery . . . the indelible memory of his own family's fate . . .

"No, Cletus!" Pettibone shouted. He made a grab for Buckhart's hand, but the angry nineteen-year-old slapped his friend aside and leveled the revolver. Cavasos stood his ground, too old to run, and too proud. Snake-Eye Gandy bounded down the slope and batted the Ranger's gun hand aside just as the barrel blossomed flame. A chunk of limestone exploded, and the bullet ricocheted off toward the trees, causing every man on the slope to duck.

Buckhart brought the gun to bear yet again. This time Gandy was in reach. He caught Buckhart by the left shoulder, swung the man around and snatched the revolver from his grasp. The young Ranger's hand dropped to the Colt holstered on his left. Gandy stiff-armed him in the chest and knocked him off his feet.

"Damn it, Snake-Eye," Buckhart groaned, struggling to catch his breath. "Are you blind? Don't you see what they done?"

"I can see," Gandy replied. "One-eyed I may be, but I damn sure see clearer than you."

"Goddamn Najera anyway," said another Ranger; a stubbled, hell-for-leather rider named Blue Napier. Approximately the same age as Gandy, he had ridden the border for as many years as the sergeant. He tilted his sombrero back off his forehead. His salt and pepper hair glistened with sweat. "What kind of man would do such a thing?"

"Najera seeks to put fear in your hearts," Cavasos said. "Fear and hatred make a man do foolish things." The goatherd nodded his thanks to Gandy. He owed this man with the devil's eye his life, and the hermit of the hills decided to repay the debt.

"Besides the two scouts, there was another survivor. The officer also escaped," Cavasos said. His words had the desired effect on Gandy, whose whole body seemed to coil like a spring. "He reached the creek below and hid among the broken trees. After the general departed, I climbed down, but when I reached the creekbed, the norteamericano was gone. Who can say what became of him?" The goat keeper turned and started walking across the hillside, picking his way among the bones and heading for the trees.

"Hey, just where do you think you're going?" Buckhart managed to yell despite his lack of wind.

"I am going home. Shoot me if you must," Cavasos said over his shoulder.

"Where can I find General Najera?" Gandy called out. His gravely voice reverberated across the barren ground.

"Saltillo. With his army of almost a thousand men . . . or so a little bird told me. Go with God, gringo. And I don't envy God." The shadows beneath the trees seemed to reach out and swallow up the old hermit, receiving him into the heart of the wild and the free.

"Maybe Cletus is right," Pettibone said, rubbing his bruised biceps where his friend had struck him with the Patterson Colt, "and we shouldn't have let the old bastard leave."

"There was a day when that old-timer was much man, mark my words," Gandy said, staring at the

woods. "I'd have hated to brace him in his prime."
He touched the brim of his sombrero as if saluting
the goatherd. Then Gandy sighed, returned the gun
he had taken from Buckhart, and studied the faces of
the men around him.

"Reckon I'll take me a little ride over to Saltillo
and pay this General Najera a visit." Snake-Eye
Gandy remounted, his trouser leg slapping leather as
he settled in the saddle. "I might even keep a lookout
for Ben McQueen. Maybe even the turncoats who
betrayed these men." Small and wiry and every inch
of him fire and brimstone, pure poison with gun or
knife, Gandy checked his guns, then pointed his
horse south. Dodging patrols and maybe traveling at
night, Gandy figured he just might make it. Behind
the sergeant, every Ranger appeared to have the same
idea. As far as they were concerned, Najera had not
left a warning, but an invitation.

It was Cletus Buckhart who voiced their
thoughts. "A thousand to our twenty-five," he
drawled. "Seems just about a fair fight."

No one heard any arguments. Out of the valley
rode twenty-five men, sobered by what they had
seen, grieving for the slain and riding for vengeance.

Chapter Ten

Ben woke screaming. Zion, shaving three day's growth of beard at a water bucket over by the tack room, jumped and nearly slit his own throat with the straight razor. He hadn't noticed Ben asleep in the stall, otherwise he might have been prepared for some kind of outburst. The man called Alacron rarely slept without being besieged by horrifying nightmares that often left him shaken and depressed.

Josefina, her features pale and filled with concern, appeared in the barn doorway. She wore a bonnet and carried a basket of jicama roots she had just gathered from the meadow surrounding the hacienda. A few briars clung to her apron, and her blouse was matted with perspiration and molded to her bosom. She made no effort to hide her concern for the tall, rangy americano who sheepishly muttered an apology to both parties.

A couple of days had passed since Ben and Zion had returned to Ventana with the horses. After long hours in the saddle, scouring the brush country and driving the scattered cattle down out of the hills and onto the valley floor, they were ready for a home-cooked meal. They'd worked from "can see to can't" and risked life and limb chasing strays out of le-chugilla thickets and down steep-sided arroyos.

General Najera had only confiscated the live-stock that could be easily driven back to Saltillo. Riding the chaparral country was much more diffi-cult and Najera had been loath to spare the men or waste any more of his valuable time. Besides, he had the bulk of the Quintero herd, and that was all he needed.

Ben sat upright and cradled his face in his hands. Each nightmare took a greater toll but brought him closer to the truth than the one before. His breathing, labored at first, became normal. The im-ages that flooded his mind parted like torn silk, yet vestiges remained, a "patch" of dying men, a "ten-dril" of gunfire and death, a "thread" of two men, Tolliver and Dobbs, astride their horses. Tolliver raised his arms and gestured for Ben to join them. Then confused images, dust and heat and powder smoke. Screams of the dying . . . the sound welled in him and demanded to be heard.

"Damn, I wish you'd give me some kind of warning before you haul off and cut loose," Zion growled.

"Sorry," Ben said, standing. He walked out of the stall where he'd been dozing on a bed of straw and headed for the sunlight. Emerging from the shadowy interior of the barn, he encountered Jose-fina, who handed him the basket of freshly dug roots.

"Carry these to the house for me?" she asked.

"Yes, ma'am," Ben said, and took the basket from her hands. Elena would cut them into chunks and put them in her stew. The jicama, once peeled, had much the same color and crispness as a raw potato and could be eaten raw, mashed, or boiled in soups and stews. Ben was surprised when Josefina fell in step alongside him. He glanced aside and met her warm, friendly gaze.

"What is it?" she asked.

"Nothing."

"You men," she said, and shook her head. "You'd rather wrestle a steer than a handful of words."

"All right." Ben grinned. "What will Elena think . . . you walking with one of the hired hands?"

"First of all, I am walking with a friend," Josefina corrected. She lifted her hem over a prickly pear cactus.

"You don't even know my name."

"I know all I need to. I have seen you fierce, dangerous, driven. I have seen you frightened and lost like me. I think we have much in common, Senor Alacron. But you are more than a scorpion, for there is gentleness in you. I sense this. The gentle . . . and the deadly."

Ben studied the woman, marveling at the change a couple of days had made. She seemed clearheaded now, and he suspected she was no longer depending on the narcotic he had once spied her taking on the journey to Saltillo. The proximity of the pretty widow got the better of him, and for a moment Ben lowered his eyes to the woman's sweat-soaked blouse and the rise and fall of her chest with every breath. He caught himself and shifted his appraisal to the widow's high cheekbones. She was a rare beauty. He found himself envying the late Don Sebastien. Ben was about to speak that very thought when he spied a plume of dust trailing in the air. Someone was approaching from the direction of the town. He froze for a moment, and Josefina, seeing his reaction, turned to see the telltale brown smear against the pristine horizon.

"I think we are about to entertain guests," Josefina remarked. "I'll have Elena set the dining room table with coffee and some of her honey cakes."

Ben returned her basket. That much dust indicated several riders were on the way. He guessed General Najera must be coming to pay his respects. "Perhaps I ought to make myself scarce."

Josefina understood. She took the basket but allowed her hand to close over Ben's scarred knuckles. "I am glad you remained with us, my nameless friend. We have much in common." She read the confusion in his eyes. "Our loneliness."

Before Ben could reply, the woman left his side and hurried on to the house, leaving him with yet another question for which he had no answer.

A dozen riders watered their mounts and lounged around the well in the center of the ranchyard while Elena moved among them bearing a tray of corn tortillas wrapped around shredded pork, and refritos seasoned with chili peppers. Najera's soldiers were hungry and eagerly helped themselves to the contents of the tray.

Ben crouched behind the adobe wall on the roof of the barn and peered at the soldiers below. Najera's carriage had been left in front of the hacienda. Nino, Isabella's fearless canine guardian, had crawled beneath the carriage and was carefully scrutinizing the intruders in the ranchyard. The animal's face was a patch of darkness glimpsed from between the wheel spokes.

Raul Salcedo, Rincon, and Angel walked their mounts over to the barn. Ben recognized the youthful gunman. Zion was standing in the doorway down below, and Ben could easily overhear the conversation that followed.

The black man was blocking Raul's path and did

not appear ready to move. Raul met the segundo's belligerent stare with his own icy resolve. Clouds like puffs of war smoke drifted across the sun and left shadows on the land.

"You look tired, my friend," Raul said. "I think such a large rancho like Ventana is too much work for an hombre like yourself."

"I suspect you're right," Zion replied. "Maybe you'd like to talk to the general and tell him to cut some of my vaqueros loose from his damn army and send them on back home." Zion folded his burly arms across his chest.

"We might have another solution, amigo," Mariano Rincon said. The mestizo slapped at a bothersome horsefly that kept diving toward his leathery features.

"What would that be?" said Zion.

"You could pack your bag and leave," Raul replied.

"I used to think one day I wanted to saddle up my old hammerhead gray and ride this world and find me somewhere to be. A place I could call my own." The black man kicked at the dirt. "But I reckon right here will do."

"Poor choice, *negro*," Angel said. Brash as Raul, he was not content to remain in the gunman's shadow. "Mexico is our country. Your mistress is a gringo and you are a gringo's slave. Better for you both if you ride north."

"Any one of these fine horses I see in the corral could make the journey," Raul interjected as he maneuvered his mount past his associates and approached the wooden fence. His experienced eyes quickly appraised the stock. "I wonder where they came from?"

"Can't see why it should concern you. After all,

General Najera has already taken the best of the stock." Zion's tone was decidedly unfriendly.

"All the ranchos contributed. The general has sacrificed much to supply his troops, but all will be returned once the americanos are driven from our land." Raul eased back in the saddle and motioned for Angel and the mestizo to retrieve the animals. "We can always use a few more horses."

"Now you hold it right there. These horses stay put." Zion brushed past Raul's gelding and climbed up on the fence until he was on the same level as the horsemen. His hand dropped to the pistol at his waist. Angel and Rincon reined in their mounts and glanced at Raul for instructions. The dragoons by the well were too busy gorging themselves on Elena's tamales to notice the confrontation brewing in front of the corral.

"You have no lack of courage, amigo. But we are three and you are alone."

"Not hardly." Ben's voice drifted down from above. "He isn't any more alone than he was that time in the arroyo a couple of weeks ago."

The three men looked up with a start, but Ben remained out of sight. Raul searched the roof line, suddenly less confidant now that there was a man behind him, possibly armed, and with a clear shot at any man in the ranchyard.

"Who are you?" Raul hissed. "Show yourself."

Zion was as shocked as any of them by Ben's behavior. The norteamericano's words were even more puzzling until he glanced down at the scarlet-and-black-striped serape draped across Raul's gelding, just behind the saddle. He remembered the flash of color as the gunman had scrambled for cover. "It *was* you there in the creekbed outside Monterrey."

Raul ignored him and rode along the front of the

adobe barn. "I have asked you a question, hombre. Who are you?"

"El angel de muerte," Ben said. "The angel of your death if you try for the horses."

"And if I summon my *soldados* . . ."

"You will be dead. I and my vaqueros are no strangers to powder smoke. Return to your compadres and enjoy Senora Quintero's hospitality. But know you'll be in our sights until you've left Ventana."

"Did Najera send you to stop us? Why?" Zion asked, reaching for the reins of Salcedo's horse.

Raul pulled away. "You are loco, amigo. Ask any of these men, ask the general, he will tell you. I rode with him to fight the gringos." Raul glanced at Angel and Rincon, who were more concerned by the presence of a hidden marksman than verifying Raul's story. They watched the roof with apprehension and shifted nervously on horseback. Angel imagined he saw movement on the hacienda and the bunkhouse. The whole damn ranchyard was ringed by these fortresslike buildings. How many more riflemen were concealed behind their battlements? There were four horses in the corral. Another four vaqueros armed with pistols and rifled muskets could cut the horsemen in the yard to pieces.

Raul motioned for his companions to rejoin the dragoons as they waited for Najera to end his visit. The mestizo saluted and swung his horse around. His hard, fierce eyes searched the surrounding buildings for some sign of a threat. Angel rode at his side, shoulders hunched. He imagined a dozen rifles had drawn a bead on him. Even Raul Salcedo appeared anxious. What should have been a simple situation had grown terribly complicated. It was time to cut his losses and live to fight another day. The gunman looked down at the black hand still clutching the reins by the bridle.

"Were you after me or the widow, Salcedo?" Zion snarled.

"You misjudge me, amigo."

"Maybe so, maybe not," the segundo said. He realized that with the odds stacked against them, now was not the time or place to set matters aright. His voice was filled with menace. "You're mighty loose with those 'amigos,' but you better know, we aren't friends, Raul. We never were and never will be. Now get out before I let El Alacron up there or one of his men part your hair with a bullet."

"*Bueno*," Raul said, and pulled free of Zion's grasp. At last he had a name for the man who was continuously intruding in matters that were none of his concern. The gunman looked up at the roof. "Come to Saltillo again, Senor Alacron. I do not fear your sting." The boy-faced killer touched the brim of his sombrero and joined the riders at the well. There was still some food left, but for all his bravado, Raul Salcedo had suddenly lost his appetite.

Valentin Najera scolded himself. He had been a fool to send Raul after the Quinteros. This was much better, seated across from his old friend's charming widow. No matter that she was a norteamericano, her beauty transcended the bitter hostilities that divided their countries. And her availability made her all the more lovely.

"The news of Don Sebastien's death struck deep in my soul," he said, finishing his second glass of wine. He shooed a fly away from the honey cake on his plate. The general's brows knitted and his features contorted with grief, then he shook his head and sighed. "Such a waste. Such a waste." Don Sebastien had been his closest friend. Everyone in and around Saltillo knew that. The two men had struggled side by side against Comanches, Apaches, drought, flood, and bitter winters, to maintain their ranchos and secure what they had inherited from their fathers. Najera's first act on arriving at Ventana had been to place a bouquet of desert flowers on Don Sebastien's grave. Milking the moment for all it was worth, the general bowed his head, his shoulders shook, and he appeared to weep silently for the loss of his compadre.

"When he came to see me that night in town, and we shared a bottle of brandy at the Casa del Noche, I had this feeling." He placed his hand over his heart. Movement in the opposite room caught his attention. "Ah, my little sister," he exclaimed. Isabella, caught, stepped through the doorway and entered the dining room. Najera held out his arms as if to embrace the girl, but she hurried past her father's friend and stood by Josefina's chair at the opposite end of the table.

"My dear, my poor little one, I understand your shyness. But the hurt you feel will pass. I would be honored if you thought of me as your father now. You can always come to me with your problems." Najera lowered his outstretched arms and took a morsel of honey cake. He cleared his throat and smiled. "You both stare at me as if I were no longer welcome in the house of Quintero. Have you forgotten Don Sebastien was like a brother to me?"

"If you are so much a friend, why did you steal our cattle?" Isabella blurted out. Josefina instantly regretted discussing anything to do with Ventana's precarious financial situation in front of the precocious ten-year-old. A leaden silence seemed to fill the room. Najera's gaze hardened. Josefina was perceptive enough to realize how dangerous a man her husband's friend really was.

"Nonsense, my dear," she said, gently chiding the child. "All the haciendados have sacrificed for the good of Mexico."

Her words had the desired effect; her gracious acceptance soothed his anger, and the imperious smile once more radiated from his dignified countenance. "Listen to your stepmother, little one. You'll find wisdom in her words. Our country is in peril. An army needs more than guns to fight a war. My men must eat. I am forced to find food for my soldiers wherever I can."

"Perhaps you had best leave us, child, and wait for me in your room. Unless you've finished the reading I assigned you." Josefina had never stopped tutoring the girl, despite her marriage to Don Sebastien. Isabella was at the moment working her way through *Don Quixote*. The book currently lay on an end table alongside her bed. The girl made a face to show her displeasure, then continued on out of the dining room and made her way to the rear of the hacienda.

The general chuckled and sighed. "She is her father's daughter. Don Sebastien never held anything back. He also spoke his mind." Najera leaned forward, his elbows on the table. He glanced toward the door to the pantry. He could hear Elena bustling around the kitchen, preparing another platter of food for his soldiers. For the moment the couple in the dining room were alone. "And as my friend was wont to do, so shall I speak my mind." Najera rose from his chair, walked down the length of the table and took his place at the corner by Josefina. The woman willed herself to remain still, though something in his touch upon her arm made her want to recoil.

"Ventana was not meant to be run by a woman," the general said. "Especially a woman alone. And you are alone, my dear. In these troubled times, there are many who find you suspect. They whisper 'norteamericano' behind your back, and will not lift a hand to help you."

"But you are not one of these?" Josefina looked demure in the afternoon light. Her yellow hair seemed to glow with a brilliance all its own. She smelled of lilac and rosewater.

"No. Never. My dear Josefina, I have always had a special feeling for you." Valentin Najera spoke in silken tones, his aristocratic bearing lending credence to his words. A lie would never grace the lips of such a man. "Ever since Don Sebastien brought you to Ventana. And when I had gathered the courage to speak what was in my heart, Don Sebastien had already asked you to be his wife."

"General Najera . . . this is hardly the time or place. My husband has only been dead for a couple of weeks."

"He was dead to you longer than that."

"Sir?"

"Your husband, my good friend, confided in me about everything. We were like brothers. He told me of his inability to . . . perform intimately. The trouble had plagued him ever since the pain began in his back. How long? Seven months. Eight months. A long time to be without love."

"My personal matters are none of your concern," Josefina protested. "But I can assure you I was never without love in this house."

"Yes. Of a spiritual kind," Najera said, tightening his grip. "But you deserved more. Much more."

"Really, Senor Najera, you overstep yourself."

"Only when the treasure is worth the risk." The general eased back in his chair. "I speak of such things so that you will understand the depth of the feelings I have kept locked away for so long." He stood and walked behind the woman and placed his hands on her shoulders.

"Please . . . Valentin . . . no," Josefina protested. "For the sake of our friendship and the esteem you felt for my husband."

The hands dropped away and he crossed around and sat again at the table, close at hand. The diminutive soldier smoothed his silver hair, then stroked his chin.

"As you wish, dear lady. My affection for you makes me your humble and obedient servant. I can wait. Perhaps it is too soon. In another week or two you will see things differently. I will come again. You will find I can be most persuasive."

"And the war?"

"The war will happen whether I visit you or not," Najera said. He reached for her hand, lifted it to his lips and brushed her knuckles with a kiss. "Don Sebastien would not wish you to pine away, senora. Or sacrifice your beauty on the altar of sorrow. Without cattle and vaqueros to work the range, you cannot last here. You need me." He stood and bowed. "Think about it, my dear. I can do much for you. With my influence, your every wish will be satisfied. Join Ventana to what I have built, and we will have an empire that we can rule together. An empire greater than any in all of northern Mexico."

General Valentin Najera retrieved his lancer's helmet and brushed its scarlet plume with the palm of his hand. His polished thigh-length leather boots click-clacked across the stoneware tile floor. Josefina tried to show him to the door but the general was in a hurry and outdistanced her. Indeed, her movements were awkward, so caught off guard was she by what for all intent was the general's proposal of marriage.

The dragoons came to attention as Najera left the

house and briskly strode to his carriage. Nino crawled out from under the carriage and started toward Najera, who sent the dog packing with a well-placed kick to the rib cage. The general climbed into his carriage and drove out into the ranchyard while his men mounted up and resumed formation. Raul rode up alongside the general and as briefly as possible explained what had happened by the barn. Najera listened intently without looking right or left to inspect the buildings surrounding them. If Senora Quintero had found men to ride for Ventana, the general wanted to know. He issued his instructions, keeping his voice low, and then with a flick of the reins led the way out through the gate. The dragoons formed a column behind the carriage and departed in a cloud of dust.

"Are you certain Raul Salcedo was the man with the Comanche breeds who tried to kill us?" Zion asked, a cup of hot coffee in his hand. He propped an elbow on a bookshelf in Don Sebastien's study, a place where Josefina often took her afternoon tea. Though Najera and his soldiers had departed, they left behind a legacy of tension that permeated the hacienda.

Quintero's widow was still reeling from the shock of Najera's marriage proposal. She looked from her segundo to Ben McQueen. Once again he had acted on their behalf. His intervention had averted bloodshed.

"I may not know who the hell I am," Ben growled, "but I sure as hell remember him. It was Raul Salcedo who tried to kill you. But I doubt he was acting all alone."

"I don't understand. Surely Valentin wouldn't be a part of this. The general was my husband's closest friend."

"Not anymore," Zion said. He had never particularly trusted Najera. Now he was convinced his misgivings had been well-founded. "Why'd he come here, if you don't mind me asking, senora?"

"He wanted me to marry him."

Zion's eyes widened. "Marry him?!"

Josefina ignored his outburst. She poured a cup of tea for herself and waved a hand toward the tray, inviting Ben to help himself. He declined and, having said his piece, excused himself from the study. It was obvious he was a troubled young man and preoccupied with his own problems. He had nothing else to add.

Zion finished his coffee and watched the americano disappear through the front door. "Never known the like of such a man," he said. He scratched his chin with a thumbnail then drained his cup. "What the devil is Najera after?" he muttered, dismissing Ben from his mind.

"Ventana, of course," Josefina said. "My husband was the sole inheritor of his sister's estate. Her death gave him complete ownership of the ranch. Everything belonged to him. And now it is passed on to Isabella and myself. We are all that stands between Najera and his 'empire.'"

"Hell, he's got us by the balls! Uh, sorry, ma'am. Pardon my colorful—uh, I mean poor choice of words." Zion coughed and looked away. Josefina's half smile made him fume even more. "What I'm trying to say is, the general just about has everything his way. He's taken our men, our horses, and there isn't enough cattle to drive to the markets in Guadalajara. You aren't gonna be able to winter here without some kind of income. He must know sooner or later you'll have to leave. What's making him so damn impatient?"

"He must want title to the Ventana, free and clear," she said.

"And want it bad enough to marry you or get you out of the way permanently," Zion finished. A breeze lifted the curtains, and the segundo lowered his face and closed his eyes as the sudden, welcome gust cooled his features. "There's something else. Why act now and not years ago? I wonder what Najera's up to. What does he know that we don't?"

Josefina patted the extensive ledgers and notebooks her husband had kept. Another stack of documents itemized the estate of his notorious sister, Theresa, who had lived a life of promiscuity and shocking immorality until her recent death. Josefina remembered Don Sebastien had talked recently of buying out his sister's share of the Ventana. Theresa had inherited a stretch of land on the northwest border of the ranch, in the foothills of the cordillera. It was worthless mountain country, yet the trouble had begun with her death and Don Sebastien's acquisition of his unmarried sister's estate. Perhaps the answer could be found among the lonely silent hills.

There was only one way to find out.

Sitting atop a wooded ridge north of the hacienda, Angel Perez scratched at the scraggly growth he proudly had trimmed into a goatee, yawned, then stood and stretched the stiffness out of his lean, wiry frame. He had taken the first watch. Squat, solid Mariano Rincon lowered the spyglass through which he had studied the hacienda, barn, and bunkhouse for the last few hours. Now with night coming on, both men were preparing to end their vigil.

"What do you see?" Angel muttered, reaching for his canteen, a clay jug with a cork stopper.

"The same as you. One man, this Alacron, and the segundo. No vaqueros. Just *el negro* and Alacron." Rincon rolled over, sat up and proceeded to fumble in his pocket for the brittle stub of a cigar that resembled a length of twig snapped from a tree. Tobacco in hand, he struck a match, lit the tip and proceeded to enjoy this simplest of pleasures. The aroma stank like burning rubbish. Angel wrinkled his nose and grabbed up the spyglass, working the focus until the man called Alacron appeared in the eyepiece. Ben was standing by the well in the ranch-yard, facing north, one leg crooked on the edge of the well as he braided a length of hemp rope.

"The son of a bitch bluffed us," Angel snapped.

"And sent us packing with our tails tucked between our legs." Rincon chuckled.

"You think it is funny?" Angel said, glowering at the mestizo.

"You are too proud, my headstrong friend." Rincon blew a cloud of smoke into the air.

"And you have no pride at all," Angel retorted. He tossed the spyglass on the ground next to Rincon and began to pace the narrow confines of the clearing. To the west a fading glow brought the day to a close. Shadows quickly deepened on the hilltop beneath the dry pine and oaks. Bats began to swarm across the night sky. Rincon finished the remaining inch of his cigar and crushed the glowing remains against a chunk of limestone. He unrolled his blankets and, helping himself to the supply of beef jerky, crawled into his bedroll.

Angel turned back his blanket and started to get comfortable, then jumped up and swatted at the ground. "Bastard!" He brushed a scorpion from his bedroll. The insect attempted to scuttle to safety but lost its race with death. Angel took a flat rock and crushed the meddlesome intruder.

"Ah . . . now you have your revenge. Let it end there." The mestizo's stomach growled. "Never kill a man for anything but money. Pride . . . revenge . . . love, these things can put a man in an early grave." Rincon rubbed his paunch and gnawed at a leathery strip of jerky. He wondered what Senora Montenez was serving at the Casa del Noche. Perhaps roasted prairie quail with potatoes and wild onions, smothered in gravy, or her stuffed chili rellenos. He began to salivate.

Food was the furthest thing from Angel's mind. His thoughts had taken a darker turn. For too many months he had walked in Raul Salcedo's shadow. He glanced down at the rock in his fist and the smear that had been the scorpion. It was time he proved his own worth, to Raul and to *El Jefe*, Valentin Najera. Angel tossed the rock aside. His lips curled back in a semblance of a smile. He began to formulate a plan.

Night and a breeze like a whisper from God turned the blades on a windmill out in the meadow east of the hacienda. Water drawn from an underground aquifer trickled into a cattle tank. The lowing cattle, vague silhouettes in the darkness, added their voices to the chorus of evening sounds. Starlight brought a chill as the earth relinquished its borrowed warmth. Ben's breath clouded the air. He needed a coat but lacked the will to retrace his steps to the bunkhouse and retrieve one. Zion would be there, and Ben simply wished to avoid the segundo for the moment. The americano wanted to be left alone. At least those were his thoughts until Josefina arrived from the hacienda. Her long, shining, unbound hair lent an air of ethereal beauty to the woman, which transcended the reality of their situation. The lantern dangling from her hand was turned low, its amber glow highlighting her slender neck and delicate features. In the distance, the call of a coyote went unanswered. The animal would sleep lonely tonight.

"The rancho reminds me of a ghost town. I have never known it so quiet." Josefina approached the man seated on the wall by the gate, his lariat coiled and looped over his left shoulder. "It seems only yesterday that the barracks were noisy with the rough camaraderie of men. Vaqueros sat in the ranchyard and serenaded the moon. There were cattle everywhere, and horses. Something was always happening. War has a habit of ruining things, doesn't it?" She wore a gaily dyed blanket wrapped around her shoulders.

"War . . . ? Yes, ma'am."

"You left so abruptly, I didn't have time to thank you. Once again you saved us. If you hadn't bluffed Najera's men, Zion might have been killed. Without him, Isabella and I would be truly finished." She glanced over her shoulder at the hacienda. "I watched you from the study window." She swung a leg up on the wall and kept her other foot on the ground for balance. "You can have part of this blanket. There is room I think for us both."

"You had best be careful, ma'am. An offer to share a blanket is akin to a marriage proposal among the Choctaw." The words slipped out before Ben could think. But his eyes widened the minute they were spoken. The Choctaw! What did he know of such matters? He was so excited by the information he had blurted that it took him a moment to realize Josefina's embarrassment.

"One proposal is enough for today," the widow said.

"I suppose so, senora. I spoke without thinking."

"I accept your apology, but if you wish to truly make amends, perhaps you will accompany me tomorrow." Her eyes were round and limpid by starlight.

"Where?"

"Out there." She gestured to the western horizon where the cordillera loomed. "I may have discovered what General Najera is really after."

Ben watched as the woman set the lantern on the wall and turned up the flames. She brought a small, ornately carved walnut box out from beneath the blanket and set it beside the lantern.

"I found this in a concealed drawer in my husband's desk. I discovered it quite by accident." She unlatched the box and revealed its contents, a piece of parchment bearing a map crudely drawn by Don Sebastien's own hand, and a small buckskin bag. The map indicated a creekbed and a mountain that lay to the west of the hacienda.

"Check the pouch," Josefina said.

Ben obeyed her instructions and emptied the pouch into the palm of his hand. He sucked in his breath. It was a nugget the size of a goose egg.

And damn near solid gold!

Chapter Eleven

The ten-year-old girl rode as well as any vaquero. Isabella had learned to sit a horse at an early
age, and given the opportunity, would rather ride
than walk any day of the week. Her dog Nino
charged among the cattle, scattering the remnants of
the herd. With Nino's help, Isabella cut the calf away
from its mother and drove the frightened animal
toward the segundo. Zion caught the little animal's
front hooves with a well-timed toss of his lariat,
looped the rope around the saddle horn, dismounted
and jerked the calf to the ground. He ran up to the
struggling animal and quickly tied off the calf's
flailing hooves with a piggin string. Then he dragged
the squalling critter over to the fire.

Zion raised the branding iron and spit on its
surface. The moisture sizzled on contact. He knelt on
the calf's neck and applied the iron to its left flank.
The smell of singed hair and flesh momentarily
filled the air. The entire ordeal lasted but a few
seconds, and the calf was released to run bawling
back to its mother. Isabella watched the entire scene
unmoved. Such things were a common occurrence at

the rancho; however, the branding usually involved more than three calves.

Zion straightened and dabbed at his brow with the bandanna he wore about his neck, then stood and surveyed the puny excuse for a herd. Thirty head spread over hundreds of acres could hardly be construed as a thriving enterprise. Isabella's great-grandfather had begun the ranch with about the same size herd. It had taken many years and much sacrifice to establish Ventana and see it become the largest rancho in all of Coahuila. Zion wondered if Quintero's widow was up to a task most men would hesitate to undertake. Of course gold ought to make rebuilding a herd somewhat easier. If there was indeed a seam of gold in the cave above Turtle Creek, as Don Sebastien's map had indicated, Senora Quintero could mine enough ore to buy breeding stock from the ranchos to the south and speed up the process of replenishing the herd. Zion shook his head and sighed. Who would have thought it? Gold. How sadly ironic that such a find, while possibly saving Ventana, might well have cost the haciendado his life.

Zion's thoughts drifted back to the previous evening, when Josefina and Ben had awakened him in the bunkhouse and shown him the nugget and the map the widow had discovered. Zion immediately recognized the drawings, although he could recall no cave above Turtle Creek. He did point out that the discovery was on the section of Ventana deeded to Theresa Quintero, Don Sebastien's errant sister. No doubt this was the reason Josefina's husband had refrained from confiding in the rest of the family. He wanted to be certain of ownership.

Zion immediately surmised that General Najera must have found out about the possibility of gold in the hills west of the valley. Perhaps Don Sebastien had confided in his closest friend while attempting to figure out a way to wrest control of the land from his sister, Theresa.

The segundo, standing on the plain with the branding iron still gripped in his gloved hand, pictured the forest-lined ravine and the cliff from whose base the spring had flowed. Zion had not ridden up into the western hills since the ground tremors earlier in the spring. The shifting earth just might have revealed an entrance heretofore concealed. According to the haciendado's notes, Turtle Creek was no longer the lovely spring-fed watercourse that had provided water for the cattle as they grazed their way up into the high country. Evidently the quake had been strong enough to alter the water table up in the hills, for the spring had ceased to flow, leaving a dry, rubble-strewn creekbed in which Don Sebastien had quite by chance found the gold nugget and supposedly tracked it to its source.

"How long do you think they will be gone? I don't know why Josefina refused to allow me to come along. I might have been of help." Isabella crossed her hands on the saddle pommel and pouted.

"Yes'm. As much help as a snakebite," Zion said while kicking dirt into the fire and shoving the branding iron into the sod until it had cooled enough to carry back to the barn. He reached over, snatched the hat from Isabella's head and sent it sailing through the air. Isabella grinned and tried to return the favor, but Zion was too quick for her and sidestepped as she grabbed for his sombrero. She lost her balance and slipped from the saddle. But the segundo was close at hand and caught her, depositing her on the ground.

"You ought to try and keep your hat on, girl." Zion grinned. "And that's a saddle, not a rocking chair, you know."

Isabella tried to scowl but couldn't maintain the pretense and chuckled despite herself. A gust of wind lifted the girl's flat-crowned hat and propelled it even farther away. Quintero's daughter had to retrieve it on the run and then, facing northwest, eyed with some trepidation the line of thunderheads that darkened the horizon. Earlier in the morning the clouds had been but a thin smear of color above the crest of the cordillera. She glanced around at Zion, who was also watching the sky.

"Reckon we better head back to the hacienda and see if we can rustle up any more of Elena's corn fritters and honey butter," he said to the girl. Though half a mile down the valley, they still had plenty of time to get to shelter before the approaching storm could reach them.

"What about Josefina? And Senor Alacron?"

"There's plenty of caves up in the hills. I reckon they can pick one and wait out the rain," Zion replied as he led both horses over to Isabella. His nonchalant attitude had a calming effect on the girl. Standing alongside her mount, he caught the girl around the waist and lifted her into the saddle.

"Race you to the barn," Isabella exclaimed, and then to ensure she had an adequate head start, snatched the segundo's sombrero before he had time to react and sent it spinning over the chino grama grass. She jabbed her boot heels into her horse's flanks; the animal broke from Zion's grasp and dashed off across the trampled earth.

"Hey!" But he had to grin, and to himself added, "I reckon turnabout is fair play." He trudged through a field of short-stemmed grass and clusters of pink and yellow wildflowers. Grasshoppers vaulted before him, startled into irregular flight as he approached. Reaching down, he gingerly pried his sombrero from the hungry clutches of a prickly pear cactus. Thankfully, the hat had landed upside down, else donning it would have been akin to fitting his head with a crown of thorns.

Zion picked out what barbs he could find and started back to the mean-tempered gray who balefully pawed the earth. The gelding sensed the approaching storm and was anxious to retrace its steps to the hacienda. Zion took up the reins and muttered for the gelding to be patient.

"Never met a horse yet that was so all-fired touchy about a little rain," he complained. "There's nothing to worry about, you ugly sack of bones." Zion's gaze drifted to the western horizon and the trail Josefina had taken, accompanied by a man with no past. As if trying to convince himself, he repeated, "Nothing at all."

"We could kill them now. Right here," said Angel Perez as he entered the clearing in the oak thicket overlooking Turtle Creek. The dry creekbed lay about fifty yards farther along the timbered trail.

"*El Jefe* ordered us to report back to him. We are to tell him what the senora is up to. Nothing more," said Mariano Rincon, a few paces ahead of his hotheaded companion. Ever the pragmatist, he saw no profit in taking unnecessary chances. Najera's orders had been simple and to the point. How many men had the widow hired and what was she up to? Rincon had seen enough. He shot the gun-metal-gray sky a wary glance and then proceeded on to his ground-tethered horse.

"We could sneak up on them. That bastard

Alacron wouldn't know what was happening until it was too late." Angel pulled a pepperbox pistol from his belt and checked the loads in each of the five barrels, but Rincon did not even waver from his course. The mestizo was set on leaving.

"Go on." Angel halted in his tracks. "I am not afraid of a little rain or the widow and her hireling." He and Rincon had followed the couple all morning without incident. Angel saw no reason why he should begin to worry all of a sudden. The senora and the vaquero were too busy with their map to notice they were being followed.

"*Imbecil!* You are no Apache," Rincon finally blurted out. "This vaquero called Alacron troubles me. I think he is a dangerous man. Try to ambush him and you will give yourself away. He will hear you and you will die."

"You talk like a frightened old woman. Wait and see. I will bring General Najera his head. They will write songs about my bravery."

Rincon shrugged in dismay. Arguing with a vain and vengeful youth like Perez was a waste of time. He was tired and hungry and was looking at a long ride back to Saltillo. "I am finished talking," he said. The advice he offered was born of age and wisdom. If it fell on deaf ears, so be it. The mestizo waved farewell, caught up the reins of his gelding and vaulted into the saddle. By the time he had turned, Angel had already started back toward Turtle Creek.

An owl broke from the sanctuary of the trees and glided on ashen wings along the perimeter of pine, cedar, and oak until it had distanced itself from the intruders who had disturbed the bird's tranquility. Squirrels chittered from the branches, as if scolding the humans for their effrontery. Jays added to the chorus, voicing their raucous warnings to the wild-life that continued to call the barren banks of Turtle Creek home. Josefina Quintero dismounted on the banks of the dry creekbed and walked out across the pebble-strewn remains of what had once been a pristine, spring-fed stream flowing out of the rocky battlements, about fifty yards directly ahead.

Ben led his own mount, a blaze-face gelding, along the perimeter of the dry watercourse. He picked his way among the boulders and the profusion of weeds and wildflowers that added color to the barren watercourse. He surmised that the water table had been severely disrupted or possibly re-routed underground by the spring quake. The changing earth had shrugged, and here in the cordillera the mountain had reacted by reclaiming its waters. Perhaps farther along the cliff or even on the opposite side of the ridge, a fresh seepage had begun to wear a path down the slope. Ben tilted his sombrero back on his forehead and studied the battlements. The limestone cliff was scarred with cracks and crevices. Along the crest of the ridge several oaks clung precariously close to a two hundred foot drop, while on the slope that skirted the battlements, the shattered remains of trees, like the bones of slaughtered buffalo driven over the cliff in days past, lay visible among the boulders.

Thunder rumbled, and Ben turned his attention to the sky. It was already past noon. If the storm came on through, he and the widow could still reach Ventana before nightfall. But they'd certainly need shelter. To the north, sheet lightning shimmered in the black iron bowels of an enormous thunderhead that continued to threaten the cordillera with the chance of a drenching downpour and the danger of flash floods.

"Alacron! I've found something!" Josefina excitedly called out. She was on her knees among the water-smoothed pebbles, and motioned for him to join her. By the time Ben reached the woman, she had climbed to her feet and was literally trembling. Ben dismounted and stood at her side. She opened her hand and revealed several pea-sized pebbles of gold. Ben slowly exhaled, his own pulse quickened at the sight of the ore. It was like being hit by lightning, a shock that commanded one's attention and could prove lethal.

"Where does it come from?" Josefina asked, dropping the nuggets into a pouch dangling from her belt. She was dressed like a vaquero, in a flannel shirt, canvas pants, and a broad-brimmed, flat-crowned hat. She wore her blond hair in a single braid down her back.

"Up yonder," Ben said. "The spring could have washed it out from an underground chamber. But the map there has a cave circled." He took care to study the hillside and the cliff, and noted a gash at the base of the ridge, which appeared to be the mouth of a cave. That had to be the cave indicated on Don Sebastien's map. "Perhaps we better get under cover." He took up the reins of both horses and led the animals up the slope toward the opening, which on closer examination appeared to have been created when the outer wall of a chamber had literally crumbled away. Don Sebastien's cave offered the best available shelter. At least it was good enough for Josefina, who was more than anxious to avoid the oncoming storm. Ben quickened his pace up the incline as the first heavy droplets began to fall. Behind Ben, a pair of wild turkeys broke from the underbrush and darted across the streambed, only to vanish in the underbrush lining the opposite bank.

Ben turned and drew his revolver. Josefina stopped in her tracks. "What?"

Ben held his finger to his lips and continued to watch their back trail. Minutes crawled past slower than any of the turtles that had once populated the creek. Ben watched the last of the turkeys disappear. Something or someone had startled the normally reclusive creatures. However, as neither man nor beast revealed themselves, Ben resumed his climb to the cave. Along the way the americano scanned the surrounding forest. He'd been too damn occupied with the woman and the map, and scolded himself for not being more vigilant, although there was probably nothing to worry about.

The wind picked up and thunder rumbled yet again and more droplets fell. Ben was the first to reach the cave, an opening about fifteen feet in height and nearly thirty feet across. The rocky ceiling overhead gradually angled down until a man would have to walk at a crouch to reach the back wall. The tremors had literally obliterated the outer wall of the cavern, allowing access to the front chamber all along its length. Ben tethered the horses in the front chamber and faced them toward the rear of the cave, then left to gather firewood, of which there was plenty among the rocks. The sky darkened until it seemed as if night itself was upon the land. As the heavy raindrops began to spatter against the stone, pockets of dust erupted on impact like miniature explosions. A few of the droplets stung Ben's knuckles and convinced him he had enough firewood. He darted up the slope, entered the open-sided cavern, and deposited his load of wood. He noticed Josefina, still clutching her husband's map, standing at the rear of the chamber and staring at a seam in the back wall of the cave.

Ben stacked the wood and started a campfire. Flames quickly devoured the dry timber. Soon a circle of light illuminated the chamber, leaping flames casting gyrating shadows on the walls, whorled pillars and jagged stalactites taking on the semblance of motion. The effect was disconcerting for it seemed as if they had made camp in the jaws of some monstrous beast. Ben didn't need to ask about the seam, he had seen the map. It had not been on a whim that Don Sebastien had sketched in the creek-bed and the cave. He had drawn a circle around the crudely penciled representation to indicate its importance. From what Ben could tell, Senora Quintero was a very rich widow.

The rain began to fall in earnest now, great slanting sheets of gray water that masked the chamber from the rest of the ravine. Josefina approached the fire and knelt in the circle of warmth on the blankets Ben had spread. She watched in silence as he spooned coffee into a tin pot, added water from his canteen, and placed the pot in the coals on the periphery of the fire.

"These hills used to belong to my sister-in-law, Theresa Quintero. For more than a month my husband had been trying to acquire it from her. I could not understand why he was so desperate to buy her out of the estate. Now I know." Josefina sighed and folded her hands in her lap. "Poor Sebastien. He must have been horrified at the very notion that Theresa would have wound up with a gold mine." Josefina brushed the dust from her trouser legs and sat back on her heels. "Sebastien loved his sister despite the fact she caused him a great deal of pain. One scandal after another . . . We all were relieved when she moved to Linares. When news reached us she had died of pneumonia, he was saddened, and yet I wonder if he felt some secret, guilty joy. After all, Ventana was completely his." The widow leaned into Ben and added, "And it didn't even cost him a single centavo."

The woman's gaze grew distant. She had been alone for so long. Even before her husband's accident, he had been dead below the belt. Accident? Perhaps Zion was right. "Poor Sebastien . . . he probably thought his discovery was a blessing. But it was a curse." She lowered her head and cupped her face in her hands. Her shoulders bowed forward, and in that moment Ben was moved to pity. He eased up alongside her and, kneeling on the blankets at her side, put his arm around the woman to comfort her. She turned and pressed against him and gradually the tears subsided. He found himself staring into the fathomless pools of her eyes. Josefina reached up, placed a hand on the back of his neck and drew him to her. Her mouth covered his in a feverish kiss. Now her arms were around him, her weight against his chest causing him to lose his balance. Ben's shoulder struck the blanket and he pulled her atop him. Her fingers fumbled with the buttons on his shirt. When his chest was bare, she rose up and pulled off her own blouse.

Ben was speechless. A gentleman ought to stop this before things got out of hand. However, even if he had been able to think of the words, he wouldn't have said them. The taste of her, the animal heat radiating from her, aroused his own primal instincts. Her passion had ignited his. Right or wrong had nothing to do with what happened next. Josefina and Ben were drawn together out of loneliness. There was no turning back. Storm-tossed on a sea of sorrow, they clung to one another. Clothes were hurriedly cast aside, and in the union, quickly consummated, they found not love, but healing.

Lulled by the rain, the two drifted into sleep, a man without a memory, a woman who remembered too much.

Angel Perez brushed against a cedar branch and showered himself with cold droplets of rain. A droning downpour continued to fall in rippling silvery sheets from the brooding sky. The slim, dark-haired gunman had waited long enough. He'd lost track of time, but he figured at least an hour or so had passed since the storm began. Turtle Creek was flowing with runoff as he crossed the once dry bed and started up the slick slope toward the cave. The odor of wood smoke permeated the air. That suited him fine. If the widow and the vaquero had pitched camp, they wouldn't be expecting trouble. Angel grinned and pulled the pistol from his belt. It had served him well.

At first Angel had considered waiting, concealed among the trees, and with his rifle, bringing down the one who called himself Alacron. But the gunman wanted the hireling to see his killer's face and to know that, although Angel Perez might have been driven off from the rancho, he had returned to exact a price.

The gunman picked his way among the rocks. Once, he slipped, fell to one knee and dislodged a handful of pebbles into the creek. He checked the mouth of the cave and saw nothing but the horses and a ribbon of smoke curling out from the opening. Angel held his pistol beneath his serape to keep the weapon dry. Rivulets spilled from the brim of his high-crowned sombrero. He licked his lips and continued up the hillside, anxious to have the senora and Alacron under the gun. Rincon should have stayed, Angel thought. The mestizo was a coward.

He had no use for men who lacked courage. No use at all. It was time he and Raul were rid of the likes of Mariano Rincon. High time indeed.

Angel reached the cave and carefully entered the chamber. The loud, peculiar sound of the rain pattering against his sombrero instantly ceased. Funny, he hadn't noticed the noise before. The mestizo's warning nibbled on the periphery of his thoughts. Supposing Alacron had heard? Angel dismissed the notion and started past the two horses, who stirred as he approached.

The animals shifted their stances and swung their heads to watch the stranger with round-eyed suspicion. The crackle of the campfire and the flickering light dispelling the storm's gray gloom lured Angel onward. He rounded the geldings, reassuring them with a touch of his hand. He had always been good with horses and had gentled many of Najera's wild stock. But where was the gold or glory in breaking horses? Angel brought up his pistol. He hesitated, inhaled, then darted into the center of the chamber and brought the pistol to bear on a rumpled blanket, a discarded shirt, a pair of woman's riding boots. Mariano Rincon's final warning suddenly reverberated in Angel's mind. *He will hear you and you will die.*

The unmistakable sound of a gun being cocked and a hasty glance toward the rear of the chamber revealed the man and woman Angel Perez had come to kill. Josefina was only half dressed; she wore canvas pants and clutched a shirt to her naked bosom. She was barefoot as well. Quintero's widow was a study in confusion and alarm as she peered over Alacron's shoulder.

Ben McQueen was shirtless. In the firelight his muscled torso gleamed with perspiration. His trousers were hitched around his waist with a wide leather belt from which dangled a pouch containing powder and shot and a spare cylinder for the Patterson Colt he was aiming at the intruder outlined against a backdrop of rainfall and mist-shrouded ridge.

"Scorpion . . ." Angel hissed, and his gun hand snapped up.

Ben fired, and the gun boomed loud as a cannon in the cavern. The bullet struck Angel in the shoulder and slammed him back into the rain. He lost his footing and tumbled down the slope. Ben followed the wounded man out from the cave. The downpour pelted him, washing the dye from his muscled physique and from his hair. Ben spied Angel about twenty feet farther down the hill. The gunman was smeared with mud and had struggled to his knees. He was trying to bring his pistol into play with his left hand now, for his right arm hung useless. The pain of his shattered shoulder fueled his efforts.

Ben picked his way down the hillside, and by the time he reached Angel's side, the rain had for the most part washed away his disguise. Angel's jaw dropped and his gaze hardened.

"A gringo!" he said through clenched teeth. The gun in his left hand swept up. Ben's well-placed kick sent the pepperbox spinning from the gunman's grasp. He placed the smoking, blued-steel muzzle of his Patterson Colt against the wounded man's temple and thumbed the hammer back. Angel grew pale, and fear replaced the pain in his eyes. He began to tremble as he beheld his own death.

For what seemed an eternity, the tableau held. Then Ben changed his mind. He grabbed Angel by the front of his serape, hauled him to his feet and, putting his face close to the gunman's, spoke in a hushed but ominous voice.

"Get out of here! *Comprende?* Don't look back. I give you your life . . . for the last time. Ride north, south, I don't give a damn. But keep riding, away from Saltillo, away from Ventana, and away from me." Ben contemptuously released his hold. Angel staggered and momentarily lost his footing as Ben turned his back on the humiliated young man and started up the hillside.

Angel blinked back tears of rage, his shoulders sagging, his breathing coming in coarse and ragged gasps. *Driven off like a whipped dog! No! Not again! The shame was unbearable.*

"You bastard gringo!" he screamed. "It is not ended. One day we shall meet again. And I will kill you. Do you hear me? I swear on the grave of my mother, it is not finished between us."

"The hell it isn't!" Ben said. He turned and shot Angel Perez between the eyes. The gunman's body flopped back and slid a yard, then rolled down the slope and came to rest in Turtle Creek. A trace of silt, caught by the runoff, washed into the dead man's gaping mouth.

Ben holstered his revolver and returned to the cave. When he entered the chamber, he found Josefina dressed and obviously in a hurry to be on her way, no matter what the weather. She drew back as he approached. The woman seemed afraid of him, as if he were the dead man in the creek below. Ben tried to hold her, but she retreated from his outstretched arms.

"You shot him. In cold blood. Like swatting a fly. It didn't even bother you. What kind of man . . . who are you?" She shrank back toward her horse.

Anger flashed in Ben's eyes, and he caught her

by the arm and forced her to face him. "I am no one. A blank. The scorpion when you need me to sting. I am the man who lay with you on that blanket, and there is no going back from it."

He released his hold, and she turned and bit her lower lip, suddenly embarrassed by her own weakness and wrapping herself in regret for everything that had occurred. He was the man who had saved her life. Who was she to pass judgment on him now?

"Look," Ben gently added, "Josefina . . ." But the words failed. She had seen too much death. He looked down at his hands and then left her side to stare through the lessening downpour at the crumpled body lying in the creek. Ben gasped. Images suddenly assailed him. Bodies tumbling. Men dying. Ned Tolliver waving and then disappearing into the trees. Screams and gunfire and horses breaking loose and running free. For a brief second fear had a chokehold on his heart, then the moment passed.

The dead man in the creek had left him no choice. Ben wasn't about to live his life watching his back trail for the likes of Angel Perez. He did what needed to be done. He lifted the medal that lay against his chest. Just a coin, a silver coin, scratched with the initials of George Washington. Realization struck him like a slap in the face. Another fragment of memory. He grasped for more, tried to capture the thoughts and missed, and yet what was left was a sense of purpose, a feeling . . . no . . . more than a feeling . . . a knowledge that he came from a family whose offspring were always ready "to do what needed to be done."

Ben pulled on his shirt, caught up his hat, and returned to the horses. The animals stamped and tossed their manes, anxious to be free of the cave and the acrid stench of powder smoke. He glanced aside at Josefina, who lowered her gaze.

"I don't know what . . . I'm sorry," she said.

"Don't be," Ben replied. "You found what you came looking for." He glanced down at the glowing embers. Without fuel, the fire wouldn't last. But the blaze had served its purpose, it had warmed them throughout the storm. Now was not the time or place to ask for more.

Chapter Twelve

It was said of Ned Tolliver he'd gamble with the devil if the stakes were high enough. In lieu of "Old Scratch" he'd found Valentin Najera, much to the chagrin of Lucker Dobbs, who couldn't help but be alarmed at the way Ned was winning. Serena Montenez, the proprietress of the Casa del Noche, had warned the Texans that the general was a poor loser and apt to seek retribution against those who caused him displeasure. Dobbs dabbed the perspiration from his thick, ugly features with a soiled bandanna and glanced across the courtyard at the wall, with its row of jars whose grisly contents were common knowledge. He had witnessed Najera's treatment of the dead Rangers firsthand, and had no desire to experience the same fate as the comrades he had betrayed. The brooding ex-patriot noted that Najera's personal guard, eight soldiers armed with sabers and pistols, were scattered around the courtyard, dozing peacefully. But there was no doubt a single command from *El Jefe* would snap them into action.

Seated at the table were the general and Ned Tolliver; Carlos Navarro, the mayor of Saltillo; and

Emilio Granados, a local haciendado who had brought horses and cattle and left them with his vaqueros outside of town at the main encampment. Granados's rancho was about half as large as Ventana, but he had been stricken with patriotic fervor and willingly joined the Army of Coahuila, for which he had been accorded the rank of Lieutenant Colonel. Both Navarro and Granados, weary from three and a half hours of liquor and bad luck, had folded after the general's deal, abandoning the "field of battle" to the former Ranger and Valentin Najera. The general had been losing steadily since midnight. It seemed Tolliver could do no wrong. Every card he needed came his way no matter who dealt. The current hand was no exception.

"Sorry, General," Tolliver said as he laid three queens faceup on the table. A broad self-satisfied grin crinkled his face. Easing back in his chair, Tolliver shoved his wire-rimmed spectacles back up on the bridge of his nose. "Three lovely ladies . . . for your pleasure."

Najera stared down at his own hand. He had been certain three tens would recoup his losses. The general cursed beneath his breath and glared at Tolliver as the Texan arranged his winnings in three neat stacks; an assortment of Spanish coins, currency, and Valentin Najera's latest wager, a pouch containing an assortment of gold nuggets that the general had personally recovered during a clandestine and solitary visit to Turtle Creek.

"You are a most fortunate hombre. Lady Luck has smiled upon you," Najera said.

"Not luck. You take too many chances," Tolliver replied, his narrow-eyed stare hidden behind the glint of lantern light off the lenses of his spectacles.

"A man who does not take chances cannot lead or command the respect of his men," Najera replied, leaning back. Marita had been seated directly behind the general ever since her paramour had moved the game outside and away from the smoky interior of the cantina. She immediately leaned forward and began nibbling his ear. He brushed her away as one would a troublesome insect. Marita pouted, tossed her head like a wild colt and stalked out of the courtyard, long black hair trailing in the breeze. "That is the difference between us, I think," Najera added, "and why you will never be any more than what you are at this moment."

"Seems like the difference between us is that I have this here stack of coins in front of me that once belonged to you." Ned grinned. "And what I am, General, sir, is winning, which suits me just fine."

Dobbs groaned and gulped the pulque he had brought out from the cantina. The fiery liquid did little to placate his misgivings; still, false courage was better than none at all. He allowed his hand to drop to the butt of his Patterson Colt as he eased back into the shadowy corner where the low wrought-iron railing joined the wall of the Casa del Noche. The intricately designed railing separated the courtyard from the *mercado*, devoid of merchants now, as the hour was approaching a quarter past one in the morning. The amber glare of the oil lamps failed to reach where Dobbs took up position. If trouble developed, it was every man for himself. Ned Tolliver was on his own and partnership be damned.

"Easy on the gun, gringo." Dobbs recognized the stuporous voice of Raul Salcedo. The gunman was seated before an open window where he could keep watch on the entire courtyard and, most especially, the general's back. The aroma of chili and freshly warmed tortillas trailed Raul's quiet warning through the open window.

Dobbs allowed his hand to sweep past his gun.

"Ain't no need to get riled, Mex. I'm just scratching my ass." The turncoat Ranger clawed at the seat of his britches and flashed a broken-tooth grin. Dobbs shifted his stance and made a show of stretching and yawning.

"Reckon I'll catch me some shut-eye." Dobbs caught a glimmer of lightning off to the northwest. "Storm coming." He shoved clear of the wall, touched a hand to the brim of his hat, and nodded to the silhouette in the window. "Reckon I'll mosey on home."

Tolliver and Dobbs shared a jacal a few blocks off Market Square. They had chosen not to bed down in the hotel or one of the bordellos, as neither of the americanos wished to announce his comings and goings to Najera's guard. Tolliver's poker winnings were the first real money either man had seen, although Najera kept assuring them both they would be paid for their recent treachery. Tolliver trusted no man. If Najera should decide he no longer needed the service of the former Rangers, the two men wanted at least a chance to slip away from the town unnoticed.

Raul wasn't about to let the man out of his sight until the general had finished with both of the Texans.

"I think you had better return to the side of your compadre," Raul said, punctuating his advice by cocking the twin hammers on a double-barreled percussion pistol gripped in his right hand. "Sit with him in the light where I can see you. Perhaps you will bring him luck, eh?"

"Younker, you got a habit of getting on a man's nerves."

Raul merely leaned forward, allowing Dobbs to see the menacing twin barrels of the gun he held. It was a heavy-bore weapon, probably .54 caliber, from what Dobbs could tell. The gun packed enough punch to cut a man off at the waist, even one with as much of a gut as Lucker Dobbs.

"Reckon I ain't as tired as I thought." Dobbs did as he was ordered. The big man lowered his weight into a chair at a table alongside the one occupied by Ned Tolliver and Valentin Najera.

Mayor Navarro nodded to the americano then lifted his clay mug and scowled to find it empty. He set the mug aside, licked his dry lips and tried to remember just how much he had drunk. Ah, but his head felt as if it were stuffed with straw, and the immediate past hidden behind a blur of cards, pluque, and tobacco smoke. Granados reached for the cards, it was his deal, but the general caught the haciendado's wrist and pulled his hand away from the deck.

"I have had enough, my friends!" the general snapped. Then he smiled and thanked them both for the pleasure of their company. "The hour is late and you have families who no doubt resent your absence."

"Soon as we get under way, the better," Granados said. "My Chiquita has done nothing but weep and carry on ever since I told her I was going off to fight the gringos." The haciendado was a wiry man in his middle thirties, tough as whipcord, the kind of man who looks forward to a good fight. Both mayor and rancher rose from the poker table and bid the general a good night. The mayor, a portly dark-haired man with an officious bearing copied after the general's, led the way out of the courtyard. Navarro, for one, was grateful to be out of harm's way. Najera had a mercurial temper; only a fool would cross him. The gringo was playing a dangerous game. The general was gunpowder with a short fuse, and Tolliver an open flame. Sooner or later he'd press his luck too far, and the mayor did not want to be around for the explosion.

Najera waited until both men had departed, then he motioned for Tolliver to remain and sent one of his dragoons to bring coffee and fried bread from the hotel's kitchen. Senora Montenez had sent her serving girls home and retired for the evening, but the proprietress always left a platter of fried bread, honey, and a large pot of coffee hanging over the coal in the fireplace. The general watched as Ned Tolliver palmed his coins into a leather pouch.

"You are a wealthy man now," Najera dryly observed. "I am forced to consider the best way to recoup my loses." He stroked his chin as if giving the matter some thought. His eyes darted from Tolliver to Dobbs. He motioned for another of his dragoons, a gruff-looking individual, grizzled, with eyes like black marble, and sent the man to the wall to retrieve one of the jars. A few moments later the man returned bearing a jar that the general ordered him to leave on the table. Najera leaned forward and opened the lid. The strong scent of oil permeated the air. Najera shook the jar and something inside sloshed and bumped against the inside walls of the stoneware container. The muffled sound was made all the more hideous for knowing its source. "Now what do you think the Rangers would do if they ever found out who betrayed them to me? How much would such information be worth?"

"Now that ain't funny, General, sir," Dobbs remarked, nervously studying the jar. He noticed Najera wasn't laughing.

Ned Tolliver wasn't about to be bluffed. "I reckon Captain Pepper and Snake-Eye Gandy would give just about anything to learn it was me and Lucker. But since your lancers with their pig stickers took no prisoners, I reckon the Rangers won't ever know."

Tolliver glanced over at the jar on the table. He reached inside, grabbed a handful of hair and lifted the severed head out for all to see. One of the dragoons in the courtyard, a youthful good-natured vaquero, doubled over and headed for the alley. "And I doubt this poor bastard will talk."

"Christ almighty, Ned." Dobbs grimaced and looked away.

The former Ranger lowered the head back into the oil and stared across the open jar at Najera, whose thoughts were concealed beneath an aristocratic facade. "Still, if old Pete Baxter here could talk, I wonder which name'd be the first on his lips, General . . . yours or mine."

Najera calmly replaced the lid and slid the jar across the table to Ned Tolliver. "A gift . . . something to remember me by should we be separated in Monterrey," the general said. "I am a river to my people. But to my enemies . . ." He tapped the side of the jar.

"We got business in Monterrey?" Dobbs asked. His expression was one of complete revulsion toward the gift Najera had bestowed. But this new information had him worried. The last place Lucker Dobbs wanted to be was closer to General Zachary Taylor's army and its contingent of Texas Rangers. He wasn't liking any of this at all.

"I will be marching north in a few days to combine my forces with those of General Arista in Monterrey. Word has come that a number of americanos deserted General Taylor's army after the fall of Matamoros and have been imprisoned by Arista. You will take command of them when we arrive and form a troop of your fellow countrymen to join us in throwing Taylor's army back across the border."

Najera chuckled and added, "I may make an officer out of you yet, Senor Tolliver."

"Now see here. I don't—" Dobbs started to protest, but Tolliver silenced him with a glance.

"We will do our best, General," he said. "I assume we will be paid for our services?"

"Arrangements have been made," Najera said. "But tell me, do you not have enough gold?"

"There is never enough," Tolliver pointed out.

The general nodded. "Si. In this we are of agreement." His thoughts drifted back to Don Sebastien, the friend who had shared a confidence and awakened in Valentin Najera jealousy and a malevolent lust for wealth. For one single fleeting instant Najera experienced a pang of regret for what was lost. But the moment passed and nothing was changed. Najera had buried the truth of his betrayal beneath layers of self-deceit, and actually believed he had acted for the good of Mexico.

The dragoon dispensed to the cantina reappeared bearing a platter of fried bread, honey, and coffee, and placed the humble repast on the table in front of the general.

"You know," Najera said to Tolliver, "for a moment there I considered having you shot for your insolence." He picked up a piece of fried bread and began to chew.

"Why didn't you?" Tolliver asked.

"Because I have need of a man like you."

"And when you have no need of a man like me?"

"Then I'll have you shot," Najera replied, rocking with laughter. He had to spit out the bread to keep from choking. The sound of his voice alerted the other uniformed men in the courtyard, who sat up sharply and rubbed the sleep from their eyes.

Ned Tolliver was less than amused and started

to voice his thoughts on the matter when Mariano Rincon entered from the street. His clothes were disheveled and stuck damply to his skin. He had ridden through three storms after leaving the foothills west of Ventana, and was nearly out on his feet from the ordeal. Yet he wavered only slightly as he approached the general's table and saluted.

"We kept watch as you ordered, *Jefe*. There is but one vaquero to help the segundo," Rincon said after the general gave him permission to make his report.

"As I expected," Najera replied. "That news could have waited. You did not need to brave the storms to tell me tonight."

"That is not why I have come," the mestizo explained. His gaze drifted to a clay pitcher of pulque. Najera nodded his permission, and the breed grabbed the pitcher and emptied its contents down his gullet. The milky white liquor sloshed out from the corners of his mouth, dribbled down his stubbled chin, and added another layer of stains to his bedraggled attire. When he'd drained the last drop, Rincon set the pitcher aside and continued.

"The senora Quintero left this morning accompanied by the drifter who calls himself Alacron. Angel and I trailed them. It was easy enough, for the widow and her vaquero were paying more attention to the map than their back trail."

"A map?" Najera repeated, intrigued and obviously concerned.

"Si. And I think they found what they were looking for. A dry creekbed in the foothills of the cordillera west of the hacienda and the grazing land." Rincon gestured toward the fried bread, and the general allowed the man to help himself. Najera found Rincon's story most interesting. "Before heading out for Saltillo, I rode up the ridge and watched them through my spyglass. Yes, they both seemed very excited. Especially the woman. I could see Angel watching them from the trees. He chose to remain at the creek, but I thought you would want to hear about the widow's strange behavior."

"You have done well," Najera remarked, sliding back in his chair and standing. He glanced around the courtyard, his expression one of blatant displeasure and concern. He seemed to look right through Ned Tolliver and Lucker Dobbs, seated across from him. Tolliver's winnings meant nothing to the general now. Where was Marita? he wondered. Oh yes, he had sent her off to the hotel. No doubt she was waiting for him in his room. Her attentions were the last thing he needed. He must be alone, to think, to plan. The widow had found the gold. Curse Don Sebastien for leaving a map.

Valentin Najera had known it was only a matter of time before someone from the rancho, either the woman or the segundo, rode west and discovered what the shifting earth had uncovered. The general had hoped to acquire Ventana before the truth came out. Now something else would have to be done, another course followed.

"Get some rest, Rincon," Najera said, brushing past the mestizo and heading for the hotel. Time was running out. General Arista was expecting him in Monterrey along with the nearly thousand men camped a few miles from town. Najera's mind began to wrestle with the dilemma that would occupy his thoughts for the remainder of the night.

The general's departure acted as a signal to the uniformed men in the courtyard that they too were free to retire. Soon, Tolliver and Dobbs were alone. Flies began to hover above the platter of fried bread. Dobbs shooed them away and tucked several of the greasy chunks in his pockets for breakfast.

"What the hell is so all-fired important about some damn creek?" Dobbs said as he emptied the platter.

"Oh, maybe what 'some damn creek' has washed down out of the hills," Tolliver replied, holding up the leather pouch of nuggets recently acquired from the general. Now here was an answer Tolliver was determined to uncover. His gaze settled on the receding figure of Mariano Rincon, shambling across Market Square. "And I know just where to begin."

Marita was confused. She knew the general, her lover, was troubled, and she wanted to help by giving herself to him. But Najera had sent her from the room. Pausing in the doorway, she looked back and saw Valentin Najera seated in a chair before the window overlooking Market Square and the night-shrouded town. The horizon flickered with lightning and the wind picked up before the approaching storm and moaned as it seeped in through a crack in the windowpane.

Najera felt her presence, yet made no overture toward the girl. He sat in his chair and studied the storm, but his mind was far removed from the marvels of nature. It was as if the ghost of Don Sebastien were reaching out from the grave and trying to thwart his ambitions. Smoke curled from the tip of a brittle-looking black cigar Najera held in his right hand. From time to time he lifted the cigar to his lips, took a slow, lazy drag and exhaled a harsh-smelling cloud that billowed up to the ceiling.

"Mi querida," Marita said.

"Leave me." Najera never stirred. His voice drifted to her across a gulf the likes of which she ached to cross. But such a feat was impossible. He was the general, a man of station, and the only way to enter his world was to be invited.

"Let me be with you, *mi querida.*"

"Are you deaf as well as ignorant?"

His words bit as deep as a bullwhip. The fifteen-year-old winced and drew back into the hall, quietly closing the door as she left. Marita turned and felt her way down the darkened corridor, as some idiot had extinguished the lamps. Suddenly a hand gripped her wrist and pulled her into the bedroom across the hall and a couple of doors down from Najera's quarters. Marita started to cry out, but a hand covered her mouth. Raul's voice whispered in her ear, ordering her to be quiet. The glare of lightning filled the window, enabling her to discern the gunman's wiry torso. He had discarded his shirt. His sweaty body smelled of sage and tequila as he leaned against her, forcing the girl against the wall alongside the door. His hands cupped her breasts, then ran along her side and down to her thighs, pulling the hem of her flowery cotton dress to her waist.

"No" she whispered. But her tone was hardly convincing. Angered as she was by Najera's treatment, the notion of giving herself to his trusted lieutenant smacked of sweet retaliation. In the past, she had teased Raul and smiled flirtatiously whenever the general wasn't looking. It had made her feel powerful to exert her influence over as dangerous a man as Salcedo. And though he would never be considered handsome, there was a quality Raul possessed that Marita found attractive. The other soldiers gave him a wide berth for he was the general's enforcer and no one wanted his kind of trouble. She resisted just long enough to preserve her dignity and then opened to him, drawing him into her, feeding on his fire and fury.

Outside the walls, the thunder rumbled. The

dogs in the alleyways of Saltillo began to howl and bay. Shutters were closed with a bang and hastily latched. A storm was raging in the distance, battering the black horizons to the north and west. It would be here soon.

Chapter Thirteen

By noon of the following day the sky over Ventana was a deep and brilliant azure and cloudless from the crest of the cordillera to the rolling plains, with their lush carpet of pale green grasses. Standing pools of water dotted the meadow, attracting countless swarms of birds diving and swooping on wings of scarlet and blue, tufted grays and browns, borne on the spring breeze, their every movement a joyous celebration of rebirth and renewal. Sunlight turned the puddles into ponds of molten gold and warmed the earth underfoot, bringing life forth from burrow, den, and nest.

Hours earlier, in that night of storms, Josefina and the americano had returned to the warmth and safety of the hacienda. Once in the ranchyard, the couple had awkwardly bid one another a good night, then parted company, Ben to the bunkhouse and Josefina to her bedroom. Zion, waiting up by the stove in the bunkhouse, had insisted that "Senor Alacron" tell him everything that had happened and what they had found. Ben had recounted as briefly as possible all that he had seen, including the gunfight with Angel Perez, but discreetly omitted what had transpired between Josefina and himself. Whatever misgivings the segundo had felt concerning the death of Perez had been more than allayed by Ben's description of the formerly concealed seam of gold that the collapsed cavern had revealed. Zion had dreamt of gold all that night, and by midmorning he was already organizing a plan for extracting enough of the ore to restore Ventana to its former prosperity.

Anxious to continue the conversation begun the previous night, Zion was displeased when Ben refused to join him for breakfast. With a strange, almost haunted expression on his face, "Scorpion" quietly but firmly stated he had more important business, saddled a horse and rode off toward the north ridge overlooking the hacienda. Zion's fervent objections went ignored, a fact that mightily displeased him. He mentioned as much to Elena when he arrived for breakfast and took his usual seat at the table in the summer kitchen. Elena lent him a sympathetic ear as she poured him a cup of coffee.

"Senor Alacron is a strange one. None of his conduct surprises me," said the tall, thin woman whose severe countenance hid the real affection she held for the segundo. She shrugged then poured a cup of coffee for herself. There always seemed to be a pleasant breeze here in the shade of the covered walkway that joined the kitchen to the rear of the hacienda. The peace was abruptly shattered by a quarrelsome pair. Pedro Gallegos ambled around the corner of the kitchen, leading Nino at the end of a rope. The scruffy-looking hound fought the ranchero every step of the way, growling and snapping while Pedro harangued him with a litany of epithets.

"C'mon, you blasted thief, you flea-ridden son of a sow-bellied alley slut, you worthless bag of skin and bones," Pedro cursed in rapid-fire Spanish that

Zion had trouble completely understanding. However, Pedro's temperament presented a clear translation.

"Mind your tongue, husband!" Elena ordered. She struck an imposing figure with her silver-streaked black hair, and massive hands folded on the tabletop.

"I caught Nino in the smokehouse again!" For the past few months Pedro and the mongrel hound had engaged in a running battle for ownership of the smokehouse. Nino considered the delectable array of smoked meats his personal larder.

"Then make a bigger latch or replace the bricks the dog has dug through, but I will not have you use such language with a child in the house." Elena glared at the dog and the animal fell silent.

"Wife, this is a ranch, not Father Rudolfo's church." Pedro proceeded to secure the dog to a round wooden beam six inches in diameter that supported the walkway's brush roof. "And besides, Isabella left half an hour ago."

"Isabella . . . gone?" Josefina interjected from the shadowy interior of the house. She appeared in the rear doorway wearing a dressing gown, a robe, and slippers of brushed buckskin that one of Father Rudolfo's mission Indians, old Esteban, had presented to her as a gift of thanks for nursing one of his daughters through a fever. "Where?"

Pedro shrugged. "I cannot say for certain, senora, but I got the impression she was tagging after the americano." He pointed to the pine oak forest lining the north ridge.

Zion sensed Josefina's discomfort when the talk turned to Senor Alacron. His own expression grew serious. "You want me to go after them, Miss Josefina?" he asked.

Josefina shook her head and took a seat on the

bench across from the segundo. "She will be all right. I'm just a little anxious after all that has happened." She nodded her thanks when Elena brought her a cup of strong black coffee.

"You have a right to be. No telling what Valentin Najera is apt to try next," Zion said. "Sure as God made green apples, I swear that man is more crooked than a wagonload of rattlesnakes."

"Then you know what happened at Turtle Creek?" Josefina asked, hoping he didn't know everything.

Zion nodded. "Perez may have needed killing, but that won't matter to the general."

"Perhaps if we went to the authorities," Josefina suggested.

"Madre de Dios," Elena said. "Valentin Najera *is* the authorities!" She sighed. "Poor Mexico. What terrible times are yours." She rose from the table and returned to the kitchen hearth. She gingerly raised the lid on a black iron pot and checked on the pinto beans she was cooking for dinner.

"If Najera wants trouble, let him come, we will be ready," Pedro said. He lifted his coat flap and patted the butt of a small caliber pepperbox that jutted from his leather belt. Nino resumed barking, alerted by Pedro's movement. The dog snapped at the ranchero as he limped past the hound.

Elena promptly walked up to the dog, untied the animal and led it off toward the front of the hacienda. "I will put the dog in the barn. See that the smokehouse is repaired." She sounded exasperated, as if both Pedro and Isabella's dog had conspired to ruin her morning. They left Josefina and Zion in an uncomfortable silence.

Josefina took a sip of coffee and hesitantly inquired, "Did he . . . say anything else? I mean, do you, uh . . ."

"About the gold? Yes, ma'am." Zion studied her as he would tracks left by an unknown intruder. His was a shrewd, perceptive stare. "I'm right glad for you. But sorry for the trouble it might bring. Is there something else I ought to know about?"

Josefina allowed her gaze to wander to the sun-washed crest of the north ridge. A banner of smoke drifted up above a flat precipice jutting out from the trees like the bow of a ship. He was there, this man with no name. And he was in her heart. Zion was waiting for an answer.

"No," she said, watching the gossamer wisp climb toward the sun. "Nothing."

Isabella dismounted well back from the naked precipice upon which the man called Alacron had built his fire. The girl crept quietly through the woods, taking care to avoid the wayward brittle branch and patch of dry sotel sprouting from the crevices among the rocks. She heard his voice. He seemed to be singing or at least chanting like some Comanche. Curiosity overwhelmed her, and she continued to maneuver through the pines and stunted oaks that topped the ridge. She crawled forward to a lightning-split oak, which allowed her to watch the americano from a distance of about twenty feet. The chanting man had stripped off his shirt and sat on his heels by the campfire. Now this was most peculiar behavior. She hunkered down and waited, silent as a shadow. What followed left her puzzled and even a little frightened.

The flames lapped greedily at the dry branches. The tall stranger added more kindling. Wood sizzled and popped. Soon smoke trailed skyward, on which his prayers would ride to the All-Father, as his mother had shown him.

The precipice overlooking the rancho seemed an

appropriate place. He could see both horizons. The world lay before him as if newly created, reborn from the storms. So it would be with him. And now the words, the chant, spilled from his lips, as natural as breathing. He stared into the heart of his spirit fire and repeated the prayer song.

"All-Father,
the wind is your voice,
the thunder is your heart,
the silence is your truth.
Find me as I walk the Great Circle.
Guide my steps. Trace the Sacred Path before me,
behind me, under my feet.
Let my name be on your breath.
And I will hear."

These were the words his mother, Raven, taught him long ago. In his mind's eye she was standing before him, lithe and beautiful, a Choctaw medicine woman with long black hair. And there was his father, Kit, a compact, solid-looking man beside her, a wry grin on his face and thick, curly red hair. The courage of the Scottish chiefs was his lineage. He saw two children, boys, one six and the other three. His children! Jesse Redbow, the eldest, and Daniel Pacer Wolf, for whom the day was never long enough.

The words of the chant flowed around him, echoed by voices not his own. A woman's voice was singing with him. And staring into the prayer smoke he saw a speck of black he thought was an ash increase in size, take shape, become a bird on the wing, a raven. And the voice in his head sang louder and the words of the prayer song reverberated in his soul and filled him with sight beyond seeing. Minutes passed, then an hour. He lost all track of time, but when his vision cleared, the man by the fire realized he was holding the "medal," the crown sterling bearing the initials of George Washington, in front of him at eye level. Passed from one generation to the next, this was the legacy of his family.

The flames had vanished, leaving a pile of smoldering embers in their wake. He checked the sky and was surprised to find the sun directly overhead. It had to be near noon. The entire morning had passed.

He stood, but not without effort and a wince of pain. His legs were stiff, and the lack of circulation made him clumsy as he crushed the last of the embers and pulled his shirt on over his sweat-streaked torso. Down below, the cattle called to one another as the small herd moved aimlessly across the meadow.

He could hear the approaching wind, like a train from far off, rush toward him, tug at his clothing and hair, then race onward along the ridge. He turned and spied a dab of color out of the corner of his eye, and frowning with suspicion, left his vantage point and moved swiftly, with fists clenched, toward the shattered remains of an oak tree not twenty feet away. Someone was spying on him. That someone would pay. Yet when his shadow fell across the sleeping form of the intruder, his hard gaze softened and he knelt and scooped the ten-year-old girl up in his arms. Isabella Quintero rubbed her eyes and awakened, momentarily disoriented. Then she smiled.

"Senor Alacron . . . ?"

"No," he said. Were his eyes red-rimmed and teary from the smoke or was there something more? "Ben. My name is Ben McQueen."

Chapter Fourteen

"Lieutenant Ben McQueen, is it?" Zion said, working the name until it rolled off the tongue as easily as Alacron. He tilted his ladder-backed chair against the bunkhouse wall. The two men were seated in the shade of the long porch of the bunkhouse. Ben helped himself to a third dipper of water from the olla and returned to the chair next to Zion, who looked out across Ventana, searching for the right words to say. He'd kind of gotten used to this man from the north. "Well, you'll be a dead Ben McQueen if you return to Saltillo without a disguise. Let Tolliver and Dobbs go. Why get yourself killed? Men the likes of them usually dig their own graves."

"I can't," Ben said. A whorl of vultures in the distance caught his attention. Something was dead out there on the northern edge of the meadow. The sky had been dark with vultures after General Valentin Najera's butchery. Ben couldn't get the faces of the dead and dying out of his mind. And then there was Ned Tolliver and Lucker Dobbs.

At least Najera, for all his cruelty, had acted as a soldier at war. But not the two turncoats who had sold out their companions. How much had they been paid for their treachery? What was the price of their honor? Blind luck had brought Ben down the hill alive. He had tumbled and rolled part of the way and must have appeared dead. But the creek water had revived him long enough for the young officer to crawl beneath the slide's debris and lie there wounded but concealed, and waiting for the opportunity to escape.

"I can feel the hate in you, lad. It's familiar to me. I carried plenty of it in my time. I crossed the Rio Grande full of hate. All I could think of was one day getting back at them who robbed me of my freedom and kept their damn boots on the back of my neck and never let me up. Never!" The intensity in Zion's voice caused Ben to glance aside at him. The former slave was still leaning back against the wall, but his ebony features glistened with sweat, his lips were dry, and fire burned in his eyes. His hands were trembling. "Yes . . . I know hate." Then he slowly exhaled and the fire dimmed and his eyes were those of a man at peace with what he had made of his life. "Hate's a knife without a handle. The more you cut with it, the more you get cut."

Ben nodded. He understood. "I'll take whatever I have to, but I'm bringing Tolliver and Dobbs back to Texas."

"So be it, amigo. But I reckon I'll tag along to keep you out of trouble."

"This doesn't concern you," Ben said.

"Still . . . seeing as I'm sort of responsible for you even being here . . ."

"Sort of? You're wholly responsible!"

"I didn't think you'd hold a grudge," Zion said with a laconic shrug and a show of wounded pride.

"It's a matter of pride with us McQueens."

"I like you better as Scorpion."

Both men grinned, sharing a moment of camaraderie. Then Ben nailed home his argument, pointing to Josefina and Isabella. "Your place is here, segundo. Not in Saltillo with me, and you know it."

The widow had just emerged from the house with her stepdaughter. Isabella, hearing Nino's plaintive howls coming from the barn, ran off to investigate. No doubt, in minutes Pedro's smokehouse would be under attack again.

Zion watched Don Sebastien's widow and daughter with renewed interest. Even with the gold, they needed him to make the rancho work. Oh, Josefina would learn, he was sure. But right now she needed him. And the girl. Who would protect her from the likes of Najera? The segundo shrugged and nodded. "You got a memory and a damn clever brain all at once, Ben McQueen. Reckon you win. I just hope you haven't lost your head in the process."

"Me too, segundo." He stood and stepped down from the porch as Josefina started across the yard to him. He intercepted her midway by the well. They walked together, in silence and without any conscious direction. Ironically, their steps brought them to the Quintero family plot with its garden of markers sprouting from the earth.

"Isabella is the last of her family," Josefina said, at last breaking the tension.

"She's lucky to have you, Josefina."

"Benjamin Bittercreek McQueen," Josefina continued. Isabella had revealed Ben's full name to her the minute she and Ben had returned to the ranch from the north ridge. She could not wait to inform the entire household that the man called Alacron was no more.

"The middle name was my mother's idea. I'm part Choctaw."

"And you have children . . . two boys?"

"Yes. They live with my parents on a ranch in the Indian Territory north of the Red River." He sensed where her questions were leading. "My wife died some time ago. I am a widower."

"Oh . . . I'm sorry." Josefina glanced at her husband's marker. "Then we have much in common."

"Yes, ma'am."

She noticed the formality and for a brief moment took affront, after what they had shared. Then she realized why Ben had assumed such an attitude. "You're leaving." It was a simple statement of fact.

"After I tend to some unfinished business in Saltillo."

"And I will never see you again."

"Never? Who can say?" Ben reached down and took her hand, lifted it to his lips and gently, gallantly, brushed her flesh with a kiss. "You are a good woman, Josefina Quintero. Any man would be lucky to have you at his side."

The widow smiled and blushed at the compliment, but a tear spilled down her cheek. "I'm sorry. It's just that I feel as if I betrayed him." She continued to stare at Don Sebastien's grave.

Ben shifted uncomfortably. He lifted his gaze and took in the dark browns and emerald hues of the cordillera in the distance, where the plains ended and mysteries began. A man could love this land. Ventana was something to live and die for. Another time and place, he'd want to stay, for the land and for Josefina. But his path led elsewhere . . . it led away. The woman at his side laughed softly. Ben hadn't expected that reaction.

"You're trying to figure out how to tell me good-bye. Well, just say it." A breeze sprang up and her unbound tresses streamed behind her. "You may think my tears a sign of weakness, but believe me, they'll dry. The wind brought you into our lives, and it will carry you from us. *Vaya con Dios,* friend Scorpion, go with God." She squeezed his hand and then pulled from his grasp and entered the gravesite where three generations of Quinteros awaited resurrection. Ben left her weeding the flowers she had planted at the base of her husband's marker, and bathed in the sun's golden glow.

Miles from Ventana, in the hills north of Saltillo overlooking the army encampment of Valentin Najera's Army of Coahuila, Snake-Eye Gandy estimated the force to be five hundred to a thousand men. It was difficult to say for certain. One thing he knew: there were plenty of Mexicans down there, and though they looked bored and listless, a gunshot would galvanize them into action and there'd be hell to pay.

"We take them now or wait for night?" Cletus Buckhart asked half serious. Young and full of righteous anger, he was ready for a fight. His freckles seemed more prominent as his sunburned cheeks began to peel. The two men crouched beneath a limestone boulder on which a rattler had been sunning itself until Snake-Eye grabbed the reptile behind the head and tossed its writhing body over the hillside. Even chunky, good-natured Leon Pettibone and the seasoned veteran, Blue Napier, had been impressed at the sergeant's cool confidence as they knelt on the rocky summit and assessed the situation.

The Army of Coahuila had made camp in the dogleg bend of two intersecting limestone ridges. Feeling secure in the certainty that the nearest enemy force was still near the border, the officers had posted only a scattering of guards to ride herd over the horses and cattle grazing on the prairie about a quarter of a mile from the main body of men.

"The old one said the general stays in Saltillo. We'll attack the town under cover of darkness," Gandy said, shifting his attention to the vaqueros watching the herd.

"How do we find the general, Snake-Eye?" Pettibone asked.

"Kill every Mex we come to and we're bound to find him," Buckhart growled.

"You're riding for a fall, Cletus," Gandy said. "Best you let it go. We'll get Najera, but like Texas Rangers, not some pack of animals. Fight his way, and we wind up worse than he ever was."

"Listen to this old bastard." Napier chuckled gently. "Now and then he makes sense." The grizzled Ranger was brown as a Comanche. Like Gandy, he was Texas born and reared. The frontier had left its mark on him, an indelible brand that set him apart from the likes of the city-bred officers who served in the army under General Zachary Taylor. Napier returned his attention to the vaqueros on the plain below.

"Pettibone, get on back to the rest of the men and bring them up after dark." Gandy slid on his backside across the limestone shelf and, keeping under cover, worked his way over to Napier. "Blue, after sunset we might just help ourselves to that there herd. Reckon you could take one of them vaqueros alive and make him tell us where Najera hangs his hat in town?"

"Can a hawk fly?" Napier confidently replied. "No problem, Snake-Eye." The Ranger tugged a bone-handled dagger from his boot. He ran a thumb across the razor-sharp blade and grinned.

Gandy needed to hear nothing more from the man. He found a plug of tobacco in the pocket of his greasy-looking buckskin shirt, stuffed it in the inside of his cheek and began to chew as he watched Pettibone work his way along the bluff toward a grove of oaks and cedars where they'd left their horses. Blue Napier tilted his hat low to shade his features and stretched out alongside Gandy. Cletus Buckhart glared at both men. How could they just sit here in the sun and wait? He wanted to do something, anything but wait. He slapped his fist into the palm of his hand and both of the older Rangers looked around at the nineteen-year-old as if he were some child they had to humor. Buckhart's cheeks reddened and he found an excuse to avoid meeting their eyes. He suddenly found a column of ants marching past his boot to be of immense significance.

For the young, time's always wasting, Snake-Eye thought as he studied the cluster of whitewashed adobe buildings that was Saltillo. It crawls past slower than the insects underfoot. The passing years had a way of changing a man's perspective. Now it seemed the seasons slid past on greased skids. And try as he might, there was no slowing them down. Whatever memories of childhood he held were viewed with a kind of dispassionate interest, as if his past belonged to someone else.

General Valentin Najera knew what must be done. The decision had come to him as he enjoyed an early dinner on the hotel balcony overlooking the *mercado*. Earlier in the day he had resolved to set aside his personal problems and spend the daylight hours finalizing the preparations that needed to be made before he marched his Army of Coahuila to Monterrey. A supply train needed to be put together to feed his army while it was on the move. His vaqueros had brought in a herd of mules while the remainder of his personal guard were requisitioning food and grain from the townspeople. His strategy worked. Halfway through dinner, Najera realized that the solution to his problems was really very simple.

Father Rudolfo huffed and puffed and climbed the stairs to the balcony. Despite Raul's attempts to block the padre's progress, the priest would not be denied access to the general and complained repeatedly that Najera must speak to him.

"Sorry, General," the young gunman remarked from behind the padre. Raul pointedly resisted looking at Marita, who had been invited to dine with Najera and appeared to be once more in the general's good graces, though at the moment the girl sat sullenly at his side. Najera had confided in the girl, indeed he had boasted of his intentions. To Marita's intense displeasure, she no longer figured in the general's immediate future.

Najera waved Raul aside. "All is well," Najera said. "I was about to send for the good padre anyway. Order Tolliver and Dobbs to join Major Granados and the lancers at the encampment before morning. See that the dragoons are ready to ride tonight."

Father Rudolfo gave Salcedo a look of vindication as the gunman departed. Then he turned to confront the general.

"Valentin, the people of Saltillo have given what they can spare. Why do you send your men from house to house stealing what little our people have left? The corn will not be harvested for at least another month. Food will be scarce. They need what they have. Why do you inflict such hardships on those you claim to protect?"

"Claim?" Najera glanced at the empty stalls of Market Square. Word had spread that the Army of Coahuila was preparing to march. The merchants and outlying farmers had avoided gathering in the *mercado*. No one wanted to see their goods confiscated by roving details of Najera's dragoons. As far as the townsfolk were concerned, today the soldiers had a license to take whatever they wished. Their lack of patriotism enraged the general. "Tomorrow, I and my soldiers will be marching north to join with General Arista in defeating the americanos," he said through clenched teeth, eyes smoldering. "I do this to spare Saltillo the indignity of being occupied by Taylor's troops. And yet this ungrateful populace would begrudge my men food!?"

"Save your bluster, Valentin. I knew your father. He was a good man and would never condone this treatment, especially of the campesinos and old Esteban's people, who suffer the most and have the least to spare."

"Priest, they are sheep. It is for me to shear them. That is how it has always been and will always be." Najera paused to allow the turbulent seas of his passion to grow calm. He poured a glass of wine for himself and one for his guest. "But that is not why I intended to have you brought to the hotel. Here, we drink a toast." He slid the glass of wine across the table and motioned for the priest to join him.

Father Rudolfo eyed the officer suspiciously. "What for?"

"Why . . . to wish me health and happiness on the occasion of my marriage. You will perform the ceremony before I leave to assume command of my soldiers."

"Marriage?" The general's command caught the priest completely off guard. He looked from Najera to the girl at his side. Marita sullenly stared at the untouched meal set before her. Flies had begun to circle the congealing sauces on her plate.

"Oh good heavens, no," Najera said, reading the

padre's thoughts. "Not her." Najera ran a finger along Marita's cheek and then beneath her chin. He tilted her head. She was quite lovely, and he might consider bringing her to bed for one last romp if he had the time.

"Then who?" the priest demanded.

Najera smiled, satisfied. Victorious. "Josefina Quintero."

Chapter Fifteen

Old Esteban looked up from the church steps where he had been standing for the better part of an hour, turning back the local mission Indians as they arrived for evening services. The padre always concluded his midweek liturgy by dispensing the contents of the poor box as fairly and judiciously as he could. But tonight there would be no mass. The disappointed families turned away from the church and filed toward the front gate.

Ben McQueen rode through the gate and past the faithful who headed dejectedly toward the jacals, where they lived in close proximity to the church. Ben pointed his gelding toward the church and the Yaqui maintaining his lonely vigil on the steps. Bats swept across the evening sky while an owl in the bell tower voiced its distinctive, questioning cry. Veils of silvery moonlight washed the front of the church. Overhead, a vast array of stars stretched from horizon to horizon. Old Esteban listened to the owl and shuddered as the horseman approached.

"Esteban . . ." Ben pushed back his sombrero

to reveal his features. "Do you know me?" He wore a coarsely woven, loose-fitting cotton shirt, a faded brown woolen poncho, and nankeen breeches tucked into his Army-issue boots. After a moment the Yaqui's eyes widened with recognition.

"You came here for the horses," said the old man. The Yaqui had no feelings concerning the war. His world was the mission and Father Rudolfo, who spoke to him of Jesu Christi, son of the All-Father. But he remembered that Ben had treated him courteously, with respect, and behaved the same way toward his granddaughters. "You looked different then."

"I darkened my hair and skin. My mind was clouded then, but no longer," Ben said. The gelding, a bay with three dark stockings, shifted and pawed the earth. McQueen tightened his grip on the reins and allowed the animal but a little slack. "I must speak with the padre."

"He is not here."

"Where is he? There are two men I must find. Americanos. They are bad men who must answer for their crimes."

Esteban frowned and his voice cracked as he spoke. "The padre went to the Casa del Noche to speak with General Najera. Now he and the general are both gone. They left Saltillo with the soldiers." Esteban's leathery hands trembled as he shuffled down the steps to stand alongside Ben's gelding. The old man reached up and caught one of the reins. "I looked through the window of the cantina and saw the ones you seek. Perhaps they are still there."

"*Gracias,*" Ben replied. There had been no sentries guarding the approaches to town. Although he had avoided the main road and ridden overland to reach the town, once entering the streets, it was plainly evident that something had drastically changed. "What has happened here? Even the guards are gone, and no lancers patrol the streets."

"The Army of Coahuila marches to Monterrey. They leave at dawn." Esteban shook his head. "But the padre would not go with them. His place is here. And General Najera has no use for such a good man as Father Rudolfo." The Yaqui glanced up as Ben freed the reins from the old man's grasp. Suddenly, in the distance, they heard a thunder of gunshots. Ben and old Esteban looked in the direction of the black hills where the main army was encamped.

"Now what?" Ben muttered. He was beginning to feel that there was more happening than anyone was aware of, that he had ridden into the heart of a whirlwind. He backed a few steps from the Yaqui and nodded in farewell. Even if hell were breaking loose and death waiting for him at the end of the street, so be it. There was no turning back. The medal he wore, the legacy of his family's honor, had brought him to Saltillo for the last time—not for vengeance, but justice. He heard the owl's solitary ghostly call and glanced up at the bell tower. Like the Yaqui, the Choctaw also believed the bird was the harbinger of death. Doomed was the poor soul who heard the owl call him by name.

"You know . . ." old Esteban said, sensing the americano shared the ancient beliefs.

"Yes," Ben said. "I too have walked in the old ways and danced among the bones of the rain." McQueen touched his heels to the flanks of the skittish bay, and the horse cantered off at a brisk clip, bearing its rider toward a deadly rendezvous.

Old Esteban watched the horseman disappear into the night. He blessed himself with the sign of the cross, and for added protection dug a medicine pouch out of his coat pocket and hung it around his neck. A cloud drifted across the moon's bald face, and suddenly the definition between light and darkness became less pronounced. The two merged. And the owl took flight.

A stampede is like some great beast, a juggernaut of unstoppable energy, flattening anything in its path. The life of the beast is brief but furious. At night cattle will bolt and run at the first unexpected snap of dry grass or a tumbleweed blown cross the path of a steer.

The soldiers in the encampment were roused from their sleep by a fusillade of gunfire followed by a surge of thunder. The earth shook as over a thousand head of cattle and nearly three hundred horses moved as one, surged forward, panic-stricken as Snake-Eye Gandy and his Texas Rangers opened up with their Patterson Colts. Lances of orange flame stabbed the night air. The Rangers hooted and shouted, raising a commotion akin to an army of vengeful spirits loosed from the black depths of the cordillera. By the time the officers could dispatch their skirmishers, the startled herd was well on its way to Saltillo, hounded by Gandy's men, who never let up.

Cletus Buckhart screeched and waved his saddle blanket over his head. Snake-Eye Gandy, off to the young man's left, fired his pistol and leaned low over the saddle horn, slapping the loose end of his reins across his mount's neck. The mouse-colored gelding quickened its pace and slowly brought its rider up abreast of the lead animal, a mean-tempered longhorn with a lumbering gait, who lorded over the herd despite the constant challenges of the younger steers testing the battle-scarred old bull's supremacy.

The bull seemed to sense Gandy's presence, and followed the Ranger's lead, though the one-eyed man made certain he remained off to the side. With Blue Napier to the right of the herd and even with Gandy, the stampede could be somewhat controlled. It was a tenuous situation at best, but successful. The charging herd of horses and cattle bore down on the sleepy town nestled in the flatlands of the Coahuila plain, and wouldn't slow until they hit the streets.

Serena Montenez stood in the doorway to Najera's room and watched in silence, her arms folded across her rounded bosom, while Ned Tolliver proceeded to search every drawer and wardrobe. Najera's extra clothing lay in a couple of piles in the center of the bedroom. Chests were left open, a chair and an end table had been overturned in the drawing room, Najera's desk had been ransacked, all to no avail.

"The general's fortune went to supply his army. A grand and noble gesture, eh? Would that he had felt so patriotic about his hotel bill. The gold you won the other night was supposed to go to me, to cover all the general owed for his food and lodging. He has left me nothing but debt!" Now that Valentin had officially departed to rejoin his army, Serena could allow her true feelings to be known. Angel Perez had failed to return, and she was concerned for his well-being. She suspected something terrible had happened to her young lover, and she blamed Najera for sending him away.

Ned Tolliver could not care less about the woman's troubles. Disgusted with this turn of events, he brushed past the woman and stalked down the hall, opening the first door he came to. The creak of bedsprings and a girl's muffled groans foretold what he'd find. The shutters were drawn, no lamps were lit, and only the faintest illumination seeped in through the doorway.

"Lucker, we got to get the hell out of here," Tolliver said.

"Not till I got all the general owes me out of this little *puta*."

He heard Dobbs yelp and then came the slap of a callused hand against softer, more resilient flesh.

"Try that again," Dobbs growled, "and I'll knock your pretty little teeth down your throat."

"Please, senor. No." The girl's voice was barely louder than a whisper. "No more."

"I'm leaving in five minutes," Tolliver said. "It's never taken you any longer than that."

"Go to hell," Dobbs cursed as Tolliver chuckled and shut the door.

The turncoat Ranger met Serena's smoldering gaze.

"What the hell you looking at? Just be glad its the general's tramp in there and not you. You may be next anyway." He started past her.

"Marita is young and she is foolish. But she has done nothing to deserve this," the proprietress angrily snapped. "I won't be next. No man lays a hand on me unless I wish it." The woman's eyes were cold as ice. She meant what she said, and could back up her talk with action. Tolliver tried to laugh her off but he was convinced. He walked down the hall and descended to the cantina, another room devoid of customers. A single oil lamp flickered on a table near the bottom of the stairs and cast a pool of amber light that forced the darkness to grudgingly retreat. However, the victory became more tenuous the farther one went toward the front of the cantina. Tolliver walked straight to the bar and poured himself a shot of whiskey, tossed it down his throat, then helped himself to another. He glanced along the bar at the jar Najera had given him. He had intended to leave the severed head of his former companion in the courtyard for Serena Montenez to dispose of as she saw fit. He noticed the lid was off. Funny thing that. Drink in hand, he ambled over to the jar and replaced the lid without looking inside. He turned toward the proprietress standing at the foot of the stairs.

"You handle this?" he asked.

"I was with you while you were searching the general's room."

"If not you, then who?" He had seen Senora Montenez personally dismiss her serving girls.

"Perhaps him," the woman replied, looking past the americano. Tolliver turned and for the first time noticed the silhouette of a man in a sombrero standing just beyond the perimeter of light, between a window and the front door. Tolliver dropped a hand to his gun but froze when he heard the telltale click of a hammer being thumbed back on a Patterson Colt.

"Unbuckle your belt and let it drop," Ben said.

"Who the hell are you?" Tolliver growled. He could tell by the accent this wasn't any Mexican.

"A ghost," Ben replied, and stepped into the light.

Tolliver's eyes widened behind his spectacles. "You! The lieutenant! How in the blue blazes—?" He noted McQueen's revolver was centered on his chest, then shrugged, unbuckled his gun belt and let it clatter to the floor. He kicked the gun belt aside and opened the flaps of his black frock coat to reveal he was unarmed. "How'd you escape?"

"I died," Ben sneered with ghoulish amusement.

He was trembling with rage. A few minutes ago he had entered the cantina and found the place apparently devoid of life. Resolving to search the entire hotel if need be, he had started toward the side door leading into the lobby of the Casa del Noche when he noticed the jar. The tall stoneware container was similar to the ones lining the back wall of the courtyard outside. It had only taken a moment to remove the lid and discover its terrible secret. Now he knew the meaning of the wall in the courtyard. Revulsion had turned to cold fury. There must be a reckoning. Now was the time, and here was the place, to begin. "Where is Dobbs?"

"Gone," Tolliver answered. "The yellow bastard cheated me out of my pay and took off with Najera's army."

"You're a lying dog," Ben said. "I guess some things don't change." He'd seen two horses tethered outside. And old Esteban had seen both men in the cantina.

"Look, I'm telling the truth. I swear on my mother's grave."

"The other one is upstairs," the owner of the cantina said. Serena Montenez had no idea as to the stranger's identity, but he was obviously no friend of the two americanos, and that was good enough for her. She tugged a black scarf from her bodice and dabbed at her upper lip. "He is with Marita Two Ponies, the daughter of old Esteban."

Ben glanced in Tolliver's direction. "Call him down."

"Go to hell," Tolliver said. He still couldn't believe his eyes. Lieutenant Ben McQueen alive and able to identify the two men who had sold out their compatriots! Damn McQueen. Ned Tolliver wasn't finished yet.

"Do you have any rope?" Ben asked of the proprietress. The senora shook her head.

"And I ain't going with you," Tolliver said, grinning, "so why don't you just head on upstairs and leave me here. I promise I'll stay put."

"I believe you," Ben said. Taking a step forward, he cracked the man across the skull with the gun barrel of his Colt revolver. The blow caught Tolliver off guard. He sagged against the bar and crumpled to the hardwood floor. Ben stepped over him and walked the length of the bar until he reached Serena Montenez. "Are those stairs a back entrance to the hall above?"

"Si. They will take you to the rear of the hall-way. The man you seek is in the last room on the right." She studied this red-haired americano with renewed interest, and she wondered where he had come from.

Ben nodded his thanks and moved toward the narrow stairway Tolliver and the senora had just descended. The wooden steps beneath his feet creaked as he climbed.

The hallway was dark and thick with the aroma of stale pulque, sweat, and tobacco smoke that had permeated the upper floor of the hotel over the course of several years. Ben wrinkled his nose and stifled a sneeze. With Najera's departure, the rooms were empty, awaiting a normal trade. Although the military had frequented the hotel and cantina, the citizens of Saltillo for the most part had avoided the establishment. The silence in the hall was deafening, the darkness oppressive as the grave. Gunfire, still faint, became more frequent, the rumble of thunder audible even within the walls of the Casa del Noche. Suddenly a door up ahead opened. Ben froze and brought up the Colt. A vague lumbering patch of humanity loomed in the doorway and stopped, still partly concealed. As fortune would have it, Dobbs was facing the rear end of the hall and caught a glimpse of McQueen outlined against the faint glow at the top of the stairs.

"*Quien mas?* Who is it? Ned?" Silence. Ben did not reply. "Just a second, Ned." The man disappeared into the room. The muffled sound of a struggle reached Ben, then Lucker Dobbs called out in a whiskey-soaked voice, "You ain't Ned." The turncoat appeared in the doorway again, this time holding Marita Two Ponies before him, his left arm encircling her waist. Dobbs was larger than the fifteen-year-old, but she shielded his vitals. Dobbs's right arm was extended, a Patterson Colt gripped in his iron hand. "I got the general's whore with me. Any harm come to her, and Najera will have your head." Again silence. "Damn it, who's there?" Dobbs's Colt spat flame. Ben flattened himself against the wall, but in the brief flash of gunpowder his features were revealed. Marita twisted in his grasp and sank her teeth into Dobbs's thumb. The man howled and flung her to the floor. Ben fired. Then Dobbs and Ben again. The hallway was cast in vivid relief with each muzzle flash. The gunshots came in rapid succession. Fire and shift your aim and fire again, anticipate the other man's movement, fire, and no time to wonder how many shots were left.

Marita hugged the floor, senses numb from the deadly exchange. The narrow confines of the hallway were a hellish prison of jetting flame, leaden death, and the acrid stench of burned black powder. Her eyes were watering, her ears ringing. She didn't know what was happening. Marita only wanted it to stop. She wanted to live. She wanted to run to the forgiving arms of her grandfather, and prayed to the Blessed Mother that she would get the chance.

And then, abruptly, the deadly exchange ended with a groan . . . a death rattle and a low, sibilant sigh.

Chapter Sixteen

General Valentin Najera brought his men to a halt in front of Quintero's hacienda. Twenty dragoons, each armed with saber, pepperbox pistol, and short-barreled musket, immediately arranged themselves in sharp and precise order. The entire column was proud of the reputation they had earned as the general's handpicked guard. Only the padre struggled with his mount and broke the order.

Across the ranchyard, the bunkhouse, barn, and outbuildings were silent and dark, but lantern light seeped through the shuttered windows of the hacienda. The hour was late, and Najera had expected to roust the occupants of the rancho from their beds. Every room in the house was lit. Could the widow be entertaining? Highly unlikely. Najera stroked his chin as he considered the possibilities.

Raul walked his mount forward and drew abreast of his commander. The gunman was distracted; he had Marita on his mind. And why not? General Najera no longer had any use for her. Raul, after a single night of passion, had resolved to take up where *El Jefe* left off. Marita would be his woman now. Images of her willowy charms flooded his mind with heated recollections and left little room for the task at hand.

"Well?" Najera petulantly asked. "Damn it, man, are you listening to me?"

"Sorry, *Jefe*. I didn't hear," Raul said. His cheeks reddened. It wouldn't do to anger the general, already thin-skinned and anxious to resolve his problems with the widow of Don Sebastien.

"Five men to the barn, five to the bunkhouse, and the rest remain with us here."

"And if there is trouble?"

"Tonight I will have the Ventana."

"The segundo will fight," Raul dryly observed. "And the vaquero they hired. Even the widow, I think. With its back against the wall, even a cat can become a panther."

Najera shook his head. "They will not have the stomach for it. The senora is soft. She will do as I order because she will not want to die."

Raul studied the shuttered hacienda. Lanterns were strung about the yard and across the front of the house. Piles of wood had been set ablaze around the yard, successfully illuminating the area surrounding the hacienda, providing plenty of light for hidden marksmen. He suppressed his misgivings and dispatched the men as he was ordered to. Why hadn't Angel Perez returned or joined them along the way here?

The gunman removed his serape and draped it across the saddle pommel, permitting him easy access to the twin pistols holstered at his waist, then glanced at Najera. Raul had no breeding, no station in life. If he was ever to ride in splendor through the streets of Mexico City, it would be in the service of a man like the general. But all dreams aside, astride a horse and seated in plain sight before the fortified hacienda, Raul wished he had never heard the name Quintero.

Josefina stood leaning on Zion's strong shoulder, and peered through the gun slits at the dragoons in their blue and red uniforms, who were no doubt ready to obey Najera's every command. She tucked a strand of blond hair back from her face. Her expression was serious, firelight reflected in her eyes.

"You were right, Zion, the general's back," she said.

"Yes, ma'am," the segundo replied. He had labored all day to fortify the hacienda and ensure that the rifled muskets, shotguns, and Allan revolving pistols were cleaned, primed, and loaded. Struggling until well after sunset, he and Pedro had stacked wood a lantern's throw from the hacienda, all the better to illuminate a field of fire if the need arose. "But I wish to the Almighty I'd been wrong," Zion added. What was the general up to now? Najera's effrontery continued to stagger the former slave. One thing for certain, the general hadn't come to pay a social call.

Pedro was already on the roof. Elena, a crack shot, was guarding the back of the house. Isabella, struggling to keep a brave front, stood behind Josefina, clutching her stepmother's dress. She jumped when the general's voice rang out loud and clear.

"Senora Quintero! I will talk to you."

Zion slowly exhaled. "Reckon I'll see what the good general wants."

"No. He's asked for me," Josefina said, walking across the room to the front door. Zion caught her by the arm, but she twisted free and confronted him. "Your place is on the roof with Pedro." She took up a double-barreled percussion shotgun and cradled the weapon in the crook of her left arm, then smiled at Isabella.

"I am not going to my room," the girl defiantly stated, just in case the woman harbored any intention of sending her there.

"Your father taught you to load?"

"Si. And shoot."

"Then your place is here. And whatever happens . . . I love you, Isabella."

Zion had heard about all he could take. "Goddamn it, senora—" But his argument died on his lips when Josefina waved him to silence.

"If Ventana is to belong to Isabella and myself, then it's high time I did more than wring my hands and complain." Josefina tugged the latch, opened the door and left the hacienda. Her boot heels crunched the crushed rock as she left the porch. Coyotes in the distance howled at the moon as she approached the circular drive where Najera and his dragoons waited.

"Senora! Ah, here you are." Najera sat erect on his horse. He was the epitome of formality and looked every inch the saviour of Mexico that he envisioned himself to be.

"The hour is late for you to come calling, Valentin," Josefina said. In the glare of the lantern light she seemed fragile as fine china; however, the shotgun added a darker element to the illusion.

Najera nodded to one of his orderlies, a stern-looking horseman who rode back along the column and returned with Father Rudolfo. The padre seemed thoroughly embarrassed at the part Najera was forcing him to play.

"The hour is never too late for the union of a happy couple," Najera said. "Soon I must bring my army to Monterrey. Time, unfortunately, does not allow for a proper courtship."

"What are you saying?" Josefina blurted out, confused and taken aback.

"Find a proper wedding dress, my dear. We will be married within the hour."

"You're mad," Josefina retorted. "Padre?"

Father Rudolfo held up his hands in a gesture of helplessness. "I have tried to reason with him," he said. "But he refuses to listen."

Josefina frowned and advanced on the horsemen, her features livid. She stabbed a finger at the general. "Marry you? Take in holy sacrament my husband's murderer? How dare you? Ventana will never be yours. Never!"

The woman's outburst was like a slap in the face to the general. He momentarily recoiled, then regained his composure. Her accusation, not to mention her refusal of his marriage offer, caught him off guard. His aristocratic features became more mottled and ugly the more he dwelled on her reply.

"Leave us, padre," Najera said in an ominous tone. "It seems you have no business here. Return to Saltillo."

"I don't think so." Father Rudolfo eased his great weight out of the saddle and left the horsemen. "I think my presence here is essential. I should like to hear more of what Senora Quintero has to say concerning the death of Don Sebastien." He nodded to Josefina, motioned for her to join him, and continued on into the hacienda. Josefina started to follow him, but Najera wasn't finished. The general, smiling grimly, nodded to his orderly, who unrolled a document and proceeded to proclaim its contents.

"In this time of conflict between our two nations, I, General Valentin Najera, do hereby authorize myself to act as legal guardian of Isabella Quintero and do hereby establish control over Ventana, acting in the girl's best interest and conducting the girl's affairs until Isabella comes of age and is taken in marriage. Josefina Quintero will receive safe escort to the border, where she will be delivered to the embrace of her own countrymen." The orderly sniffed and swallowed, then glanced at the dumb-struck woman over the top edge of the document.

"You'll find it properly dated," Najera said. "Your household staff and *el negro* will accompany you, of course. Raul Salcedo will deliver the girl to my rancho. I have a housekeeper who will look after Isabella in my absence."

Josefina was so astonished, words failed her. As the orderly returned to his position behind the general, a thousand arguments, hurled epithets, and defiant retorts flashed through Josefina's mind, but the only defiance the widow could offer was a simple, blunt, "No." And then stronger . . . "No!"

At a word from Najera, Raul dismounted and left the column of dragoons. Josefina turned the shotgun on him and cocked it. She retreated toward the house as he approached.

Raul never broke stride. Instead his gaze bore into the woman's eyes. The shotgun trembled in her grasp. "Senora, think how much trouble you bring on yourself. Stand in the way of *El Jefe* and you will die. And for what? Land? Look around you. It is just dirt. That's all. Just dirt. Think. You will be dead, never to feel the sun warm your face again or the wind caress your hair, eh?"

He was close now. Fifteen feet away. Then twelve, ten. Now just a pace or two. She was within his reach. His voice hypnotic, holding her entranced as he reached for the shotgun and grabbed it by the muzzle.

"Hold it right there! Najera, call off your hound!" Zion, musket in hand, leaned over the edge of the roof and took aim at the general. The segundo's warning elevated the tension. Embers crackled, dry timber split with a resounding crack as the hungry flames continued to feed among the burning stacks of timber.

"Think about it, Najera," Zion continued. "You make a pretty target in the firelight."

But Najera wasn't the only one. Raul saw his chance. The segundo's eyes were trained on Najera, leaving himself at the gunman's mercy. Raul retreated a step from Josefina and found the right angle for an easy head shot. He palmed his right pistol and took aim.

Josefina had never fired a gun, much less ever killed a man. There wasn't time to consider the moral dilemma, to wrest with the philosophical aspects on the sacredness of life. She squeezed both triggers. The shotgun roared, its recoil shoving her backward. Twin loads of buckshot nearly cut Raul Salcedo in half at the chest. He was blown out of one boot and flung several feet in the air, then slammed into the earth, dead before he hit the ground in front of the dragoon's spooked horses.

"Run, Josefina! Run!" Zion shouted. He fired but missed Najera as the dragoons scattered around the ranchyard and rushed to the general's aid.

Josefina turned and, lifting the hem of her dress, bolted toward the front door as the padre rushed out to help her. She stumbled into his arms. Shielding her with his broad, round body, the padre all but dragged the visibly shaken young widow inside the hacienda. A bullet clipped his side, a second creased his neck. Once in the comparative safety of the walls, Father Rudolfo collapsed in a cushioned parlor chair while Elena Gallegos hurried to patch his wounds, both of which were thankfully superficial.

Valentin Najera brought his startled mount under control and rode the animal out into the center of the ranchyard. His men, led by Mariano Rincon, gathered around him. The mestizo appeared visibly shaken by Salcedo's death. This was bad. This was very bad, he thought. A bullet whirred past his ear. Rincon snapped off a shot toward Zion and Pedro on the roof of the hacienda. The general drew his saber and held it aloft. After sweeping the blade in an arc, he pointed it at the hacienda as if to call down the wrath of God upon its defenders, concealed behind the shuttered windows and rooftop battlements.

"Kill them," Najera said. His expression was a mask of cold, murderous rage beneath the shiny brass visor of his lancer's helmet.

"What about the girl, *El Jefe*?" Rincon asked. He had the unsettling notion he was looking into the face of a man on the precipice of sanity with one foot poised to step over the edge.

"All," the general replied. He stood in his stirrups and his voice rang out with the intensity of a man consumed by hatred for those who had defied him. There was no question about his orders. "Kill them all!"

The townspeople of Saltillo, huddled in the safety of their homes, would never forget the night the Texas Rangers came to call. Streets and alleys were choked with cattle and horses. Jacals were flattened. Wagons were overturned and porches demolished, sheds crushed, and the few remaining chickens scattered. However, the hungry residents, their larders stripped bare by Najera's troops, thronged to the street with knives and fifty-year-old long rifles, and soon the cattle began to disappear by twos and threes. The already panicked beasts were killed and butchered where they fell. The streets ran red with blood, much to the delight of the citizens, who ignored the Texans in their haste to feed themselves and their families.

Snake-Eye Gandy, feeling like a damn fool, rode into what was left of the *mercado*. Cattle were milling among the ruined stalls. Several horses had stopped to drink at the spring-fed stone cistern in the center of Market Square. Children had emerged to watch the Rangers with a mixture of awe and curiosity before being summoned by parents to lead the livestock home. It was better than any celebration. For the first time in many weeks there was plenty of food to eat. The citizens of Saltillo were not about to pass up this opportunity. Cletus Buckhart, Blue Napier, and Leon Pettibone rode up to Gandy with their guns drawn, but no one to fight. They searched the buildings and rooflines in vain for any indication of a threat.

"What the hell's going on?" Buckhart growled, spoiling for battle. "I ain't fired at nothing but the moon."

"It appears we may be too late," Blue Napier said as he reloaded his pistol. Other Rangers were slowly entering the square.

"There's a fire by the hotel over yonder," Pettibone said. Since the oil in the jars and the grisly content each jar contained provided a perfect medium for a blaze, the back wall was completely engulfed in flames.

"That's the general's headquarters," Snake-Eye remarked. "C'mon." He led the way around the perimeter of the *mercado* and, followed by his three hard-riding companions, walked his mount up to the front of the Casa del Noche. Another half-dozen Rangers took up the flanks as the clouds of smoke drifted across the front of the hotel. The night air was already hazy with the settling dust in the aftermath of the stampede. Gandy tilted back his hat and called out in a loud, rasping voice that had all the warmth of a hacksaw.

"General Valentin Najera!"

Ten Patterson Colts were cocked as one, a distinctly ominous sound.

"He's not here, compadres," came the reply from within. Then a tall, broad-shouldered figure appeared in the doorway, rising out of the black interior into the firelight, into the hard merciless faces of the Rangers, these riders of vengeance who would not be denied.

"My God," Snake-Eye muttered when he recognized the red hair and square-jawed features of Ben McQueen.

"But I know where to find him."

Chapter Seventeen

Lieutenant Ben McQueen was back where he belonged, riding hell-for-leather across the rolling plains of Old Mexico, with Snake-Eye Gandy and the Texas Rangers at his side. Saltillo was behind them now. The Rangers had arranged themselves in a single line on horseback while Blue Napier read a psalm over the ashes of their massacred comrades. Then as one the Rangers took up the pursuit of Valentin Najera. No one attempted to impede their progress; the populace was busily replenishing their stores. Several of the townsmen, led by the mayor, had captured several of the horses and were busily driving the cattle out of town. The townsmen were determined to conceal the livestock in various arroyos, where it was hoped they would go unnoticed and serve to feed the populace when the Army of Coahuila had officially left for Monterrey.

With the wind in his face and a fresh horse beneath him, charging to the rescue of Josefina Quintero, Ben would not have changed places with anyone in the world. This was what he was born to do, this was the legacy of every McQueen. Deep in the territory of an enemy, McQueen, Gandy, and the other daredevils from Texas were out to stop a tyrant. Nothing and no one was going to stand in their way.

But even heroes have to water and rest their mounts. About an hour's hard ride from Saltillo, Ben led the Rangers to a wallow he had passed on his previous visits to town. The sides of the wallow, though slick, were gradually inclined and permitted a careful man to walk his mount down to the shallow pool of spring water, a muddy pond transformed by moonlight into a disk of incandescent silver.

"I never figured you for dead," Gandy said, dismounting at the edge of the wallow. Ben dropped down beside his irascible friend and watched the others descend past them to the spring. Ned Tolliver, dour, downcast, and nursing a bruised skull, halted in front of McQueen. Tolliver's wire-rimmed spectacles were bent and sat unevenly on the bridge of his nose. His hands were bound at the wrists, but he still paused to glare at Ben, until Leon Pettibone nudged the traitor in the back with a revolving rifle.

"I wish I hadn't filed the trigger on this here rifle of mine," said Pettibone. "It tends to go off all of a suddenlike." He nudged Tolliver a second time and the man proceeded on down to the spring.

"It was a dark day when Captain Pepper ever let the likes of him and Dobbs join up." Gandy took a swallow from his canteen, rinsed his mouth out and spat. "O'course Dobbs is answering to a higher authority now, I reckon."

An image came to mind, one of many Ben would remember all his life. Senora Montenez arrived at the top of the stairs with a lamp in hand. In its sallow glow Lucker Dobbs finished bleeding to death from gaping wounds to the chest and throat. The bearded ruffian stared unseeingly at Marita, who delivered a brutal kick between the dead man's legs. Her cheeks wet with tears, she pummeled the man as long as she had strength.

"Yeah . . . a higher authority," Ben said, "or a lower one." He pictured Dobbs dancing barefoot on brimstone.

"You think the girl was telling the truth about Najera, that we'll find him at this ranch where you hid out?" Gandy asked.

Ben nodded. According to Senora Montenez, the general had abandoned Marita. Now the Yaqui was a woman scorned, and seeking retribution against the one who had wronged her. "She was telling the truth. Besides, from what I know of this Najera, forcing Josefina Quintero to marry him so he can legally get his hands on her gold sounds like something the general would do."

"Well, truth or lie, we'll find out before sunup." Snake-Eye searched his saddlebag for a leather-tough strip of jerky and managed to gnaw off a morsel. He offered a bite to Ben, who declined the invitation, his mood darkening. "What is it, Brass Buttons? We've faced some pretty hard times together."

With the return of his memory, Ben had been forced to confront some unpleasant facts about himself. He was beginning to miss certain aspects of his recent amnesia. There seemed no middle ground. The events of the massacre could be relived in detail now. And the facts were achingly painful to confront. His sense of exultation became suddenly tempered by the cruel realities of all that had happened and the ugly truth behind the loss of his command.

"I ran, Snake-Eye." The admission spilled out. McQueen couldn't help himself. He studied the dirt beneath his feet; it was easier than meeting Gandy's stare. "When those damn guns opened up to every side and men started toppling out of the saddle, I panicked. A bullet creased my skull and dropped me. I had my gun but I didn't even try to make a stand. All I wanted to do was live. Something snapped inside. I'd led my men into a trap. They were dying because of me, and I didn't want to be among them. I ran . . . crawled . . . I did whatever I could to reach the rocks at the bottom of the hill. I hid there until it was over."

"Hmm." Gandy chewed in silence for a moment. "The way it looks to me, Ned Tolliver and Dobbs did the leading. Still, it was your command. But as for you turning tail and skedaddling, I ain't your father confessor." His harsh tone cut through Ben's self-pity like a knife and caused the younger man to look up sharply, straighten, and pay attention. "So fearless young Ben McQueen found out he's human after all. Maybe you made a mistake, that ain't for me to judge, but live with it and go on and do what needs to be done. I figure that's what the medal you wear is all about." Snake-Eye clapped Ben on the arm and ambled on down to water his horse.

Ben remained alone with his self-recrimination and his doubts until he decided they weren't fit company. He knelt and picked up a fossilized shell. He focused on the shell and dredged from memory the words taught him by Raven McQueen, a Choctaw medicine woman and his mother.

"Into stone I place all I did not do.
Into stone I place my shame, and my dishonor.
Into stone I place my heart's pain
And cast it from me."

He tossed aside that remnant of an ancient sea and joined the Rangers at the spring. The horses were allowed a brief drink and then brought out onto the prairie, where the Rangers passed the few minutes left before remounting. Ben stood at the edge of the pool with the remaining men who had yet to water their mounts. It took him a moment to realize Tolliver was at his side.

"There'll be another day, McQueen. I'll get you for what you done."

Images again, of Angel Perez and his glowering threats. Something snapped inside Ben. He turned on the prisoner, and grabbed a revolver from his belt, shoved the weapon in Tolliver's bound hands. At the same time, Ben drew his own pistol and jabbed the barrel beneath Ned's chin, forcing his head back.

"Go ahead, you bastard," Ben growled, a crazed expression on his face. He cocked the revolver, his finger curled round the trigger. "Get me!" His breath fanned Tolliver's face as he spoke as quietly as an undertaker at a funeral. "Take the first shot."

Tolliver looked into the face of death and blinked, gulped and turned his head aside. He could blow a hole through McQueen's heart, but he'd die all the same.

"For the love of heaven, McQueen," Pettibone gasped, retreating out of harm's way.

"Ben . . . what the hell?" Gandy called out as he made his way around the pool.

"Go on!" Ben shouted in the turncoat's face. Ned jumped, then froze again. Ben McQueen lowered his revolver and contemptuously returned his gun to its holster. And still Tolliver didn't move a muscle, though for the moment he had Ben completely at his mercy. But in one swift explosive burst of temper, McQueen had broken the traitor. Ben reached out and took the revolver from the bound man's grasp. He leaned in close to Tolliver and said softly, "You aren't going to *get* anybody, Ned. You're going to cling to your wretched life right up to the moment the hangman slips a noose over your neck."

There came a collective sigh of relief from Gandy, Pettibone, and the other few men still gathered around the pool. McQueen took the reins of his mount and walked the sturdy gelding out of the wallow. When he reached the plain, he vaulted into the saddle and galloped off down the wheel-rutted road, a lone rider in the night. But not alone for long.

Chapter Eighteen

Pedro Gallegos sat with his back against the roof wall and watched with painful fascination as Zion fashioned a tourniquet out of a bandanna and a flintlock pistol, thrusting the gun barrel through a loop in the bandanna and rotating the pistol to tighten the cloth until it closed off the supply of blood to the bullet crease in Pedro's leg.

"Damn. It would be my good leg," the ranchero muttered, sweat beading his upper lip despite the cool arid air.

"Lucky for you the ricochet was just about spent," Zion said. The bullet, fired by a rifleman atop the bunkhouse minutes ago, had glanced off a corner of the wall and plowed a ragged furrow in Pedro's right leg, just above the knee.

"Ain't gonna be lucky for anybody the next time they come," Pedro said. "What the hell is the general up to?"

"He's waiting out the fires we set," Zion said. Najera had lost five men during the first attempt at storming the house. After their initial onslaught, the dragoons had fortified themselves in the bunkhouse and the barn, with a couple of marksmen behind the stone walls of the water tank in the center of the ranchyard. From these three vantage points the soldiers had kept up a sporadic assault on the hacienda, peppering the shuttered windows and the roof battlement with gunfire.

"Once the fires burn out and we can't see to shoot until they're right up on us . . ." Zion's voice trailed off. He saw no reason to go into detail. Pedro wasn't a tenderfoot. He knew as well as any man what to expect. Zion scrambled away from Pedro's side to peer over the front wall and inspect the yard. A rifle atop the bunkhouse spat flame, and a bullet struck the wall a couple of feet below the segundo. Zion cursed and answered the shot with one of his own. His rifle boomed and the man on the bunkhouse ducked out of sight. The men by the water tank opened up with their muzzle loaders and forced Zion back down behind the wall, but he'd seen enough to worry him. The fires were nearly spent, the darkness encroaching where flames nearly as tall as a man had leaped and danced and held back the night. Gunshots from the women below spattered the tank walls; geysers erupted in front of the hidden soldiers. Josefina and Elena were holding their own. The women still had plenty of fight left in them.

The trapdoor in the roof creaked open and Isabella poked her head through.

"Stay below," Zion called out.

"The rooms are full of powder smoke, it stinks downstairs," the child remarked. Her cheeks were smudged with ashes. She'd tied a bandanna around her head to hold back her hair. A second strip of cloth circled her left hand where she'd been struck by splinters from a bullet-riddled shutter. The girl lifted a canteen for Zion to take. "I brought water."

The segundo scrambled across the roof to the

trapdoor, retrieved the water, then passed the canteen to Pedro, who gratefully accepted it.

"Pedro's been hurt," Isabella exclaimed, and tried to climb out on the roof, but Zion pushed her back.

"I've looked after him."

"But I should be here," Isabella protested.

"You should do what I tell you, little one." Zion was too strong for the girl and prevented her from reaching the roof. "The soldiers on the bunkhouse won't think twice about shooting a child. It's safer for you in the hacienda."

"But Josefina and Elena won't let me do anything but load their pistols," Isabella complained. "I'm a better shot than either of them, I bet."

"Obey your stepmother," Zion said flatly, unmoved by her arguments. "Remember what you said to me, my little spitfire. It's the gentleman's duty to protect the lady."

The ten-year-old scowled, caught by her own cleverness. She looked into the segundo's kind eyes and nodded. Her expression softened. "Is General Najera going to kill us?"

"No," Zion said. Isabella continued to stare at him with those soft brown eyes that always seemed to be able to look right through him. "Now get below. And mind your footing, a couple of those rungs are slick."

"I love you, Zion," Isabella said before she ducked down and disappeared below the edge of the roof.

Zion crawled back to the adobe wall and knelt alongside Pedro. The blood had all but ceased to seep from the leg wound. The ranchero's lips were drawn back tight against his teeth. He was in pain.

"She is a brave girl. I think you convinced her," Pedro said.

Zion glanced toward the trapdoor, laughed ruefully and shook his head. "Isabella Quintero? I didn't fool her for an instant."

Josefina Quintero abandoned the study window and made her way across the house, into the sitting room where Father Rudolfo was ramming charges down the barrels of the widow's shotgun. He primed the piece and set it aside as Josefina knelt by a tin pitcher of water and poured herself another drink. As a last defense the widow, Elena, and the priest had built a makeshift barricade at the rear of the front room. Should Najera's men begin to break through the door, the hacienda's defenders would seek shelter behind the overturned tables and chairs near the back wall. Josefina hoped it wouldn't come to that, but if it did, well . . . She picked up the shotgun and nodded her thanks to the priest.

"I have never been so thirsty in my life," she said. A haze of powder smoke drifted through the house, irritating the eyes and throats of everyone inside.

"Take courage, senora. The good Lord will not abandon us," the padre said. At his side, Nino lifted his furry head and wagged his tail, waiting for a scratch behind the ears.

"Just the same, keep praying," Josefina said. "For we will need a miracle indeed."

"I prayed when the Comanche took me. Prayed every day. It kept me alive when I wanted to die," Elena replied, coming in from the dining room for another tin box of musket balls. "The Comanche squaws used to beat me, once or twice a week. They'd break off branches of ocotillo cactus and whip me bloody. That's when I quit praying and fought back and never shed a tear." The woman eased her big frame past the priest and helped herself to the water. "If we aim to walk away from this, it will take more than prayer. We must fight like she-wolves. We must get mean." She drank a cup of water and, seeing Isabella climbing down from the roof, called the girl to her side.

"Isabella, is Pedro all right?"

"He is fine, Elena," the girl lied. She saw no reason to cause the house servant undue worry. And after all, Zion was there to look after the vaquero. Isabella knelt down and petted Nino, then followed her stepmother into the study. It seemed a lifetime ago to the girl that she had visited her father here in his library. She walked around the desk and sat in the chair, her father's "throne." She tucked her legs up under herself and closed her eyes and for a moment could almost feel Don Sebastien's protecting embrace surround her. A gunshot startled her and shattered her brief reverie. A bullet thudded into the shutter. Josefina ducked out of reflex and then returned fire like a veteran. Her shoulder was bruised from the musket's recoil but she no longer even winced at the pain. She grabbed the ramrod, swabbed out the barrel, tore open a paper cartridge, poured in the charge, and finally rammed the ball and paper wadding down atop the powder. After fitting an explosive cap upon the nipple, she cocked the hammer and was ready to loose another shot. She awkwardly accomplished the entire procedure without assistance, then, realizing she had an audience, smiled at the girl.

"Can this be your tutor?" Josefina held out the powder-burned, blistered palm of one hand. "Do you remember when I taught you to play the wooden flute?" Now the widow could barely move her fingers, and a trickle of blood could be seen on the side of her neck. Isabella hurried out of the chair and ran to her stepmother's side. She took Josefina's hand and kissed the blackened palm.

"Papa would have been proud," the girl said.

"Of us both," Josefina said, holding Isabella close to her bosom. Beyond the walls of the hacienda, the world fell ominously quiet. It wouldn't be long now.

About a quarter of a mile from the hacienda, the Rangers halted to assess the situation. As Ben and Snake-Eye Gandy and the rest of the Texans looked on, the brief exchange of gunfire ceased.

"Looks like we ain't too late," Gandy said. "How tall is the wall?"

"We can clear it at a gallop," Ben said. "That is, if an old fart like you can stay in the saddle."

Gandy chuckled. "Just you try and keep up, Brass Buttons." He raised his hand and the Rangers fanned out, twelve to a side, then began to check their loads and tuck loaded cylinders into their coat pockets.

"We take 'em straight on, Snake-Eye?" Cletus Buckhart asked, breathing quick from the excitement.

"There ain't no other way." Gandy rode out in front of the Rangers, and when he spoke, his low voice carried all along the line. "General Valentin Najera's down there, lads. I don't know how many men he's got with him, but there's bound to be plenty to go around. We come here to show him that no man can do what he done and get away with it. The way I see it, back on the road to Linares when he ambushed and mutilated our compadres, it was like he throwed a glove in our faces. Let's see if he can wear it."

"Suits me. How about the rest of you boys?" old Blue Napier said in a gravelly voice. He tugged his hat down on his head and tied it off beneath his chin.

"I didn't ride all the way out here for my health," Leon Pettibone said.

"That's for damn sure," another voice added down the line. Almost everyone laughed.

"What do you aim to do with me, Gandy?" Ned Tolliver spoke up. His voice was a reminder to the others of the seriousness of their position.

"Any one of you hell-for-leather riders want to sit out the dance and nursemaid Ned?" Gandy asked. He waited for a reply, and when none was forthcoming, took the silence at face value. "Looks like you'll be joining us."

Tolliver gulped and stared down at his bound hands. "Then give me a gun for heaven's sake."

Pettibone had to laugh again. "Ned, you are a kidder."

"You can't expect me to charge them Mexicans unarmed!" Panic crept into Tolliver's voice.

"Don't worry, Ned. From what I hear, Najera's a friend of yours," Gandy said. And with that he dismissed the turncoat and was deaf to the man's protests. Snake-Eye rode on back to Ben and wheeled his horse into line, then nodded to McQueen. "The men are ready, Lieutenant."

Color crept to Ben's cheeks at the implication he should lead these men into battle. The past would take a long time to heal. There was still a part of his soul scarred with the shame of his earlier failure. "It isn't for me to lead you," Ben said.

"That's for us to say," Gandy replied. "Let me put it this way. Texas Rangers are a peculiar breed. We don't follow the uniform, we follow the man."

"Waiting on you," a voice drifted up from the ranks.

"Take the point, Ben," another man drawled.

Ben glanced to either side and saw in the moonlight the faces of those around him. They were a wild, often disreputable lot who had no use for medals or authority. But they'd charge through all Perdition to pluck the devil's beard.

"Time's wasting," said Gandy.

For Valentin Najera, the time of reckoning was at hand. It wouldn't do to keep the general waiting. Ben McQueen touched his heels to his mount, and the animal started forward and quickly broke into a canter, then a gallop, bearing its rider to victory or death.

Valentin Najera, his arms folded across his chest, studied the hacienda from the barn's darkened doorway. His black eyes never seemed to blink. Like Caesar studying the scene of his intended triumph, Najera played out in his mind the assault on the hacienda. He cursed the moon which bathed the ranchyard in silvery light. The fires had diminished, though they still served to illuminate the area around the hacienda. But time was wasting, and he was anxious to end this affair once and for all. He had given Don Sebastien's widow an opportunity to come out of this alive, and she had hurled the kindness back in his face. Only his most trusted men were with him, vaqueros whose solitary devotion to the Najera family was unquestioned. What transpired this night would be buried beneath their silence.

"Jefe?"

"What is it?" he asked without turning to look at the mestizo.

"Felipe has just died," Mariano Rincon said.

"It was to be expected. A belly wound is bad-
. . . very bad."

"The men are angry. Felipe was young and full of song," Rincon said. He scratched his belly, hooked his thumbs in his gun belt and took a step closer. The mestizo was full of misgivings now, but he could see no escaping his predicament. Things were turning out badly. Raul Salcedo was dead, and there was no telling how many of the dragoons would join him. But Rincon could not bring himself to sneak away under cover of night. Blood demanded blood. The defenders of the hacienda must be made to pay. And there was his own position to consider. Mariano Rincon had, by default, assumed Raul's place at the general's side and hoped to make the most of it.

"Then gather my soldiers," Najera said. "I grow impatient. By now the widow and her household are weary, their eyes grow leaden and their spirits dampened by fear of the inevitable."

The general stepped into the yard and, oblivious to any danger, started toward the water tank. He knew what effect this would have on his men. In the barn, half a dozen dragoons grabbed their muskets and pistols and followed Najera as he strode toward the hacienda. They went on foot, moving stealthily in the night, each man thinking of the generous reward *El Jefe* had promised them. The general and his soldiers chose their steps wisely so as not to alert the widow and her hirelings until it was too late. The soldiers on the roof of the bunkhouse scurried down to join in the attack and alerted their compañeros within, who filed out through the front door, closing ranks with the general. Najera ran at a crouch toward the water tank, where another couple of uniformed vaqueros hastily reloaded their weapons and fumbled as they tried to salute.

Najera, in the lead, motioned for the mestizo to bring the men on the run, but when he turned to address the breed, the general found the man kneeling with his hand on the ground and facing the front gate through which the column had ridden earlier in the evening.

"What is it?" the general hissed.

"Someone comes. Many horses." Rincon looked up, worried.

"You're imagining things," Najera scoffed.

"No. I can feel the earth. It does not lie. Wait. There . . . now . . . do you hear?"

Najera listened. At first he heard nothing but the wind and the silence. Then his own ears picked it up. Rincon was right. It sounded like horsemen approaching from the direction of Saltillo. His men? But why? Yet who else could it be?

A shot rang out from the roof of the hacienda and derailed his train of thought. Gunfire blossomed from the bullet-riddled windows. Lead slugs fanned the air. For a moment the dragoons looked confused, until Najera's voice rang out and gave them purpose.

"To the hacienda, mi amigos. Break down the doors!" The general ran a gauntlet of gunfire as he charged the front of the house. His soldiers, electrified by the general's command, rushed the hacienda. A couple of them staggered but kept advancing. Within a matter of seconds they had reached the porch and began to ram the shutters and front door with their rifle butts. A trio of marksmen under Rincon's command kept Zion pinned down behind the battlements. The segundo could only loose a blind shot or two through the thatch roof at the men below. His attempts proved futile at best. To actually lean over the wall and take aim meant his death.

Within the hacienda Josefina and Elena were forced to abandon their positions in the study and dining room under a hail of lead that showered both women with splinters and chunks of adobe brick. Josefina had to catch Isabella about the waist and drag her out of harm's way. The child was full of fight and refused to give an inch to the soldiers shooting point-blank into the windows. The women and Father Rudolfo retreated toward the protection of the barricade, their final redoubt. They held their fire now, saving the ammunition for their last stand. The front door continued to hold, but the bar that prevented the soldiers from entering was beginning to splinter and crack; the hinges were coming apart.

Isabella clung to Nino, who barked and bared his teeth at the men outside. Josefina took a deep breath and aimed her pistol at the front door while Elena aimed the shotgun. The widow could only hope that Valentin Najera was fool enough to be the first to enter. The padre began to recite the Lord's prayer as he reloaded the two remaining single-shot pistols. The noise outside increased, the gunfire becoming all the more furious, intensifying, as if the forces outside had swelled in number.

"My God," Josefina whispered beneath her breath. "How many of them are there?"

"Not that many," Elena shouted, to be heard above the thunder of drums. Her eyes were watering from the gun smoke.

Suddenly the hinges and wooden bar gave way and the heavy oaken door came crashing down into the room along with one of Najera's soldiers, who toppled through the doorway and sprawled on top of the door as it hit the floor. The defenders held their fire; the dragoon was already dead, his uniform torn from several wounds. From the terrible din outside, Josefina realized a battle was raging, but it wasn't the one she'd been fighting. Gunshots and war cries to rival any Comanche's reverberated in the night. Whatever else was happening, Najera's men had ceased their assault.

The trapdoor in the hall opened and Zion scrambled down into the lower reaches of the hacienda and rushed into the room, his .45 caliber pistol in hand. He quickly surveyed the women huddled behind their barricade and was relieved to find them unharmed. His expression was one of elation.

"Zion . . . what's happening?" Josefina asked.

"Deliverance!" he roared, and charged out of the room and into the melee.

Ben tightened his hold on the reins and leaned forward over the neck of the gelding as the animal took the three-foot wall in stride. He beat Gandy's mount by a nose. The other Rangers weren't far behind, riding hard and shooting straight. The Texas hellions loosed a volley from their Colts as they bore down on the Mexican soldiers bunched in front of the hacienda. Najera's men retreated from the porch and scattered out into the yard, where they returned the fire. Startled by the unexpected attack, the Mexican dragoons hoped to fight their way to the barn, where their own mounts were corralled. The exchange of gunfire and the proximity of the Rangers caused the suddenly leaderless command to change their plans and take up a formation around the water tank as the Rangers rushed to surround them like a horde of howling Comanches.

A bullet missed Ben by inches when he rode up to the hacienda. He fired at a pair of retreating figures, one of them disturbingly familiar, as they darted around the corner of the house then re-emerged to fire a volley at McQueen. From out of the corner of his eye Ben saw Snake-Eye Gandy's gelding stumble and fall. Horse and rider appeared grievously wounded. Forgetting the battle that engulfed the ranchyard, Ben leaped from the saddle and rushed to his friend's side.

"Snake-Eye!" Ben dropped to his knees next to the Ranger and put a hand to the man's chest. Gandy groaned, opened his eye and tried to focus. Gradually his vision cleared. He tried to speak. Ben lowered his ear to the man as he struggled to form words while trying to catch his wind. The Texan sucked in his breath and channeled all his strength, then tried again.

"Behind you!" Gandy managed.

McQueen twisted in time to see that one of the Mexican soldiers he had chased from the porch had returned and was brandishing a large-bore musket, aimed directly at his chest. From a distance of only a few yards, the man couldn't miss. Ben glanced toward the pistol he had foolishly tucked in his belt. The dragoon grinned, shook his head and said, "Too bad, hombre." He squeezed the trigger, but a gunshot proceeded his own. The Mexican arched his back and fired into the air, took half a step and fell face forward on the ground. Zion, his pistol trailing smoke, trotted off the porch and ran up to join McQueen.

"You boys are the prettiest sight these eyes have ever seen," Zion said. "Is he all right?" he added, looking down at the Ranger.

"I'm just pinned, and I think my ankle's twisted, but I ain't gone under yet," Gandy said, speaking for himself. He glared at Ben. "Glad to see there's someone else around here to pull you out of the fire when I ain't able to."

Ben grinned. If Snake-Eye had the energy to scold him, then the crusty old Ranger wasn't hurt too bad. He and Zion pulled Gandy out from under the horse and, using the dead animal for cover, crouched behind the carcass and fired at the dragoons clustered around the water tank.

"Stay with him," Ben said to Zion. The segundo nodded. "And thanks," he added with a glance toward the dragoon lying nearby.

"I owed you one," said Zion.

"You owe me two," Ben corrected.

"Who's counting?" the segundo replied and winked.

As Ben scrambled back toward the house, he noticed Josefina and Isabella watching him from the doorway. He stopped for a moment, outlined against a swirl of charging horses and fighting men, this tall redheaded stranger who had come to their aid once more. He waved. Josefina raised a hand.

"He came back, Josefina," Isabella said.

"Yes," the mistress of Ventana said. *This one last time. El Alacron.*

Ben skirted the melee and hurried off in pursuit of the other man who had escaped around the side of the house. A riderless horse plunged past him. He looked over his shoulder and saw two more. The dragoons, outnumbered, were putting up a desperate struggle. The Rangers would pay a dear price for victory. Most of Najera's men made their stand at the water tank, where they peppered the circling riders with gunfire. For their part, the Rangers surrounded the dragoons and fired from horseback. The Patterson Colts began to take a serious toll among Najera's men.

As Ben looked on, one of the Mexicans clutched his uniformed chest and fell backward. A second man on the opposite side of the water tank shrieked, dropped to his knees and tried to fire his gun, until another three slugs ended his efforts. A third dragoon came too late to his friend's aid, then, enraged, charged the Texans, emptying one saddle with a pistol shot and wounding another Ranger, poor Leon Pettibone, who took a saber slash to the thigh. Cletus Buckhart broke from the ranks and shot the swordsman twice in the chest. Then Cletus shuddered and clutched his shoulder as a bullet glanced off his collarbone. The young Ranger galloped out of harm's way as the air became thick with bullets. It was a grim and dirty business, the two forces like wild animals clawing and fighting, joined in a death-lock grip which only one would survive. Najera's most loyal vaqueros exhorted their compadres to fight on, proclaiming this a battle to the death. As the hope-lessness of their situation became evident, this out-cry began to wear a little thin on the less resolute.

Ben turned his back on the fray in pursuit of the second shadowy figure who had bolted from the front of the hacienda. He had caught a brief glimpse of silver hair as the man leaped from the porch, and instinct told him that whatever victory the Rangers might gain here at Ventana would be for naught if this man escaped. Ben eased past the corner of the house, searched the ranchyard and caught a glimpse of his prey racing toward the corral. Ben broke into a run, gun in hand, his long strides eating the distance between the hacienda and the barn. The Mexican reached the corral, turned and spied McQueen. He snapped off a shot, then vaulted onto the back of the nearest horse and leaned down, struggling to open the gate. Ben doubled his efforts and drew close enough to confirm his suspicions that the man in the corral was none other than Valentin Najera.

Suddenly the gate swung open and Najera made his break for freedom. Ben loosed a bloodcurdling scream, waved his sombrero over his head and emptied his revolver into the ground in front of Najera's horse. The terrified animal reared and pawed the air, glanced off part of the railing, arched its back as a shard of wood dug into its belly, then bucked and twisted and tossed Najera to the ground.

Ben tossed the revolver aside and drew his second Colt. Najera was up and running, his own pistol spewing flame and powder smoke. Ben reached the corral and would have tried a shot but the horses were in the way. The animals were milling around in a tight circle, unnerved by the gunshots and the presence of both intruders in their midst.

Ben crouched low and eased his way past a big brown mare, worked past a pair of geldings, then paused, stalling for time, trying to listen, and hearing the labored breathing of the horses and the sound of their hooves thudding upon the trampled earth. Then came the whisper of the long knife, a gleam of steel. Ben twisted, saw the saber slicing toward him, and parried the blade with the barrel of his Colt. A booted foot caught him in the belly and knocked the wind out of him. He brought up the Patterson and fired at his attacker. Najera darted away. Ben dropped to one knee and aimed, but the gun wouldn't cock; the cylinder was jammed. Najera was on the move, but the moonlight revealed his path. Ben glanced about for a weapon and spied the basket hilt of a saber jutting from a saddle scabbard on one of the geldings. He slid the weapon free, climbed the corral fence and resumed the hunt.

Ned Tolliver worked his way to the edge of the ranchyard and dismounted near the bunkhouse. He looped his mount's reins over the hitching post and with an over-the-shoulder glance to see he hadn't been followed, hurried inside the long, low-roofed adobe structure that had housed Don Sebastien's rancheros. To his relief, he found the room empty. Tolliver feverishly began to search through what few belongings had been left behind by the men Najera had pressed into his army. The hammering gunfire served to heighten his tension. None of the Rangers had seen him ride away. He could escape unnoticed.

But he wasn't about to ride off into the mountains with his hands tied.

Tolliver searched in vain. There were no knives, nothing sharp to saw loose his bonds with. Then his gaze settled on the Franklin stove in the center of the room. He crossed to its side and felt the black iron. It was warm to the touch. He opened the trap and his expression became triumphant. Coals . . . some of them still pulsing with life. He took a scoop from the side of the stove, scraped out a pile of embers onto the floor, then lay on his belly and blew on the coals until they glowed crimson. He held his wrists to the embers and bit his lips to keep from yelling at the pain. His skin began to blacken and blister. He focused his hatred on Ben McQueen, who had cheated the grave and ruined his plans. Another time and place and he would have his revenge.

"You'll pay," Tolliver said through clenched teeth, blocking the agony by concentrating on McQueen. Just at the moment when even hatred failed, the leather bonds imprisoning his wrists separated with a snap. He crawled across the room to a black-enameled pot of cold coffee on a nearby table and poured the liquid over his wrists. His great, chest-heaving sobs were the only sound save for gunfire and the cries of the wounded.

A sense of urgency swept over Tolliver. Rather than waste even a few precious seconds searching the bunkhouse for supplies, he resolved to make good his escape, steal a few necessities from some outlying farm near Saltillo and leave Mexico for healthier climes. There would be time enough to plot McQueen's comeuppance.

Tolliver headed quickly for the front door. He could see his horse at the hitching post, framed by the doorway. His wrists hurt but he'd tend to them later. Let them hurt for now; it was a price he was willing to pay to secure his escape. He plunged through the doorway and out onto the porch. An arm immediately encircled his torso, and a familiar voice whispered in his ear.

"Sorry amigo, I need your horse," Mariano Rincon said. The mestizo's right hand swept across Tolliver's throat, and steel glinted in the moonlight. The knife's deadly kiss slit Tolliver's throat from ear to ear. His wire-rimmed spectacles hit the floor, to be crushed underfoot as Tolliver struggled in vain against the mestizo's ironlike hold. The turncoat clawed at Rincon's forearm, Tolliver shoving and twisting while his lifeblood soaked the front of his shirt. He died unheralded, unmourned, too late for regrets or any saving grace.

Mariano Rincon propped the corpse upright in a chair on the porch then hurried over and untied Tolliver's horse. The mestizo's movements were fluid and very fast. There wasn't a moment to spare. Having survived a gauntlet of gunfire, the last thing Rincon wanted was to tangle with the Rangers again. Without so much as a glance toward his compadres, the mestizo led the horse around behind the bunkhouse. Only then did he climb into the saddle and ride off into the night. It was time to return to the mountains and leave this war behind. As for Ventana, he never wanted to hear the name again.

The grave markers in the Quintero family plot loomed like bone-colored tablets in the moonlight. The lone oak tree spread its heavy arms in what might pass for prayerful supplication above the final resting place of the Quinteros. It was here that the general turned when Ben McQueen called him by name.

"Najera!"

In the ranchyard the gunfire ceased as the last of

the general's personal guard, four weary soldiers, tossed down their weapons. The Rangers, oblivious at first to the confrontation in the graveyard, immediately began to tend their wounded and tally the dead. It was Snake-Eye Gandy who alerted his men to Ben's absence and the fact that the battle was far from over.

The general searched his belt in vain for the cartridge box with which to reload his pistol. He'd probably lost the damn thing when the horse threw him. No matter. He had his saber. The general tossed the pistol aside and motioned for Ben to enter the graveyard. McQueen obliged. The ghosts of those he had led into an ambush demanded this final confrontation.

"One of us will not leave here alive," Najera said, warily advancing on the americano. The general was visibly shaken, like a man who has survived a hurricane that's obliterated a lifetime of work. Where had the damn Rangers come from? How had they found him, here of all places?

He could escape, though, and live to fight another day. Only one man stood in the way. Just one . . .

Ben extended his blade until he and the general stood at sword's point. A gossamer veil of cirrus clouds drifted across the face of the moon. In the distance coyotes wailed. Then, from the branches of the oak tree in the center of the family graveyard, a gray owl took flight, its wings outstretched against a backdrop of iridescent stars.

Najera lunged. Ben parried and retreated. The general slashed, missed, lost his footing, caught himself and swung his saber. Ben caught the general's sword with his own blade, the hilts clashing together, and Ben shoved the smaller man back. Overconfident because of his size and strength, Ben moved in for a quick kill. Najera taught him the error of his ways. The general regained his balance and sliced upward, cutting Ben from belly to breast bone. Ben gasped and retreated toward the oak tree as the pain coursed through him like fire. His size only made him a bigger target, nothing more. The wound, though superficial, hurt like hell, and blood began to seep along its length. Najera pressed his advantage with a thrust toward the bowels that Ben just barely managed to avert, then a slash to right and left. Ben defended himself as best he could, cheating death once, twice, then a third time. The clang of steel on steel rang out in the stillness. Blades like silver talons flashed in the moonlight. Najera tried for a killing blow. Ben slammed against the tree and nearly knocked himself unconscious. He blocked the thrust and used the hilt of his weapon like a battering ram to deliver a savage uppercut that caught Najera flush in the mouth and sent him reeling among the graves. If Valentin Najera had drawn first blood, Ben McQueen had certainly accounted for the second. The general staggered and spat blood and bone, wiped a forearm across his puffed, ruined lips and tried to curse Ben. But the words came out garbled. Najera's front teeth were gone and his upper and lower gums were split and horribly mangled.

Najera lost control in that instant. Blinded by rage and the agony of his battered mouth, he charged forward, sword raised as if to behead Ben and in the process cleave the tree like a lightning bolt. He was unstoppable, invincible. He held the power of the gods in his right hand.

Ben stood poised, uncowed by the general's onslaught, and waited until the last possible second. Then, as Najera's blade slashed for his throat, Ben dropped to his knees. The general's sword cropped a tuft of his red hair and sank into the tree trunk with a sickening thwack. Ben rolled to the right, leaped to his feet and drove his saber into the general with all his strength.

Najera gasped and staggered back, tearing the saber from Ben's grasp. The blade, entering just below Najera's eighth rib on his left side, had passed through his vitals. Like a skewer through a chunk of meat, a foot of steel protruded from underneath his right arm. He rose up on his toes; his mouth dropped open, but he had no voice to scream. The effect was all the more horrible for the silence issuing from the mortally wounded man's contorted features. He sank to his knees, braced himself against a grave marker. Through blurring vision Najera read the name "Don Sebastien" and laughed, a horrid chortling sound, then sank to the earth.

Ben McQueen heard the gate creak open behind him and turned. Snake-Eye Gandy and Zion were standing just outside the fence. Ben stumbled toward them, his legs growing weak.

"You can lean on me," the segundo said, offering Ben a shoulder. The americano gratefully accepted.

"You all right?" Gandy asked, limping along as they left the graveyard and headed toward the hacienda.

Ben thought of all that had transpired. The loss and regaining of his memory, his honor, his own dignity. He had made mistakes, but he had tried his best . . . in both lives, as Ben McQueen and as the man called Alacron.

"It's time to bury the dead," Ben McQueen said.

General Valentin Najera sucked in a mouthful of air, found the pain unbearable, and coughed, his features contorted. He was dying. It had all been for naught. But he had made such careful plans. He had foreseen everything, except this. But how? Who had brought it all about and caused his downfall? That was his prayer, just to know a name, a face. Who?

He felt something tickle his outstretched hand. He turned his head to the right and managed by force of will to hold back the curtains of everlasting night that even now framed his sight. He tried to focus, and through a velvet, shimmering haze saw something scuttle across the palm of his hand then conceal itself beneath the leaden weight of his wrist. General Valentin Najera died without understanding that fate had provided the answer to his question.

A scorpion.

ABOUT THE AUTHOR

KERRY NEWCOMB is the best-selling author of several major frontier novels, including *Morning Star* and *Sacred Is the Wind*. He lives with his family in Fort Worth, Texas.

From the bestselling author of *Morning Star* and *Sacred Is the Wind* comes a powerful new novel of a man caught between tradition and change, a man who gives up his birthright in search of an uncertain future . . .

THE ARROW KEEPER'S SONG
by
Kerry Newcomb

Tom Sandcrane is a young Cheyenne living on the reservation in the Oklahoma Territory during the waning days of the last century. For the Southern Cheyenne, it is a time of change and uncertainty. Men like Tom's father, Seth, the keeper of the Sacred Arrows, cling to the old ways; but in the outside world, white men still covet Indian lands and the natural riches that lie therein, while the rumblings of a war on the far-off island of Cuba will intrude even into the placid life of the reservation. For Tom Sandcrane, the time of questing has begun: to find his place in this strange new world and still listen to the voices of his spirit-guides, to find his destiny and, with it, the destiny of his people.

Turn the page for an exciting preview of *The Arrow Keeper's Song* by Kerry Newcomb, coming from Bantam Books in Spring 1995.

The hand of Maheo, the All-Father, appeared in the center of a circle of old men whose stern features were etched in stark relief by the brightness of the apparition. The heartbeat of Maheo filled the air and caused the earth to tremble. The Maiyun, the spirits of those who have gone before, leaped soundlessly one moment, gyrated madly the next, as if attempting to distract the elders from their somber ritual.

Tom Sandcrane, blind to the hand of God, saw only the leaping flames from a briskly burning fire. To his ears the heartbeat of the Creator was no more than the hypnotic tap-tap-tapping of the ceremonial drums. No spirits but the tribal elders' own shadows danced upon the buffalo hide walls of the Ceremonial Lodge.

Tom stood with the other young men, apart from the ceremonial fire. His twenty-two years hardly qualified him for a place in the circle traditionally reserved for the elders of the Southern Cheyenne. Although Tom was held in high esteem throughout the Reservation, here in the Sacred Lodge, tradition and custom needed to be obeyed, he could only join the elders if summoned by one of them.

Sandcrane shifted his stance and kicked a dirt clod with the scuffed toe of his right boot. He'd been gentling a horse for Allyn Benedict, the local Indian agent. Sandcrane's hard wiry physique had taken a pounding but the money had been good and the experience had afforded him a chance to visit with Allyn's pretty daughter, Emmiline. That green-eyed beauty was worth a hard ride any day.

It was mid-December, the time of the big-hard-face-moon, the third Sunday of Advent, in the last days of 1896 and Tom Sandcrane wished he could have accepted Allyn Benedict's invitation to accompany the Indian agent and his family to church and afterward, return to the house for a late dinner. Emmiline had never looked prettier. But Tom Sandcrane had promised his father he'd attend this night's ceremony . . . so here he was. He'd spent the last hour standing in the shadows and awaiting his father's humiliation. It was difficult to be too sympathetic. The horny bastard had brought this on himself.

Tom removed his faded gray Stetson and brushed back his close-cropped black hair with the palm of his hand then settled the sweat-stained broad-brimmed hat back on his head. It was warm here in the lodge and he considered removing his wool-lined denim jacket and would have if there had been a place to set the coat aside. Tom sighed and shoved his hands in his pockets. His movements distracted Seth Sandcrane who noticed his son standing outside the circle of light. Seth appeared curiously relieved to see his son had made it to the council. The older man began to take heart. There was still hope that all wasn't lost.

Father and son were built much the same. Tom Sandcrane, cut from his father's image stood a couple inches under six feet. Like his Cheyenne forbearers, theirs was the blood of warriors, the finest light cavalry in the world who once had roamed the plains and followed the great herds of buffalo and answered to no one. Boarding school had done nothing to dull the young man's natural skills. There wasn't a horse he couldn't ride, no brag, just the plain fact. Tom was sharp as a whipcrack, leather tough, with his father's dark brown eyes.

Unlike his son who was lean and wiry, Seth Sandcrane carried an extra twenty pounds now and was beginning to show a paunch. His features were creased now not smooth like Tom's and a white crescent shaped scar marked his right cheek just below his eye but the forty five year old man could sit a horse as well as any young buck. Dressed in the traditional garb of fringed buckskin shirt and leggings, Seth's long silver-streaked hair was braided and decorated with an eagle feather bearing three notches symbolizing the times he had counted coup in battle. Usually a good-natured easy-going soul, Seth Sandcrane wore a grave expression this wintry night. By force of will alone he shielded his feelings as the elders began to speak. He would not give them the satisfaction of seeing his pain. Seth lowered his eyes to the buckskin Medicine Bundle on the ground before him. The Bundle was tied with rawhide and decorated with the sign of the hawk, the buffalo, and horse. Whorled designs of finely stitched beadwork ran along one side from the tied top to fringed bottom. No one needed to view the contents to know what the Bundle contained. These were *Mahuts*, the Sacred Arrows brought long ago to the Cheyenne by Sweet Medicine, the prophet, as a gift from the All-Father. The Arrows were the most powerful and sacred objects the tribe possessed. They nurtured and guarded the People and were as crucial to the survival of the Southern Cheyenne as the very air to breath or food to eat. Seth Sandcrane had been the Arrow Keeper for almost a decade but that honor was about to come to an end.

The majority of the tribe had learned of Seth's indiscretion through rumor and hearsay, but Tom heard the story first hand from his father's own lips. Seth had become enamored of *Kanee-estse*, Red Cherries, who was the wife of Jordan Weasel Bear, one of the elders of the tribe. Jordan, after learning of his wife's infidelity and in a fit of drunken rage, savagely beat his wife then fled on horseback into the black night. A couple of days later, the rancher's body was found alongside the carcass of his gelding. It was surmised the animal had stepped in a prairie dog mound and broken a leg and crushed Jordan as it fell. The tragedy had tarnished Seth's reputation and jeopardized his position as Keeper of the Sacred Arrows, a man who must be above reproach.

Tom shifted his stance and surveyed the circle of elders. He recognized Luthor White Bear, a crease-faced individual with steely gray hair braids that hung to his shoulders. He was approximately the same age as Seth and had made no effort to conceal the fact that he coveted the role of Arrow Keeper.

To begin the council, Luthor removed a Medicine

Pipe from a buckskin bundle in his possession and after brushing the red clay bowl with dried sage and brittle stalks of sweetgrass, lit the contents of the bowl, a mixture of tobacco and cherry bark.

Luthor's features were marked by a single white band of color painted across his eyes like a narrow mask. The elder represented the originator of life and light and was seated at the southeast point of the circle.

"I am morning, I bring new life to the people. The sun is my servant," said Luthor White Bear who smoked the pipe and then passed it to Henry Running Shadow, seated at the southwest point. The elderly warrior's traditional buckskin shirt and leggings were baggy and seemed almost comical upon his frail looking torso. He looked as if he were trying to shrink out of his clothes. The man's features were concealed behind a mask of red paint.

"Thunder lives in me. I journey from the south bringing rain and warm weather. In me the grass grows and the earth becomes green again," said Henry Running Shadow in a gravelly voice. He was fifty-seven years old and his hands had a slight tremble from the onset of palsy that would one day kill him. He smoked the pipe and handed it to the Cheyenne seated at the northwest. At fifty years of age Abe Spotted Horse had lived long enough to grow restless for the old days. Chasing buffalo and raiding the white man's villages and towns had provided plenty of opportunity for a warrior to count coup and prove his bravery. Peace had left him brooding and restless. His color was yellow, the color of the sunset.

"I am the place where the sun sleeps. I am that which is without blemish, the ripeness and beauty of the world." He smoked and again a cloud of prayer smoke billowed up above the heads of those gathered in the lodge. Abe Spotted Horse stretched out his hand and the pipe was taken by the last of the painted elders.

The face of Coby Starving Elk was smeared with a band of black paint. He too was in his mid-forties. A stocky man with a belly that overhung his beaded belt like a bay window, Coby was unflaggingly honest and could be counted on to hold a wise council.

"I will smoke this pipe," said Coby. "For I am the killing storm, the blanketing snow and the crippling cold. I am your death. I am always seated at your fire. But as you honor me I will stay my hand." He puffed on the pipe three times and paused to allow his words to ride the prayer smoke to heaven. He pointedly refrained from offering the pipe to Seth who remained sitting on his haunches close to the fire. When Coby had returned the Medicine Pipe to Luthor White Bear, Seth leaned forward and untied the bundle of brushed deerhide and mallard skin and unwrapped its contents.

The Sacred Arrows were about six inches longer than a normal hunting arrow. Each shaft was ringed with varying bands of color corresponding to the painted elders; a white arrow, a black, a yellow and a red. *Mahuts* were tipped with glassy black obsidian arrowheads. Each shaft was trimmed with eagle feathers although the arrows would never know the touch of bowstring. Their power was mystical in nature.

Tom has seen the relics before, in his father's house, the first time as a lad of thirteen when he had sneaked a peek inside the Medicine Bundle. He had been frightened then of invoking the wrath of a host of evil spirits. Now the Arrows meant no more to him than the tradition they represented. He had accompanied Allyn Benedict to the nation's capitol and had seen in the cities of the East the power of commerce and invention which had fueled the white man's conquest of the frontier. Tom had glimpsed the future, that unstoppable juggernaut, progress, which the Southern Cheyenne could either climb aboard or be ground beneath. What were a bunch of wooden sticks compared to the raw power of industry? The sooner his people left the old ways behind, the better.

Seth Sandcrane looked down at the Arrows, his features remaining impassive. He'd been a fool to become involved with Red Cherries and should have kept his pants zipped. But Red Cherries was the kind of woman who could make a boy feel like a man and an old man feel like a boy again. Seth sighed and looking up, met Luthor White Bear's icy stare. There was no love lost between the two elders. Luthor had coveted Seth's role from the moment the Bundle had been placed in Sandcrane's hands. Luthor was making no attempt to hide the disdain he felt for his rival.

Coby Starving Elk cleared his throat and with a wave of his hand, gestured for the drummers to cease. The three braves immediately complied and a silence broken only by the crackling fire filled the lodge.

"Long ago in the time of those who have gone before, *Maheo*, the All-Father sent the Sacred Arrows to us. Sweet Medicine was the first Keeper. And after his death came men like White Thunder and Rides Horse. Once there came a time when the Pawnee stole the Arrows and many Cheyenne rode the warpath to recover that which was taken. Great was the suffering. Five of those brave young warriors were killed before the Arrows were returned." Coby looked from Luthor to Henry Running Shadow and Abe Spotted Horse and then settled his gaze on his old friend Seth Sandcrane. Regret was plainly evident in Coby's expression. But sympathy could not undo what was about to transpire. Yet the two men had agreed on one way the Arrows might remain beneath Sandcrane's roof. Coby was willing to give his old friend one last chance, in a manner of speaking. "Our five grandfather's were killed recovering the Sacred Arrows," he continued, "and so it was decided that the Arrow Keeper should come from one of our families. You have been the Arrow Keeper, Seth Sandcrane, as was your father before Maheo called him by name. You have renewed *Mahuts* with your prayers and sacrifice and guarded them well."

"Until now," Luthor White Bear spoke up.

"I have done what I have done," said Seth Sandcrane. "I have brought *Mahuts* and unwrapped them so that one and all can see they have been well cared for."

"But they are heavy with your shame," Luthor replied. "It is time for another Arrow Keeper to be chosen or surely all our people will suffer for the actions of this one."

"Luthor's words are straight," Abe Spotted Horse interjected. He had often hunted with Seth, the two had shared many campfires together. He took no pleasure in bringing Seth before the council but the welfare of the Southern Cheyenne came first. The Sacred Arrows must be placed in proper hands.

"I have brought *Mahuts*. I place them upon the earth before you. My hands can no longer reach them. Let another come forward and gather them," Seth proclaimed in a voice thick with emotion.

That was all Luthor White Bear needed to hear. He rose from his place and started forward with a look of triumph in his eyes. "As Pipe Bearer, *Mahuts* must be placed in my care until the next renewal ceremony."

"Wait my brother," Coby called out, blocking Luthor's path. The Pipe Bearer was caught completely unawares. Coby turned to face Seth and winked before explaining his actions. "Ten winters ago, *Maheo* revealed to us that the Sacred Arrows should be kept in the lodge of Seth Sandcrane. Who are we to go against the will of All-Father?"

"But they cannot remain beneath his roof," Luthor protested. "This one has dishonored the Sacred Arrows!"

"His son has not," Coby said.

Seth knew what was coming and had to struggle to refrain from flashing a look of triumph at the Pipe Bearer. Thank the Great Spirit Tom had made it to the council on time. Seth watched with relish as Coby ordered the young men ringing the elders to stand back and form a path through their midst.

Tom blinked and came alert. My God what was happening? Everyone was standing aside and suddenly there was nothing but empty space between him and the ceremonial fire. A hand nudged his shoulder and he glanced back to find Willem Tangle Hair, a freckle-faced, sandy-haired twenty-four-year-old halfbreed grinning and urging him on. Willem, member of the tribal police, had worked his way around the perimeter of the lodge to stand alongside his childhood friend. It was said of Tom and Willem they were two arrows from the save quiver. They had played together as children. And in the rough and tumble days of their childhood, one was always sticking up for the other.

"Looks like they want you up front, Tom," said the blue-eyed breed.

"Damn," Tom muttered beneath his breath. What had his father gotten him into now?

"Tom Sandcrane," Coby Starving Elk called out. Beads of sweat had begun to glisten on the elder's thick features. Trails of moisture streaked the rolls of flesh beneath his chin. But his black round beady eyes glinted with crafty intelligence as he invited the son of Seth Sandcrane to join him in the center of the lodge.

All eyes were on Tom as he advanced toward the fire and gingerly approached the man who had called him by name. "I am here," Tom said. His movements were cautious, his right leg was threatening to cramp. The leaping flames highlighted the uncertainty in his eyes.

Seth stood as his son entered the circle. The Arrow Keeper's last official act was to surrender that which he treasured most. Seth placed a hand on Tom's shoulder and gave the younger man a reassuring pat then turned and walked away from the Sacred Arrows lying upon the Bundle. He held himself erect and ramrod straight with head unbowed. Seth clung to the remnants of his dignity and walked with measured steps from the circle. It soothed his battered pride to think he'd denied Luthor White Bear yet again the role of Arrow Keeper. He retraced Tom's path through the crowd of Cheyenne, walking past the leaders of the various warrior societies who were waiting for the matter to be resolved. He reached the entrance to the lodge, pulled back the flap and stepped outside.

The cold clear moonlit air greeted Seth like a slap in the face after the stifling interior of the Ceremonial Lodge. He breathed deep and exhaled slowly and managed to stifle the scream of anguish that welled up from his wounded spirit. He clenched his fists and walked to his horse and there he waited on the edge of the wooded slope overlooking the deserted, wheel-rutted streets of Cross Timbers, a Cheyenne settlement nestled between two hills near the Washita River. An amber glow filled the windows above the Mercantile but the other four buildings that constituted the center of the town were dark. Father Kenneth's Mission Church on the east end of town was ablaze with light. No doubt the choir of St. Joachim's was practicing for Midnight Mass. Lantern light also gleamed in the windows of several of the houses surrounding the settlement. He glowered at one in particular, the gray washed walls of Allyn Benedict's home, there on the north hillside. Seth had no use for the Indian agent and resented the man's influence on Tom who wasn't alone in abandoning the Old Ways.

Too many of the young men of the tribe shared Tom's sentiments. One by one the traditions and beliefs were dying. Yet there was still magic . . . still mystery . . . still power. The Sacred Arrows remained. And late last night, in the depths of the Arrow Keeper's despair, they had called his son by name.

Tom Sandcrane stared down at the Sacred Arrows while the room seemed to fill with an almost palpable silence. He still didn't understand what was expected of him.

"Gather the Arrows. And gather the People. You will be the Arrow Keeper."

"No!" Luthor White Bear blurted out. "He is too young. It is not for him to claim *Mahuts*."

"It is not for you to defy the will of *Maheo*," said Coby. The circle of Cheyenne crowding the lodge tightened around the elders as the curious struggled to hear what was being said. Henry Running Shadow stood with the assistance of a member of the Bowstring Society who lent the chief a steady arm. Henry pointed at Abe Spotted Horse.

"We have walked in a dream," he said. Then gesturing to Coby the old man repeated himself. "Him too. We walked in a dream and the *Maiyun* guided us."

Abe nodded. "Henry's words are straight. The last night of our sweat, the Spirits of Those Who Have Gone Before came to us and showed to us the will of the All-Father."

"Each of us saw what we saw," Coby added, fixing an accusatory stare on Luthor who refused to admit he had seen the same visions as his companions. However he grew less adamant and discontinued his protests. Coby, satisfied, returned his attention to Tom Sandcrane. "Pick up the Bundle."

Coby's voice sounded far away, as if he were speaking from the distant end of a tunnel. His command reverberated in Tom's mind. The faces of the crowd became a blur. The longer he stood over the Sacred Arrows, the harder it became to focus on anything else around him. He could no longer feel the warmth of the fire or hear the crackle of the logs. A loud rasping noise filled his head and he strained to identify the sound, concentrating intently until it came to him. He was listening to his own breathing, each and every breath made resonant and yet for his ears alone. No sight, no sound, save for his hammering heart that seemed to increase in volume. Didn't they hear? Why couldn't they hear?

Tom shook his head and wiped a hand across his face to clear his vision. The Arrows were not for him. He had glimpsed the future and wanted to be a part of it. He wanted to be more than a reservation Indian. These beliefs and rituals were echoes of the old ways and would only hold him back. He tried to speak but his mouth had gone quite dry. He swallowed and tried again this time and managed a hoarse reply.

"I cannot."

Coby looked stunned and retreated a step. "What?"

Tom met the gaze of each of the elders, looking from one to the other as he repeated himself. "I cannot."

"But the All-Father has spoken . . ." Coby began.

"He has not spoken to me," Tom replied. He had to be careful and had no desire to offend anyone. "I must follow a different path." The faces in the crowd were a blur as he walked from the circle of light and followed in the footsteps of his father at least as far as the night air.

Tom paused to allow his vision to adjust then breathing a sigh of relief, started toward his dun gelding. He spied Seth Sandcrane waiting for him by the ground tethered horses and dreaded what was to come. Made a widower while Tom was still a toddler, Seth had raised the boy to manhood, unaided and alone. Tom knew he owed this man more than he could ever repay. Hurting his father was the last thing in the world Tom Sandcrane wished to do but there seemed no way to avoid it. As he drew closer to the dishonored Arrow Keeper, Tom held up his hands to show they were empty. Seth's elation dimmed when he realized his son did not cradle the Bundle in the crook of his arm. He frowned and his expression became puzzled.

"Tom . . . ?"

"Now I know why you insisted I attend this . . . this ceremony. You are a wily old fox, Seth, but it didn't work. I'm sorry."

A horned owl wooshed across the night sky. It glided from the tangle of live oaks and dropped onto a small rodent attempting to cross the clearing. With the bird's prey screeching in its cruel black talons the owl lifted from earth on great gray wings and rose to the safety of the treetops where it nested in the cleft of a towering white oak and proceeded to feed.

"Coby said he would offer the Arrows to my son."

"He spoke straight, father," Tom said. "But I could not take them."

"What?" Seth staggered back as if struck. "No!"

"I'm sorry. But the Arrows should be kept by someone who knows the old ways . . . and the prayers and songs."

"I would have taught you."

"But I did not wish to learn," said Tom. "The days of the buffalo are gone. It is time to learn new ways." He placed his hand on his father's arm. "We must learn or we will die."

"I think you are already dead," said Seth in a voice thick with resentment. Now the Sacred Arrows were indeed lost to him. He would never have the power again, never sing the songs of renewal or summon the *maiyun* with a single prayer. *As my son has failed me so I have failed all who have gone before*, he bitterly reflected. Cut to the quick by Tom's betrayal, Seth Sandcrane pulled away from his son. His gaze hardened until it became an impenetrable mask without a trace of paternal familiarity. He slowly turned on his heels and with shoulders bowed by the weight of his despair, walked off through the darkness, following a trail that skirted the hill and the ceremonial lodge.

"Father . . . *ne-ho!*" Tom called out, his breath clouding the air. But the stand of timber had already swallowed Seth Sandcrane, draping the wounded man with its shadowed shrouds and hiding his hurt from prying eyes. Tom slowly exhaled and shook his head and briefly considered following the old man. What was the use? Seth was beyond listening to what Tom had to say.

Despite the guilt Tom felt, he knew he had spoken the truth. There was no returning to the past, not even if he wanted to. Perhaps it was easier for the young Cheyenne like himself to understand this, while men like Seth were still too close to what had been, to the time when the Cheyenne had been lords of the plains.

The days ahead held challenge and change. Tom Sandcrane was ready. He doubted his father ever would be. The dun gelding behind him nickered and stamped the ground. The animal was anxious to return to town and the comfort of a warm stall.

Tom gathered the reins and swung into the saddle. Just as he pointed the animal toward town a cold north wind sprang up and snatched the hat from his head. He made a futile attempt to catch it and missed. The Stetson tumbled end over end and came to rest in the underbrush surrounding a pair of live oaks, its tall crown skewered by a forked twig. The dun fought Tom's steadying hand as the wind continued to whirl about them, moaning as it rattled the dry branches and stung them with brittle leaves and grains of sand. The hairs on the back of Tom's neck rose when he noticed the other horses seemed wholly unaffected by the wind while Tom had to struggle to keep his mount from bolting as the gusts continued to buffet him with unnatural force.

Suddenly the animal reared and pawed the air and for a fleeting instant Tom spied a pair of warriors on horseback watching him from the grove where he'd lost his hat. The two warriors wore only breechclouts and leggings. Their naked torsos were swirled with red warpaint, their faces obscured by garish red designs. They carried ten-foot-long spears tipped with stone blades that appeared to have been dipped in blood and brandished war shields painted crimson as were the powerful-looking stallions they sat astride. The warriors wore buffalo-horn headdresses the tips of which glistened a gory crimson in the moonlight.

The dun came down hard and almost dislodged its rider. A lesser horseman would have been sent tumbling. Tom held on for dear life, one hand on the reins and the other tangled in the gelding's mane. Tom's breathing became labored and he felt consciousness slipping away. Then the wind ceased.

Tom gasped in a lungful of air, sat upright in the saddle and brought the gelding under control. He glanced toward the grove of oaks to challenge the two warriors to identify themselves but they had vanished without a trace.

"*He-tohe*!" Tom exclaimed, inadvertently returning to his native tongue. "What the . . . ?" He was alone outside the ceremonial lodge. He cautiously walked the dun over to the underbrush and leaning down from the saddle, retrieved the Stetson. He took note that the two warriors, whoever they were, had managed to vanish without so much as breaking a twig or leaving a single track in the underbrush.

"*Glo—ria in excelsis deo. Glo—ria in excelsis de-o.*"

The faint strains of the advent choir drifted up the slope from the gaily lit church where Father Kenneth rehearsed his songs of praise for the Christian God. The "Gloria" spoke to Tom and called him back from what he had just experienced. A gust of wind, he told himself. And his own mind playing tricks on him. He dismissed the experience and studied the church at the east end of Main Street. Father Kenneth would be there. And Allyn Benedict with his family. And there were others in the congregation, both Cheyenne and white, who had come to Cross Timbers.

The tribal drummers resumed their steady beat, two light strokes then one heavy emanated from the ceremonial lodge announcing a new Arrow Keeper had been chosen. Such matters no longer concerned Tom Sandcrane. Latin hymn mingled uncomfortably with the wailing voices of the tribal elders. Tom did not linger to appreciate the discord, but started down the road toward the settlement, a young man with his eyes on tomorrow, following the strains of an Advent chorus, and guided by the brightness of his dreams.

RECEIVE A FREE LOUIS L'AMOUR
WALL CALENDAR JUST FOR PREVIEWING
THE LOUIS L'AMOUR COLLECTION!

Experience the rugged adventure of the American Frontier portrayed in rich, authentic detail with THE LOUIS L'AMOUR COLLECTION. These riveting Collector's Editions by America's bestselling Western writer, Louis L'Amour, can be **delivered to your home about once a month.** And you can **preview each volume for 15 days RISK-FREE** before deciding whether or not to accept each book. If you do not want the book, simply return it and owe nothing.

These magnificent Home Library Collector's Editions are bound in rich Sierra brown simulated leather—**manufactured to last generations!** And just for previewing the first volume, you will receive a **FREE Louis L'Amour Wall Calendar** featuring 13 full-color Western paintings.

This **exclusive offer** cannot be found in bookstores anywhere! **Receive your first preview Collector's Edition by filling out and returning the coupon** below.

Yes. Please send me FLINT for a 15-day free examination and enroll me in The Louis L'Amour Collection. If I keep the book, I'll pay $11.95 plus postage and handling* and receive an additional volume about once a month on a fully returnable basis. There is no minimum number of volumes to buy, and I may cancel at any time. The Calendar is mine to keep no matter what I decide.

Send to: The Louis L'Amour Collection
P.O. Box 956
Hicksville, NY 11802-9829

Mr./Ms._____

Address_____

City/State_____Zip_____
* and sales tax in NY and Canada
prices subject to change; orders subject to approval
Outside the U.S., prices are generally higher.   LLBBA 41426